FROM THE GROUNDS UP

When Maggy Thorsen's coffee house, Uncommon Grounds, is virtually obliterated by a snowstorm, she and her friend Sarah resolve to reopen - and Maggy's found the perfect spot near the train station, just in time for the opening of the new commuter route. But when Sarah's uncle dies suddenly, in the first of a series of "accidents," it's clear that someone doesn't want Uncommon Grounds to reopen. Maggy, however, has no intention of yielding...

FROM THE GROUNDS UP

Sandra Balzo

Severn House Large Print
London & New York

This first large print edition published 2011
in Great Britain and the USA by
SEVERN HOUSE PUBLISHERS LTD of
9-15 High Street, Sutton, Surrey, SM1 1DF.
First world regular print edition published 2009 by
Severn House Publishers Ltd., London and New York.

British Library Cataloguing in Publication Data

Balzo, Sandra.
    From the grounds up.
    1. Thorsen, Maggy (Fictitious character)--Fiction.
    2. Coffeehouses--Wisconsin--Milwaukee--Fiction.
    3. Businesswomen--Wisconsin--Milwaukee--Fiction.
    4. Detective and mystery stories. 5. Large type books.
    I. Title
    813.6-dc22

    ISBN-13: 978-0-7278-7920-2

Severn House Publishers support The Forest Stewardship Council
[FSC], the leading international forest certification organisation. All
our titles that are printed on Greenpeace-approved FSC-certified paper
carry the FSC logo.

MIX
Paper from
responsible sources
FSC® C018575

Printed and bound in Great Britain by the
MPG Books Group, Bodmin, Cornwall.

To Jerry, for the second half

Acknowledgements

Thanks to Vickie Strachota, tennis partner and retired sheriff's deputy, for her help and support both in the books and in life. If I have anything wrong, it's because I didn't listen to her ... or lost the e-mail. Miss you kid.

Thanks, too, to my brother Robert Fischer, who dropped everything, not only to research a 1975 Firebird, but to take a sometimes harrowing ride south with his little sister. Love you, Bob. And Judi, too.

And Sandi Solomon, who cued me in on the best way to carry a cellphone. She does it with a whole lot more aplomb than I do – as she does with life. You're my role model, Sandi with an 'i'.

Can't forget my old writers' group (as in former, though they're ancient, too ...), Gary Niebuhr and Ted Hertel. You have no idea how much I miss you both.

And, finally, to my son and daughter, Michael Balzo and Lisa Balzo, who 'love me forever, like me for always'. I am so proud of you. And grateful. And Tony Balzo, one of the best human beings I know. Thank you.

One

'When one door closes, another's probably getting ready to smack you in the ass.'

Nice. My Brookhills coffeehouse, Uncommon Grounds, had been reduced to rubble by a freak but devastating blizzard. The very livelihood of Maggy Thorsen was in serious jeopardy. If another door closed on me, I'd need at least a window to jump out of.

'That's a glass half-empty kind of thing to say, don't you think?' I asked, following my friend Sarah Kingston through the doors of another unsuitable storefront located in yet another unprofitable strip mall.

Halfway out I stopped short, the stress of the last two weeks – and a full day spent with Sarah – overtaking me. 'I'd think that you, of all people, would want to put a positive spin on this. As my real estate agent you stand to make money if you find us a new location.'

'If' being the operative word. If Sarah found a new place we could afford. And if gourmet coffee survived the economic downturn. Hell, even Starbucks—

'You are an idiot, Maggy, you know that?'

Sarah, who had already been heading to the car, turned back to me. 'I meant...'

Slap. The screen door she had just exited slammed shut, trapping me in the 'airlock' between that door and the more solid one swinging closed behind me.

Which, of course, smacked me in the butt.

Sarah opened the screen door to let me out. 'Sorry, but I warned you.'

I rubbed my rump, which was going numb. 'Sorry my ass.'

'Exactly.' She raised her eyebrows at me, 'I suppose you hate this one, too?'

I stepped off the sidewalk and into the parking lot to survey the long, squat brick building, fronted with dark square windows. 'It's characterless. Not to mention,' some feeling was returning to my butt, 'dangerous.'

'It's perfect.' Sarah snatched the listing sheet from me and stuffed it into her briefcase. 'My cousin Ronny is a contractor and he can fix that door in ten minutes. The space is already outfitted as a coffeehouse. Hell, what do you want? You and Caron would just have to move in. No build-out, no new equipment, no nothing.'

'That's because it *was* a coffeehouse,' I said. 'This is the middle of an industrial park, which is why Perk 'n Stew couldn't survive. Once the people working in the area realized they could not *really* get "stewed" here, the place went belly-up. What makes you think a resurrected Uncommon Grounds wouldn't do the same?'

'This is a perfectly good location,' Sarah said, a defensive tone seeping into her voice. 'Besides, you and Caron know how to market yourselves.'

I looked around. 'FOR LEASE' signs filled the windows of not just the building we'd been in, but half the factories and wholesale businesses on the two blocks I could see. The strip mall itself was set well back, barely noticeable from the street.

The only positive was plenty of parking. Which we wouldn't need, because nobody was likely to find us. 'It's crap.'

Sarah seemed almost – *almost* – hurt. 'And you're complaining about my attitude? You're not exactly Little Mary Sunshine yourself this morning.'

I sighed and sat down gingerly on the curb, thinking about last night's telephone conversation with my partner, Caron Egan. Caron had been 'too busy' to hunt for new locations with me. After two weeks of ducking my calls, she'd finally fessed up.

Patting my palms on the thighs of my jeans, I said, 'Caron wants out.'

Sarah started to join me at the curb, but glanced down at her usual uniform of baggy trousers and flapping jacket and thought better of it. 'Wants out of what? Her marriage again? Tell her to find another boy-toy and purge the urge from her system.'

Ah, if only it were that simple. A dalliance

with an acned mini-mart clerk and Caron would come running back to me and our coffeehouse.

'This time it's Uncommon Grounds she wants to dump,' I said. 'She claims our first year was tough enough, without having to start all over again.'

Three or four murders, a couple of betrayals. The occasional natural disaster. What had Caron expected? We were small-business owners in America's Heartland.

'Maybe they're having money troubles.'

I looked up sharply at Sarah, who was digging in her pockets, likely for a phantom cigarette. She'd given them up months ago, but the reflex was still there.

'Bernie and Caron?' I asked. 'Why? What do you know?'

Sarah shrugged, but didn't answer the question.

Caron's husband, Bernie the attorney (yes, yes – I know), seemed to be doing quite well, even on our country's economic roller coaster. The couple had a lovely home on an acre or...

'They're selling?' I asked my real estate friend. 'Did Caron ask you to list their house?'

Sarah wouldn't meet my eyes. 'I can't say.'

'You just did.' Sort of. 'Besides, all I have to do is check the advertisements.'

'It's not on the market yet,' Sarah said. 'That's all I can tell you.'

Yet.

'FOR SALE' signs dotted lawns all across

12

south-eastern Wisconsin. Milwaukee and its nearest suburbs had been hit hardest, but even Brookhills, farther west, was feeling the cash-flow pinch. The little exurb, as its residents like to think of it, was relatively affluent, but it wasn't recession-proof. Nor was anyone in it.

'Times are tough,' Sarah was saying. 'Good thing you bought that little shit-box of yours and didn't overreach.'

She was right, though I thought 'shit-box' was a bit cruel, despite my blue, stucco walls and puke-green toilet. 'Amen to that. I was just lucky I could pay cash thanks to my divorce settlement with Ted.'

Because I damn well couldn't qualify for a mortgage. There was always that pesky question about last year's income. Negative numbers need not apply.

Which brought me full circle to my current problem. Opening a business had been costly and I didn't have much cash left to draw upon. Happily, I also didn't have many expenses. Taxes, sure. Wine, but of course. And some food. Mostly Frank's.

Frank is my son's sheepdog. A furry stomach on four feet. And he drooled, even when nothing edible was in sight.

When Eric took English Lit, he suggested renaming the sheepdog: 'We should have called him "Dickens". He's the best of times, the worst of slimes.'

True on both counts. I'd given up mopping

sheepdog saliva off my glass-topped coffee table and taken to using a bath towel as a table runner. On the other hand, the hairy lug had made the 663 days since Eric left home for the University of Minnesota (and Ted, for his slut in the big house) bearable. Truth is, I missed the kid far more than the cad.

But if something good had come out of Ted's affair and our subsequent divorce, it was that my life had already been forcibly downsized by the time the recession hit.

A cloud with a tin-can lining. Can't lose what you don't have anymore.

The 'haves', though, had lost a lot. If Caron's hesitation at re-opening UG was because Bernie's specialty – trademark and copyright law – was on the skids, I couldn't try to talk her into doing something that might prove devastating for them.

Still ... 'Caron can't be broke,' I wailed. 'I can't afford her to be. Nobody could do this on her own.'

Sarah started to say something. Then, apparently thinking better of it, she clamped her mouth closed and looked away.

'What?' I got up from the curb and dusted off my tender butt. 'I'm going to have a bruise the size of a grapefruit.'

But my friend had already started back toward her car, a yellow 1975 Firebird.

With a last glance at the loser of a mall, I scurried after her.

'Wait up,' I called.

Sarah stopped short of the car and turned. 'Listen, I was thinking...' She paused again.

'Will you spit it out?' I demanded. 'Since when are you afraid to say what you think?'

She blushed.

Sarah. Blushing.

I felt a twinge of unease. Was she sick? Or were Caron and Bernie worse than broke? Maybe one of *them* was sick. I eyed Sarah. She didn't usually mince words or shrink from bad news. Especially somebody else's bad news.

So I waited.

'Umm...' Sarah pressed the toe of her shoe into the asphalt and twisted it, like she was grinding out a lit cigarette. She gave me the impression of a shy kid at recess, staring down at the ground while desperately hoping someone would ask her to play.

She started over. 'I was just thinking. Maybe...' Another twist of the shoe.

I waited some more.

Sarah Kingston finally took a deep breath and looked up.

'Maybe *I* could be your partner, Maggy.'

Two

Partnering with Sarah would be like starting a business with my mother. No amount of red wine – or Valium – could take the edge off that.

'You?' I squeaked, trying not to convey my misgivings. 'You're much too busy. I mean, your real estate business, the kids. When would you ever—'

But Sarah cut off my argument before I had a chance to elaborate on it.

'I knew it!' She stamped her foot. Ants went scurrying, pebbles flying. 'I don't know why I even try to help.'

Sarah stormed around the car to the driver's side.

I trailed after her, belatedly ashamed of my reaction.

'Listen,' I said. 'I appreciate your offer, believe me. It's just that—'

'It's just what?' Sarah threw open the driver's door of the Firebird, nearly clocking me.

I stepped back, barely in time. 'Only that...' It occurred to me I didn't really know what 'it' was. My response had been entirely emotional. Knee-jerk reaction, driven by abject terror.

The truth? If Caron was rethinking our partnership, I was in big trouble. She had been the majority investor and after Uncommon Grounds' collapse, the insurance settlement was peanuts ('act of God' plus underinsured landlord – need to hear more?).

I couldn't come up with enough capital to refit a new store on my own. I already paid the salary of Amy, our rainbow-haired, multiply pierced rock-star barista, so she wouldn't leave us while we were getting back on our feet.

Not to mention that with Caron no longer working all the hours she had, I'd need to hire another employee. Either that, or I'd have to work even more...

'I'd *love* to have you as a partner,' I said, linking arms with Sarah. 'What did you have in mind?'

What Sarah had in mind was far better than I could have imagined. But then, I tend to prepare for the worst.

'Oh, my God,' I said, hand to my mouth. 'This is perfect. Absolutely perfect.'

We'd driven to 'Brookhills Junction', the oldest section of our town. In the mid-1800s, Brookhills had been a depot stop on the railroad that ran between Chicago and Seattle. Businesses had sprung up around the train station creating a small, but vibrant, downtown area surrounded by charming little houses.

But when the train had stopped ... stopping, in

favor of Milwaukee just fifteen miles east of us, the Junction had been forgotten, twentieth and twenty-first century settlers also preferring to 'Go West' – if only as far as the acres of farmland readily available down the road. There they could build their sprawling homes on acreplus lots, rather than trying to shoehorn Mc-Mansions into the Junction's tiny plot.

Over the years I'd lived in Brookhills, a mishmash of small businesses had occupied the original buildings around the obsolete station. None of them was particularly remarkable. Or long-lived.

But the depot still stood. And Sarah and I, in turn, were now standing in front of it.

'This building is in amazingly good shape,' I said, climbing the steps to a balustraded porch that wrapped around the front and side of the building. The veranda was empty except for an oversized recliner covered in burgundy Naugahyde and patched with gray duct tape. 'What's it been used for lately?'

Sarah followed me up. 'An antiques shop and, most recently, a cafe.'

I didn't remember either of them, which meant they couldn't have lasted very long. A bit of doubt crept back into my mind. Don't business collapses, like death and bad news, come in threes?

Still, when I looked around, I couldn't help but picture the white-railed porch fitted with cafe tables and cushy easy chairs. And those seats filled with free-spending Brookhills Barbies and caffeine-needy soccer moms.

Just because we built it, though, didn't mean they would come. The Junction was a good mile north of the old Uncommon Grounds and far from the elementary schools and churches, soccer fields and tennis courts around which life in Brookhills revolved. Leaving a trail of muffin crumbs and coffee grounds wasn't going to get them here. It would take some real work.

But ... the depot was just so damned *cute*. I tried to peer in a window. The slanting light of early evening allowed me to barely make out three round clocks on the opposite wall and what looked like the original ticket windows below them.

Amy, our free-thinking barista, would love working in this place. I could already imagine her behind the ticket window, latte-ing and cappuccino-ing. Maybe we'd have frequent-buyer cards that looked like train tickets to be punched.

Here I'd pretty much lifted my leg on the idea of the strip mall Sarah had showed me, but now I was getting lyrical, internally at least, about an abandoned train station even farther off the beaten track.

OK. Down, girl.

I turned to Sarah. 'I take it the recent businesses didn't do well?'

'The antiques shop was fine for a while, but they were drawing only from the immediate area, with not a lot of repeat customers. The cafe, now, did fairly well, from what I understand. I'm not sure what happened. It just closed.'

Uncommon Grounds would have to do a whole lot better than 'fairly well'. 'Tell me again why you think we can succeed. Because of our marketing expertise?'

I knew Sarah had been playing me back at the nondescript strip mall. Now here I was, practically begging for a repeat of the hard sell. I wanted to believe.

'Nah,' Sarah said. 'I just fed you a line at the industrial park. As the listing broker for that space, I'd have gotten the whole commission if you committed to it.'

A commission. And she was pitching again, trying to get me excited without my even setting foot in the place. To recalibrate myself, I gave the railing a little shove. Damn. Solid as a rock.

'Rebuilt not five years ago,' my real estate agent said.

I even liked the ugly old recliner. I wanted the depot. I couldn't afford it, but I wanted it. The American way.

I folded my arms. I wanted to stomp my foot like Sarah had done earlier. Or, better yet, kick her in the shins.

'Why did you even show this to me?' I said unhappily. 'We'd have to increase our sales by fifty per cent just to cover the overhead.'

'No, we wouldn't.'

'And why is that?'

Sarah smiled. 'Because I own it.'

'You *own* the depot?' Hope burned bright for a moment, but I fought it. Just because we wouldn't have to pay rent didn't mean we could generate the income needed in a classically low-traffic location.

'I own the depot,' she repeated, the Cheshire cat grin getting bigger. Sarah had a set of choppers that made dentists wish they could charge by the acre. 'I inherited half from my father years ago and the rest when my Auntie Vi died last week.'

'I'm sorry,' I said automatically.

'About what?' Sarah asked, looking confused.

'Your aunt. Her recent passing?'

Never one for sentimentality, Sarah waved the subject aside. 'Vi was in her nineties and ready to go. Now, what do you think about the depot?'

'I think it's great,' I said honestly. 'But even without rent, we'd still have a ton of expenses. An abandoned train station isn't—'

'It's not exactly abandoned,' Sarah interrupted.

'Not technically, I suppose, if we moved in. But—'

'Don't you read the newspapers? Watch the local news?'

'Of course I do.' Occasionally. 'Why do you ask?' I did a three-sixty spin without seeing any ground-breakings. 'Is there a plan to develop this area?'

'No.'

Enough. 'Sarah, I refuse to ask if it's bigger than a breadbox. *Or* whether we're talking animal, vegetable or mineral.'

'Suit yourself, but the answer is worthy of the build-up.'

My eyes narrowed. 'Spill it.'

'Brookhills Junction resumes service as an official train stop on September first.'

Sarah Kingston's smile rivaled the sun.

Three

September first.

And it was now mid-May. Three and a half months. Not a lot of time to outfit the place and turn it into a gourmet coffee shop with all the bells and whistles that caffeine-fiends had come to expect. God knew what kind of problems lurked behind the walls. The building was nearly a century and a half old.

But Sarah *owned* the property. And as a real estate agent, she had connections all over town. Inspectors. Contractors. Hell, her cousin Ronny even was one.

We could do it. If we moved fast.

'How much work does the interior need?' I asked her. 'Is the kitchen from the cafe still there?'

'Let's find out.'

Sarah held up a key. It was enormous by modern standards. A skeleton key, my mom had called them, though I was never sure if that was because the old locks looked like skulls or the keys themselves were long and skinny like skeletons.

As Sarah struggled to open the station's main

entrance, I looked around again. The front of the depot bordered directly on Junction Road, one of the few thoroughfares in Brookhills that ran on an angle, north-east to south-west. Much to the disgust of current city planners, who raised ninety-degree grids to the level of religion.

To make the depot area even more of a throwback, the buildings in the Junction fronted directly on the sidewalk, with nothing but a couple of parallel parking spaces between the storefronts and traffic. There were no parking lots in front (like modern Brookhills businesses were required to provide), or even in back. The depot and the store-owners that lined the two blocks north of the tracks were 'grandfathered', meaning they didn't have to comply with current codes, or at least not all of them.

As I faced the front door of the depot, to the left were the railroad tracks. To the right and across a gravel driveway was a florist shop, now closed for the evening.

On the opposite side of the street was PartyPeople, which looked like a caterer. Penn and Ink – maybe a studio or an artists' supply shop – next to them. Tucked in closest to the tracks and directly across from the depot, was a storefront advertising piano lessons.

An eclectic collection of small businesses. We'd fit right in. Sarah, Amy and me. Should Caron change her mind and commit, Uncommon Grounds would be about as eclectic as you could get.

As Sarah finally bested the lock and went to swing open the door, I snuck a glance around the corner to the track side of the building. Four angled parking spots and beyond them at the back of the building, a big lot that looked like it had recently been cleared.

'What's going in behind the depot?' I asked as I followed Sarah into the building.

'Parking.' Sarah slipped the big key back into her jacket pocket. 'People need somewhere to leave their cars before they take the train down-town to work.'

'Of course,' I said absently, trying to get my head around nearly unlimited parking provided to us and to our customers for the magic word: 'free'.

Later, I would count the parking spaces and multiply that by the cost of a latte. The number would be inflated, but hey, a girl can dream, can't she?

Right now, though, I was eager to go over the interior layout of the depot itself. In front of me were three ticket windows. Happily the previous businesses had left them untouched, probably willing to forgo extra space for the charm the counter provided.

The three clocks I'd glimpsed from outside were labeled: 'Seattle', 'Brookhills' and 'New York City'. The Brookhills entry in the center was clean though hanging a little askew, like someone had just finished polishing it. The time, best as I could tell, seemed right – a quarter to eight. In contrast, the bracketing Seattle and New York clocks looked forgotten. To my eye, they read ten after ten and six o'clock, but given the dusky light inside the station and the sheen of dust that covered their faces, ten minutes to two and twelve-thirty were also possibilities. Whatever, they were wrong and would have to be fixed if ...

'Wait a second,' I said, turning to Sarah who was busy looking for a light switch. 'Did you say people needed to park their cars so they could go to work in downtown Milwaukee?'

'Of course. What do you think they're going to do? Walk? Even if they lived a block away, they'd take their car. This is Brookhills, not Manhattan.'

I still didn't understand. 'But this line runs between Seattle and Chicago and stops in Milwaukee and Minneapolis.'

I knew this because Eric sometimes took Amtrak home from school in Minnesota and I would pick him up at the Milwaukee stop. There were only two trains each day – one heading west at eight fifteen a.m., and one east at eight fifteen p.m. 'Why would anyone take a long-distance train to work just fifteen miles away?'

Light finally dawned, even as the setting sun squeezed through the windows.

I squinted at Sarah. 'Are you telling me this will be a commuter train?'

Over the years, there had been talk of a train running between the western outskirts and the business district of Milwaukee. I was even vaguely aware that a vote had been scheduled. What I didn't know, having been preoccupied with my own problems the prior couple of weeks, was how that vote had gone.

Now I grabbed Sarah, who was grinning at me, and shook her. 'People will be coming through here to take the train to work in Milwaukee?'

'And home again. Every morning and afternoon, weekdays anyway,' Sarah confirmed. 'Sort of comes with the territory.'

I didn't rise to the bait because I was too busy imagining hundreds of riders carrying to-go cups emblazoned with 'Uncommon Grounds', humming their sleep-muzzied way into Milwaukee each a.m. and their work-befuddled way back home every p.m. We'd have to add staff in the morning so we could get them in and out quickly. Efficient, friendly service, that was the key.

'Did you hear me?' Sarah was looking disappointed that I hadn't reacted the way she expected. But then she wasn't acting the way I was accustomed to either. Since when had Sarah needed positive reinforcement?

Her expression changed. 'Wait a second. You're already planning the store in your head.' At that moment, Sarah knew she had me hooked.

So why pretend otherwise? 'You bet I am.'

I led her to the ticket counter. 'We'll serve from all three windows, though one should be an express line. That way, straight coffee-drinkers don't have to wait behind triple-nonfat-no-foam-latte types.'

'We'll bill it as the "UG Express",' Sarah said, warming to the subject. 'Like a train.'

'I love it. And how about railroad-themed drinks, like Chattanooga Chai Tea?'

'Cute,' Sarah said, 'if we were in Chattanooga. Or if Chai Tea sounded anything like "Choo-choo".'

She was frowning at the crooked Brookhills clock. Sarah might not concern herself with fashion – the baggy trousers and jacket not an aberration, but a wardrobe constant. However, she did demand symmetry in her real estate. In fact, the Victorian house she owned was a showplace. How she managed to keep it that way with two teenagers – the children of a dead friend to whom Sarah proved an even better friend – in the house, I didn't know.

Unable to straighten out the 'Brookhills' clock by telekinesis, she moved over and shifted it so '12' was back on top.

'You'll forgive me if I take a little locomotive license,' I said, before Ms Perfect could start cleaning the other two timepieces. 'We're brainstorming. No fair poking fun, though we should be taking notes.'

'Good idea.'

I looked around. 'Do you see any paper?'

Sarah's answer was trampled by the sound of a door being swung open. Hard.

I turned to see a man of about eighty, white beard and close-cropped hair, standing in the doorway. He didn't look happy. 'This is private property. Who let you in?'

Sarah stepped around me. 'Who let *you* out?'

The old man peered at Sarah. 'Identify yourself.'

'It's me,' she said, moving closer.

'Not so "itsy",' he said gruffly. 'You're fat. Who are you?'

Sarah looked affronted. She had put on a few pounds after quitting the cigarettes and then tennis. Smoking she'd participated in for thirty years. Tennis, thirty days. Food, a lifetime.

'I didn't say "itsy", you deaf old fart,' she growled. 'I said, "It's me." Sarah.'

She turned my way. 'This is Kornell Eisvogel. He was married to Auntie Vi. In addition to not hearing well, he's blind as a bat and mean as a snake.'

'Snakes aren't mean. Just misunderstood.' I stuck my hand out to the old man. 'I'm Maggy Thorsen. It's nice to meet you.'

Eisvogel ignored my gesture. In fairness, though, I wasn't sure he saw it through his cataract-clouded eyes.

Instead, he pointed a bony finger at Sarah. 'You're Vi's brother Roger's girl.'

'Once upon a time. My father has been dead

for more than ten years.'

Eisvogel didn't seem to care. 'What are you doing here?'

'I asked you first. You know you're not supposed to drive at night. Ronny will hide your car.'

'That son of mine don't know jack-shit. Still can't even close a door.'

'Are you on that again, Kornell?' Sarah snapped. 'Ronny was five at the time. Leave him alone.'

I didn't see the big deal. Even at nearly twenty, my Eric left doors open, including the one shielding the refrigerator. All of that paled in comparison to the time he traced the television image of *Barney the Purple Dinosaur* on the screen with a Sharpie. When they say 'permanent marker', they're not kidding.

'Damn right he was five.' Spittle flew from Eisvogel's lips. 'Old enough to know better. His brother was only three, rest his poor baby soul.'

'Ronny's brother?' I asked.

Eisvogel didn't answer, but Sarah leaned in. 'It was before Vi and Kornell got together, but I guess the three-year-old wandered out of the house and into the street after a ball.'

The old man swiped at tears. 'My Tommy, gone. His brother was supposed to be taking care of him.'

'Not Ronny's fault,' Sarah said in a tone that indicated they'd had this conversation before. 'You just want to blame him because you were the one who should have been watching both boys.'

Ouch. Eisvogel looked like he'd been punched. 'Ronny knew damn well not to go out,' he said, lashing back. 'They was supposed to be taking naps.'

I could understand why Eisvogel would want to hold someone else responsible for the tragedy. Knowing that it was your fault a child died had to be devastating. But to blame another, slightly older son? Inconceivable to me.

'Yeah, yeah, yeah,' Sarah was saying, holding up her hands. 'I've heard it all before, Kornell. Now don't you think it's time to leave?'

'I'll leave when I damn well please. Besides,' Eisvogel gestured toward the clocks, 'it ain't sundown yet. The sun sets at seven minutes past eight tonight. I keep that middle one there set just right.'

So it had been Sarah's uncle who cleaned her clock.

Sarah didn't seem to appreciate the gesture. 'If you get caught driving at night, you'll lose your license. For good this time.'

I turned. Three minutes to eight o'clock on the Brookhills clock. The hands on the other two hadn't budged. Judging by the old man and the ancient Buick I could see parked on the street, he'd best get rolling.

'The sun is getting pretty low out there.' I pointed out the windows. 'Do you need a ride

31

home?'

'Hey, now, who are you?' Eisvogel said, like he'd just noticed me. 'You ain't looking to buy this place, are you?' As he spoke he moved menacingly toward me.

I reflexively took a step back and then held my ground. He was eighty, mostly blind and deaf. I should be able to take him.

But he confronted Sarah instead. 'You know you can't sell this place. Your aunt left everything to me before the accident.'

'The "accident"?' Sarah asked. 'You mean the one you caused?'

She turned to me. 'Vi was getting out of the car. She still had hold of the door handle when this idiot pulled away. The fall broke her hip.'

'Tweren't my fault,' Eisvogel protested. 'Vi was too slow.'

'Vi was ninety-two.'

'What I get for marrying an older woman,' he said, some pride creeping back into his voice. 'Can't help it if I've always had a thing for bobcats.' One rheumy eye winked at me.

'I think you mean "cougars".'

'Don't encourage him.' Sarah turned on Eisvogel. 'I told you yesterday. The station was Vi's and my father's. His half came to me when he died. Her half reverted to me when *she* died.'

'Right,' the old man said, 'because you're common.'

Sarah rolled her eyes. 'My father and Vi were "tenants in common". That means that each of them owned a half-interest that they could will to their survivors. My father gave his half to me.'

Eisvogel poked himself in the chest with his thumb. 'And I'm Vi's survivor.'

Sarah looked like she'd love the chance to abandon him on a desert island. 'Kornell, just before you and Vi were married, she and I changed our title to "joint tenancy".'

Eisvogel started to interrupt, but Sarah held up her hand. 'Meaning that if either Vi or I died, that half would go to the other of us.'

Trying to help, I said, 'To keep the property in the family.'

'*I'm* family,' Eisvogel protested. 'And don't forget about Ronny.'

'Ronny is your son, not Vi's.'

'Your aunt loved Ronny.' Now the old man placed a hand over his heart. 'The woman was a saint to that boy. I haven't had the brass to break this to him.'

'You haven't told Ronny that Vi's dead?' I asked.

'Don't be stupid. What he don't know is about this place and the miscarriage of justice.'

'I like Ronny,' Sarah said, 'and I know Vi and he were close. But Ronny isn't a Kingston.'

'Kingston, Schmingston.' Eisvogel snuck me a leering look, but it was Sarah he advanced toward. 'This isn't going to stand up in court, you'll see. Your aunt wasn't in her right mind.'

'Who would be, Kornell, married to you?'

33

Sarah had moved, too, close enough to bite him.

'You watch your mouth now.' He raised his hand, as if to slap her.

I wedged myself between the two of them and pointed toward the working clock. 'It's eight, Mr Eisvogel. If you leave now, you might be home before dark. *If* a train doesn't come and back up traffic.' I added the last to light a figurative fire under him.

He glared first at me, then at the clock and, finally, at Sarah.

Then Eisvogel pulled a worn key case from his pocket. 'If I leave at eight-oh-three, I'll be at Brookhills Manor at eight-oh-six. The sun goes down at eight-oh-seven. Durn train doesn't come through until eight fifteen. By then, I'll be sitting home in my underwear, drinking schnapps.'

Well, that was good. The 'Manor' part, not the image of the old man, in his cups while in his drawers.

Brookhills Senior Manor was just two blocks away – why had he even bothered to drive? Then again, like Sarah had said, this was Brookhills. No one walked.

Since the Buick was already pointed in the right direction, once Eisvogel got up and over the tracks, he could practically coast down Junction Road, across Poplar Creek Drive and roll to a stop in the parking lot of the senior home.

With luck, the shriveled warlock wouldn't

encounter anyone on the way or in the parking lot. The seniors who lived at the Manor, including my friend Henry Wested, were hopefully tucked in for the evening.

With maddening meticulousness, Eisvogel folded open his leather key case and tucked in a skeleton key that was a duplicate of the one Sarah had. He went to snap the dog-eared case closed, but remembered to shake out the Buick key first.

Then he turned to look at the clock.

As if on cue, the minute hand on the Brookhills' clock moved one tick to the right. Three minutes after the hour. Seattle and New York stood pat.

When I turned back, Eisvogel was gone, leaving Sarah alone, silhouetted against the big side window.

'Wow. Your uncle is a loony.' I had to use my hand to shield my eyes from the fast-sinking sun. Outside, the Buick started with a hiccupping growl.

'Kornell's *not* my uncle, he's my aunt's husband. And she's dead. That means he's nothing to me.'

If I hadn't seen him raise his hand to Sarah, it would have seemed a cruel way to talk about the old lech. 'Did he ever hit—'

A spitting of gravel by tires signaled Eisvogel's departure, followed by a rumble. I waited for the noise to subside so I could continue, but instead it seemed to grow.

A whistle sounded in the distance, low and steady at first and then more shrill and even frantic as it neared. The fingers-down-the-blackboard screech of air-brakes. Finally, a sickening thud and the prolonged, wrenching scream of metal on metal.

The eight fifteen Seattle to Chicago – by way of Minot, North Dakota; Minneapolis, Minnesota; and Brookhills, Wisconsin – was ahead of schedule.

Four

The clocks on the wall shook. Hell, everything shook.

Sarah and I looked at each other and then made for the door.

The train had managed to stop, but not until only its last car was even with the station. We ran alongside to reach the front, even as passengers slid open their windows in an attempt to find out what had happened. Or, maybe, give themselves an emergency escape route.

'What's going on?' one man asked. Drops of blood trickled down his brows and cheeks from a bright red gash on his forehead, presumably from hitting the seat in front of him when the train braked abruptly.

'Did we hit something?' from a woman, eyeglasses bent at the bridge of her nose.

'A deer, probably,' another man ventured.

'Could be they're rutting,' a fourth voice contributed.

Rutting season, that time of year when sex-crazed bucks run blindly into cars and their doe counterparts temporarily abandon fawns in favor of a roll in the hay, is in autumn. Before I could point that out, a loud command from inside the train drew the passengers back in like so many turtle heads. Probably the conductor, making sure they weren't decapitated.

As we rounded the locomotive, the setting sun nearly blinded us. I shaded my eyes again.

The old Buick stood next to the tracks, its tires shredded and rims bent. The car apparently had been T-boned and carried down the tracks by the engine before some law of physics shrugged it aside on to the gravel right of way. You could still tell the mangled hulk had been an automobile, but barely.

The engineer and conductor were climbing down off the train, followed by a guy in a white chef's outfit. Sirens were already sounding around us. Equipment from probably half a dozen municipalities would show up. But they couldn't be much help to Sarah's step-uncle.

Kornell Eisvogel's upper torso was draped over the sill of the Buick's driver's window, his head turned sideways, cataract-cloudy eyes wide open. Blood dribbled from the corner of his mouth to the ground below.

I looked at Sarah. I'd seen more than my share of bodies – one or two with her. Still, none of the corpses had been family, at least according to my friend's narrow definition of same.

Sarah's face was white and her substantial jaw was trembling. I put my hand on one shoulder. 'We should move away.'

38

She just stared. A tear pooled in her right eye and then escaped down her cheek. Sarah swiped at it furiously with a fist. 'I hated the old shit.'

'I know,' I said softly. 'It's OK.'

And we moved away.

I was right about the six municipalities, give or take a few. The Brookhills police and fire rescue responded first, followed closely by the Brookhills County Sheriff's Department. That wasn't necessarily good news, since I knew the Brookhills County Sheriff. Knew, in the biblical sense – finally, hallelujah and thank the Lord. It had taken us long enough to get to that point, though life, and the more than occasional violent death, often still got in the way.

Jake Pavlik was not in the first county cruiser that responded. Nor even the second. Third, though, was the charm. I guessed it was his car, not because it differed from the other responding units in design, but rather because, while its red and blue lights were flashing, the sirens weren't blaring.

Like the coroner, Pavlik wasn't a first responder under normal circumstances. If this were baseball, he'd be more the clean-up batter. The game wasn't over, but if everyone prior to him had done his or her job, Pavlik could do his more efficiently and effectively.

I watched as the sheriff climbed out of his cruiser and strode over to the knot of officers and EMTs surrounding the Buick. As he reached them, two firefighters with a hydraulic spreader went to work on the driver's door of Eisvogel's car.

'Jaws of Life, huh?' Sarah said over the industrial whine, gesturing vaguely at the equipment.

I guessed what she was thinking. That the description 'life' was wrong in this case. That the line between it and death had been crossed by Kornell Eisvogel, and that no fancy tool, act of heroism or medical marvel was ever, ever going to bring him back.

Or maybe she was just making conversation.

'Can't they simply pull him out the window?' Sarah asked me.

'Maybe he's ... stuck.'

'So, like I said, *pull*. It's not like he's going to notice.'

We were standing about thirty feet off the railroad bed. The police had moved us away from the Buick when they'd arrived. Sarah hadn't identified herself. Or Kornell, for that matter. When I'd started to, she'd shot me a look that stopped me.

Sarah wasn't exactly a joiner, but she was going to have to get involved, like it or not. Me, too, and I really didn't fancy Pavlik catching me at the scene of yet another emergency. My timing – or lack thereof – had gotten to be a joke between us, but I feared the humor was wearing thin for him. I knew it was for me, and

40

I wasn't surrounded by crime constantly, like he was. The last thing a cop needed was to be dating a death magnet.

I didn't want Pavlik to see me, at least right then. I got some unexpected help in that area from the tenants of the Junction. They joined us now, providing cover for me.

'How in the hell did this happen?' a grizzled man built like a toad asked. 'Did the driver go right through the gates?' As he waved his hand toward what was left of the Buick, I noticed his fingers were as long and tapered as his body was short and squat.

'Look for yourself.' The little redhead next to me gestured toward the splintered railway crossing gates. She still wore an apron and yellow rubber gloves, so I pegged her as the caterer. The toady guy was the piano teacher, of course. The hands were a dead giveaway.

The third of our new neighbors, a pretty brunette, shook her head. 'I wouldn't be surprised if he never saw the gates. The tracks are on a little rise and when you're heading south-west this time of day, the sun is right in your eyes.'

'But what about the engineer's whistle?' the tall, blonde guy next to her asked. 'We certainly heard it. Wouldn't the driver?'

'He was deaf,' Sarah said, not even bothering to look at the speaker.

He cocked his head. 'I'm sorry. Do you know...' An awkward pause, 'the deceased?'

Sarah didn't respond, so I tried to answer their

questions.

'I'm Maggy Thorsen,' I said, 'and this is Sarah Kingston. Sarah was showing me the depot when her Uncle Kornell stopped by.'

Four heads swiveled toward the Buick, where the snarl of the hydraulic jaws had stopped. As we watched, the car door fell away.

'That's Crazy Kornell?' the brunette said, and then clapped a hand over her mouth.

'I apologize for my partner.' Blonde Guy laid his palm on Sarah's shoulder. 'I'm sure you were very fond of your uncle.'

'Not really,' Sarah said. She looked at his hand, seeming to notice him for the first time. 'Who are you?'

Blonde Guy blushed. It was adorable, and so was he. 'I'm Michael Ink. And this,' he drew the brunette over, 'is Rebecca Penn.'

Penn and Ink, from their sign.

'You're kidding, right?' Sarah said. My friend was obviously regaining steam. A good thing for her, not so much for the rest of the world.

Ink got redder. 'Well, actually, my name is Inkel.'

Penn and Inkel. Didn't have quite the same ring.

'Are you artists?' I asked.

'Rebecca is a graphic artist,' Michael said, turning his attention to me. 'I'm a writer.'

I love writers.

Sarah, though, had lost interest in our neighbors. She was watching Pavlik, looking on as

42

Eisvogel's body was loaded on to a gurney.

As the gurney was wheeled to an ambulance, Pavlik glanced toward the train's crew, now being questioned by a couple of guys in suits. From there, his eyes swept past the clustering passengers to the depot and the surrounding stores.

And then he settled on us.

Sarah said, 'Bull's eye.'

Sure enough. We were in his cross-hairs.

She waved.

'Feeling social all of a sudden?' I asked, mildly perturbed.

Pavlik looked more than mildly perturbed. He looked downright put out. Which probably meant he wouldn't. Put out, that is. At least not tonight.

Thing was, though, Pavlik was so attractive when irritated that any grief he gave me was almost worth it. He had the most beautiful sunny blue eyes when he was happy. But, when less than pleased with me or a suspect, which on occasion had meant the same thing, his eyes turned gray. Dirty Chevy gray, I called them the first time I met him. Now I thought of them as 'stormy'.

When he was truly angry, though, Pavlik's eyes went so black you could barely make out the pupil at the center. It was a little scary, actually, something that probably came in handy when the sheriff was talking to 'perps' and 'skels'.

Me? I'd tell him anything he wanted if his eyes got that stormy. Hell, I'd tell him anything, period, just to tangle my fingers in his black curly hair or, even better, run my hand over the buttery leather jacket he wore when riding his Harley.

Sadly, though, the May weather had turned warm and the jacket had been retired for the season. Or so Pavlik claimed. I feared he suspected something unnatural was going on between his lambskin and me.

'Who's that?' the redhead asked, rubbing her gloved hands together.

'The sheriff, and he's trouble,' Sarah growled. She looked the other woman up and down like she'd just noticed her, too. 'Who the hell are you?'

The woman answered Sarah automatically. Yet another thing I didn't get. The more audacious Sarah acted, the quicker people yielded to her will. It wasn't fair.

'Christy Wrigley.' The redhead stuck out her gloved hand.

Sarah just looked at it.

I took it. Beat meeting Pavlik's eyes as he approached. 'Maggy Thorsen,' I told her. 'Are you with PartyPeople?'

The grizzled man, who'd been avidly watching the action at the train, stiffened. 'Don't be ridiculous. I'm PartyPeople. Art Jenada, master caterer.'

'You cook?' Sarah asked. I don't think she

registered surprise that the little, round hairy guy cooked. I think she was astounded anyone cooked. Sarah and her teenage charges survived on carryout.

Jenada bristled. 'Cook? I'm a chef. I ran the restaurant there,' he pointed at the station, *my* station, 'until a couple of months back.'

I glanced at Sarah. Why hadn't she told me Jenada had been her tenant?

'What happened?' I asked Jenada.

'Him.' He nodded at the ambulance, its door still standing open, Eisvogel lying lifeless inside.

'Kornell?' Sarah asked. She seemed to know as little about all this as I did.

'You bet. Cra ... I mean, your uncle talked your aunt out of renewing my lease. If Vi had a backbone she would have stood up to him.' His eyes narrowed. 'The minute it looked like I might be able to succeed, I was out.'

'But Kornell didn't own the depot,' I said to Sarah. 'Why was he involved in the leasing?'

'Vi let him,' Sarah said. 'I didn't become part of the day-to-day management until after she died, and then, whether Kornell liked it or not, it became mine.' She shook her fist at the ambulance like the old man was going to argue the point from the beyond.

There was a crisp crack of thunder and I jumped.

'Sorry.' The little redhead was not more than a foot behind me. 'I had dust on my gloves.'

45

She clapped the big yellow rubber gloves together again – once, twice, three times – and then held them up in front of her like a surgeon about to go into the operating room.

'Christy is the piano teacher.' Jenada said. Behind her back, he pointed his finger at his head and made air circles, the universal sign for 'the woman's crazy as a bedbug'.

'The woman's crazy as a bedbug,' he said, in case I hadn't caught his pantomime.

Since knowing Sarah, I'd come to appreciate frankness. I wasn't sure Christy would feel the same.

To my surprise, though, she didn't take offense. Instead, she shivered. 'Bedbugs are not a problem if you maintain proper hygiene. I sanitize my mattress and flip it once a week.' Christy was wringing her hands as she spoke, the yellow rubber of her gloves making squeak-squeak noises. 'Everyone should.'

I was lucky to rotate my *sheets* that often, much less my mattress. 'Of course.'

'Of course,' Sarah parroted. 'But only if you're a germ freak.'

'I have to be.' Christy's green eyes widened. 'Not just at home, but at work, too.' She gestured toward the music studio. 'Do you have any idea how much bacteria even a small child can carry?'

Twice his own body weight, if I correctly remembered my son Eric's early years.

'Little buggers dirty up your piano?' Sarah

was enjoying this now.

'It's terrible. Parents will spend a hundred dollars for a pair of sneakers. What's wrong with investing pocket change in a good anti-bacterial hand-cleanser?' Christy tsk-tsked. 'I have to disinfect the piano after each student.'

'Cotton swabs?' Sarah asked. 'To get between the keys?'

'And toothpicks, for those truly hard to reach places.'

I didn't want to ask how she made the disinfectant stick to the toothpick.

'How does the disinfectant—' Sarah started.

'Maggy.'

I jumped as I had with Christy, then reluctantly turned. 'Pavlik. I mean, Sheriff.'

He'd been 'Pavlik' to me ever since we met. Even during our most intimate moments, I had to sort through 'Pavlik' and 'Sheriff' to get to 'Jake'. I think it amused him.

Though by the look on his face, amusement wasn't what he was feeling right now.

'Just passing by?' he asked.

'No. That...' I pointed to the ambulance, which was pulling away, no lights, no siren, no hurry, '...is Sarah's uncle.'

She said, 'Make that *"was"*.' Leave it to Sarah to quibble at a time like this. 'And at most he was my uncle-in-law,' she added. 'My aunt died last week, so Kornell and I haven't been related for some days now.'

'Sorry,' Pavlik said, looking like he wasn't

47

quite sure what to make of all that. Hell, I was familiar with the situation, and even I couldn't gauge Sarah's mood.

The sheriff pulled a notebook from the pocket of his sports jacket. 'Were you with Mr Eisvogel before the accident?'

'I guess you could say that.' Sarah sounded cautious.

Pavlik looked in my direction.

'Me, too,' I chirped. 'Together. All of us.' I'd found it best to put alibis front and center. Not that it should be important this time. The man had driven into the path of a long-haul train. 'Why do you ask? It was an accident, obviously.'

Pavlik seemed surprised at the question. 'The death certainly involved a train. But that means everybody and their brother – State Department of Transportation, National Transportation Safety Board, Federal Railroad Administration – will all be here.'

'Good. Let them come,' Art Jenada injected. 'I'll give them an earful. If this wasn't a "quiet zone", that man might not be dead. Another example of the government capitulating to the rich at the expense of the poor working man.'

Power to the people. The guy did look like a regenerate hippie. 'What does he mean?' I asked.

Christy smoothed her apron. 'A number of railroad crossings in Brookhills are in quiet zones. Municipalities have the right to designate that.'

'Quiet? You mean they don't blow their horns?' I said. 'But this one did. I heard it.'

'Sure,' Jenada said. 'When it was too late.'

'The man was deaf anyway,' Sarah muttered crossly. 'And nearly blind.'

'The setting sun is awful this time of year,' Rebecca Penn said, redundantly. The woman had been so quiet since our introduction that I'd forgotten she was there. 'It certainly could have wrecked his vision.'

'No "vision" to "wreck",' Sarah said. 'Cataracts.'

'What a shame.' I wasn't thinking about cataracts, I was thinking about fate. Chance. 'If Uncle Kornell,' which earned me a cutting glance from Sarah. 'If Mr Eisvogel,' I corrected, 'had left a fraction sooner. If the train hadn't been early—'

'Early?' The question came in quadruplicate from Art, Rebecca, Michael and Christy.

Pavlik expanded it. 'The train was ahead of schedule? By how much?'

'I'm not sure, exactly. Kornell left at three minutes after eight and the train wasn't due until eight fifteen. He didn't leave at a dead run,' I felt myself flush at my choice of words, 'but it certainly wouldn't have taken him twelve minutes to start the car and drive the half-block to the tracks.'

The train's conductor was standing about twenty feet away, talking with a deputy. Pavlik

49

waved them over. 'Why didn't you tell me the train was early?'

The conductor looked surprised. 'Because it wasn't. We were right on schedule.'

I turned to Sarah for support. 'Your uncle left at three minutes past the hour, right?'

Sarah shrugged. Probably ticked because I still referred to the deceased as her 'uncle'.

I turned back to Pavlik. 'Before he left, Eisvogel checked the Brookhills wall clock.'

'Figures.' This from Art Jenada.

We all looked at him.

He shrugged. 'Every day, when I ran the place, Crazy would "stop by to check the time". It was just an excuse. Bad enough the old man was too cheap to get a watch or have the other two clocks fixed like I asked him, but then he expected me to feed him, too. Acted like he owned the place.'

Which, to give the devil his due, Eisvogel thought he did.

'The decedent's license was restricted to daylight driving, sir,' the deputy contributed, as if none of us were there.

'Kornell Eisvogel,' I said, 'told us he'd be home by sunset. He seemed to have it all timed out, like he did this on a regular basis.'

'He sure as hell did.' Jenada rubbed his bristled face. 'I closed at eight and Crazy'd shoot out of there right after that, carrying any leftovers he could score.'

'Where was the deceased's home?' Pavlik

asked his deputy.

The deputy opened a notebook. 'Brookhills Manor, according to his driver's license. It's just down the street. And they're right, the old man would have made it if he'd left a couple of minutes earlier.'

'Or the train had been on time,' I added, sneaking a peek at the conductor.

'We were on time,' he said testily. 'Check our log.'

'I'll do that,' Pavlik said. 'It's most likely, though, that the depot's clock is wrong.'

'Clocks,' I corrected. 'There are three of them, but like Art says, only one of them keeps time. I'll show you now if you'd like.'

Pavlik let me lead the way. The rest of the group had already broken up and Sarah was nowhere in sight. Art Jenada and Christy Wrigley were walking diagonally toward their establishments. Michael Inkel and Rebecca Penn were heading parallel to the train about ten yards ahead of us and talking in low voices.

Occasionally I could make out a word or so. 'Why did—', 'I warned—', 'You always—'

Definitely a couple.

I started to say something, but Pavlik put up a warning finger.

When Rebecca and Michael turned off and were out of earshot, Pavlik said, 'Must you be at every unattended death in my jurisdiction?'

'It's not any fault of mine,' I protested. 'It just happens. Like a curse.'

51

His look made it clear he thought *I* might be the curse. 'People are starting to notice.'

'Notice?'

'That you show up whenever somebody crumps.'

'Oh.' I could see the awkward side of that. 'Did you explain it's just a coincidence?'

'No. I told them you're my stalker.' His eyes flared blue for a second, accompanied by the slightest trace of a grin.

Seemingly, we were OK.

Continuing toward the caboose of the train, I could see vehicles of every shape and size backed up on Junction Road. I wondered if Sarah's Firebird was wading through that mess.

Pavlik approached another of his deputies. 'Re-route traffic through the neighborhoods and over to Poplar Creek Road.'

My house is on Poplar Creek, a narrow two-lane street. Given the sheriff's order, getting home wasn't going to be easy. 'How long will this road be closed?' I asked.

'The train can't be moved until the other agencies arrive, investigate and release it as an accident – or worse, crime — scene.' Pavlik was ahead of me now, striding toward the depot.

'Crime scene?' I was trying to keep up. 'Eisvogel's car was on a railroad track and got hit by a train. It was an accident.'

'Maybe, but that's not my call. There have been way too many transit incidents resulting in fatalities lately and all of this needs to be by the book. The agencies will take a while.'

I thought I knew what Pavlik was referring to. There had been a recent rash of crashes – buses, trains, automobiles – caused by drivers talking on cellphones or texting. The authorities were really cracking down and prosecuting the people responsible. Assuming they survived.

I broke into a trot and caught Pavlik on the steps up to the station. I was digging through my handbag for my own cellphone. 'Listen, we can compare the time on my phone to the depot clock.'

I found my cell just as Pavlik swung open the door. 'It's ... nine twenty-seven,' I said. 'If the conductor was right about being on schedule, the wall clock should be about ten minutes slow. So—'

I stopped, cellphone in hand, staring at the Brookhills clock. Twenty-seven minutes after the hour.

On the button.

Five

'You're absolutely sure the train was on time,' I said to Pavlik much later.

'Logs, conductor, engineer, passengers – even the chef in the dining car. They're all in agreement.'

'I don't understand. It's as if I lost ten minutes of my life.'

'Alien abduction?'

'Funny.'

We were sitting on the back stoop of my little house, watching sheepdog Frank water the trees and bushes. He'd been cooped up much longer than usual that day. It had taken me only about twenty minutes to get home, mostly because I walked it. Sarah and I drove to the depot together earlier, but she'd left without me. Not that I minded. The walk was definitely preferable to sitting in the re-routed traffic.

Pavlik pulled in just as I let Frank out the door, but not even the arrival of my dog's best friend could stay the furrier from the not-so-swift completion of his appointed rounds. Frank lifted his leg on my peony bush, sniffed twice, and diversified to a birch tree.

Frank had been testy ever since Eric came home for a week after final exams, only to return to his job in Minneapolis for the summer. Somehow, in the sheepdog's mind, I was to blame for this.

On the one hand, I was glad Eric was working, but I missed my son. I'm sure Frank did, too, only, in his pique, he had substituted Pavlik. Fickle, thy name is sheepdog.

Frank finished his circuit, sat down next to Pavlik and licked himself.

Pavlik scratched the dog somewhere in the vicinity of his ear. With all Frank's hair, a person would need GPS to locate specific body parts.

'You probably just lost track of time, in your excitement.' He sneaked me a dirty grin. 'Did I understand Sarah is your new partner?'

I lifted my chin. 'Don't underestimate Sarah. I think she'll be great.'

'What I think is that the two of you will drive each other nuts. It's going to ruin your friendship.'

'Such as it is,' I mumbled under my breath.

'You have to admit,' Pavlik insisted, 'that Sarah is your closest friend, other than Frank and me.' The dog leaned into the sheriff's knee and slid down to the ground with a 'harrumph'.

I considered Pavlik more than a friend – with or without benefits. Still, I didn't think it was a very good time for a where-is-our-relationship-going talk. In my experience there was no better way to send a potential life-mate running for the exits.

Wish I'd known that when I was dating Ted. A twenty-minute 'We need to talk' could have saved me twenty years. On the other hand, then there'd have been no Eric and that was unthinkable.

'If Sarah and I are truly friends,' I said now, 'we'll be able to withstand anything. Even working together.'

'Spoken like a woman who has never gone into business with a friend.'

'And a man who has,' I said, slipping my arm into his.

He ran a thumbnail across the palm of my hand. His fingers were long and sensitive. Pavlik should have been the pianist instead of prissy-Christy.

He said, 'I just remember what it was like when I was promoted in the sheriff's office. Suddenly my friends were reporting to me. It gets tricky.'

'Well, Sarah wouldn't be working for me or vice versa. We'd be partners.'

'You don't think she'll order you around?'

'No.'

Pavlik snickered. 'She already does.'

'Sarah facilitates.'

He looked at me.

I squirmed. 'OK, she nags.' I was willing to take a whole lot of nagging from Sarah in order to get my hands on that train station.

'She owns the depot,' I heard myself whining.

Pavlik laughed. 'You sound like a little girl who wants a pony for Christmas.'

I nodded at Frank, who had resumed his ablutions, lying on the ground, back paws waving in the air. 'Already got one.'

'Sarah didn't seem too broken up by her uncle's death. I assume there was bad blood?' Pavlik said it casually.

'Why do you think that?' I asked.

He grinned. 'Answering a question with a question is *my* shtick, remember?'

'Think of me as a fast learner.' I leaned my head against him, but didn't add anything. It was another tactic I'd learned from Pavlik. Don't rush to fill the silence. Let it just sit there. And molder.

Finally, Pavlik sighed. 'OK, you win. So how about a different question: Know of any reason Mr Eisvogel might have wanted to end his life?'

I sat up. 'Suicide?'

'You're doing it again.'

'Why would you think he killed himself?'

'And again.' Pavlik shook his head. 'Could you just answer a question?'

'Can you?'

Pavlik's voice lowered. 'The train was on time. Eisvogel knew what the train schedule was, yet he apparently drove on to the tracks and stopped.'

'He *stopped* on the tracks?'

57

Pavlik looked threatening.

I figured I'd pushed the sheriff's envelope as far as I could. 'No, I don't know of any reason Kornell would have for committing suicide.'

'I understand his wife died just last week,' Pavlik said. 'Did he seem despondent?'

'Despondent?' I shook my head. 'Not in the least. The only thing he seemed concerned about was his wife's wi—' I stopped.

But not soon enough. 'Her will?'

'Yes.' Like it or not, I was back to filling the silence.

'What about her will?' Pavlik shifted so we were nose to nose.

Frank grunted at being disturbed and switched legs. There'd be no help, distraction-wise, from that quarter.

'You know, what she left him.'

'I know what a will is, Maggy. What did she leave him?' Pavlik peered at me. 'Or should I ask about what she *didn't* leave him?'

Damn. The sheriff had me. I couldn't lie outright. I wasn't even sure why I wanted to. After all, Kornell Eisvogel's death was an accident. Or, at worst, a suicide. What it wasn't, though, was a murder. Which meant that I wouldn't be getting myself – or any of my friends – in trouble.

'The depot,' I said. 'It wasn't part of Vi's will. She and Sarah owned it halfsies somehow and, when Aunt Vi died, the whole thing went to her niece Sarah.'

58

As I spoke, Pavlik's cellphone rang. He flipped it open. 'Sheriff here ... Yes? ... Yes ... Damn! ... No, OK. And thanks.'

He closed the phone carefully, like it was a particularly sharp-bladed pocketknife.

'Don't tell me,' I said.

Pavlik didn't. He pulled his notepad from his jacket pocket and jotted something down.

I gave in. 'OK, so tell me.'

'The Buick's gas line had been disconnected. Someone tampered with the car so Kornell Eisvogel would stall.'

On the railroad tracks.

Six

'Wait a second,' I demanded. 'Couldn't the fuel line have "disconnected" in the crash?'

'You saw the car,' Pavlik said, standing up. 'The train T-boned it at the doors. The rest was pretty twisted, but intact.'

Unlike Eisvogel. 'Are you saying someone wanted the Buick stuck on the tracks? How could they be sure of achieving that?'

'The car would start and run until the gas was out of the line. Someone who knew what they were doing might be able to predict it by micro-measuring the fuel required.'

'And predict a train would come at that moment as well?'

'Trains have schedules. And we know this one was on time.'

'But no one could know when Kornell would...' I stopped.

'What?' Pavlik asked. Frank begged for a belly rub by pedaling all four paws in the air, but his good friend was otherwise occupied.

I tried to be logical. And chronological. 'The clock in the depot. If somebody knew what Kornell's routine was, it could have been set

60

back to make it seem like it was eight-oh-three, when it was really eight thirteen – just two minutes before the train would barrel through the Brookhills stop.'

Pavlik yielded to my groveling dog. If writhing on his back, rather than his stomach, could be considered 'groveling'. But I did get the impression my favorite sheriff was weaving what I'd guessed into what he'd established.

Pavlik said, 'That would explain your "lost ten minutes". But for you to be right, that same somebody had to go back into the station and reset the time before my team and the other responders got there.'

'Which makes the killing of Kornell Eisvogel diabolical.'

'Or at least a little goofy.' Pavlik's hand abandoned Frank's belly to draw his car keys from a pocket. 'There are easier, more certain ways to kill a person. Eisvogel was an old man. The killer could have hit him in the head or shot him through the heart.'

'But then you'd be sure it was homicide, a murder to be investigated.'

Pavlik shrugged. 'So shove him down the stairs. Or in front of a bus.'

'Yikes,' I said with a shiver. 'Remind me never to get on your bad side.'

'Too late,' Pavlik said, kissing the top of my head. 'And speaking of late, I'd better go.'

I stood up. 'Already?'

'Already? It's nearly midnight and I have an

early meeting.' He cupped my face in the hand without the keys. 'I'd like to see you tomorrow, but not at one of my crime scenes, *capice*?'

'You're not Italian.' I ignored his 'understand?'

'But as you may recall, I am a cunning linguist.' He kissed me on the lips, taking his time. How was it that hours after his morning shower, Pavlik could still smell like soap and aftershave?

'Old joke,' I managed, 'but I like the thought beneath it.'

'Me, too.' He pulled back. I was still standing on a step and Pavlik on the grass, so we were eye-to-eye. 'But you didn't answer my question.'

'I'd love to see you tomorrow.' I sounded chirpy, even to me.

'But not while looming over a dead body, understood?'

Stubborn male. 'Understood.' I was fairly certain I could keep that promise. After all, who stumbled over a corpse two days in a row?

'Great. I'll call you in the morning and we'll figure out what to do.' Another quick kiss and he was gone.

Frank sat up and looked at me.

'I know,' I said. 'I was hoping he'd stay over, too.'

I opened the door and Frank brushed past me and into the house, managing to sniff disdainfully at my jeans and ballet flats. It had been a long day. Pavlik may have managed to stay fresh, but I sported a fine sheen of sweat melding a patina of dust from the railroad bed.

'OK, so maybe I wasn't at my most alluring,' I admitted, following the dog inside. 'But you didn't exactly impress. What was all that licking about?'

Frank didn't bother to answer. Instead, he padded through the living room and into the kitchen. He bypassed his full water dish and nosed the empty food bowl.

'Sorry,' I told him. 'The vet says you'll get fat if I leave food out for you all day.'

Frank eyed me. When he turned away again, he laid one big, furry paw on the rim of the full water dish and flipped it.

'Petulance does *not* become you,' I said, grabbing a roll of paper towels.

The sheepdog apparently had forgiven me by the next morning, because I woke up pinned to the mattress by his head resting on my back.

'Get off me,' I said, struggling. 'The phone is ringing.'

Frank lifted his head to listen. I seized the opportunity to wriggle out from under and lunge for the phone.

'Hello?' Waiting for an answer, I pulled at the back of my T-shirt, which was sticking to me. I came away with a palmful of canine slobber. 'Oh, for God's sake—'

'Don't get your undies in a bundle,' Sarah's

63

voice said, 'I was just taking a snort of coffee.'

'I wasn't talking to you,' I said. 'The "for God's sake" was directed at my chronically salivating hound.' Frank was asleep again, now drooling on my pillow instead of me.

'You have to stop talking to that dog,' Sarah said. 'You treat him like a person.'

Actually, I treated him better than I treated *most* persons. But then, he didn't give me nearly as much shit.

At least the figurative kind.

'Listen, Maggy,' Sarah said. 'I want to meet with my cousin Ronny, the contractor, to talk about renovations at the depot.'

'Cousin? You mean Kornell Eisvogel's son? Isn't that a bit cold? His father died yesterday.'

'We have only a little more than three months to opening. Nobody else would do it in that time. Besides, you heard Kornell. There was no love lost between the two of them. It was step-mom/Auntie Vi who Ronny loved.'

Which explained why Sarah refused to call her aunt's husband 'uncle', but had no trouble referring to Kornell's son as 'cousin'. She actually *liked* Ronny.

'But we talked about this just yesterday – your being a new partner and all. We haven't had a chance to formalize the agreement or even—'

'Do you want to open Uncommon Grounds in the depot?'

'Yes, but—'

'Then this is a limited time offer.' Sarah looked at her watch. 'And it's going, going—'

'What time are we meeting your cousin?'

We settled on shooting for ten a.m. but when I pulled up in my Ford Escape, Sarah was already waiting in repose on the depot's porch.

'You're late,' she said, heaving herself out of the recliner.

'No, I'm not.' I held up my cellphone. 'It's ten on the nose.'

'Then Ronny is late.' Sarah dug in her pocket and came up with the skeleton key.

'Thirty seconds,' I said. 'He probably has things to do. His father died yesterday.'

'So did my uncle.' She turned the key in the door. 'And I'm here on time.'

'Right. *Now* play the uncle card. Yesterday you didn't want anything to do with him.'

'Yesterday he was a live pain in the ass. Today,' Sarah palmed the door open with a flourish, 'he's just an unpleasant memory.'

I can't claim to understand Sarah. But then, if I ever could, I'd really be worried.

A change of subject seemed in order. 'How much have you told your cousin?'

'I—'

'Hellllooo?' A slight man of about forty stuck his head in the door. 'You here, Cuz?'

Who calls anyone 'Cuz' anymore? Ronny, though, did look like a throwback of sorts. Slicked back hair, cleats on the heels of his shoes, comb in the back pocket of his too-tight jeans, bulge in the center-front of them. Oh, and a cardigan sweater.

West Side Story meets Mr Rogers.

The metal cleats made click-clack noises as Ronny crossed the wooden floor. I almost screamed 'You're going to scratch up the surface,' but managed to restrain myself. After all, if he did damage the wood, he could fix it. Secondly, it was hard to imagine any more damage than already had been done to the planks over the last century and a half.

Ronny gave Sarah a hug. She kept her elbows locked and air-kissed, but it still was the closest thing to a physical expression of affection I'd ever seen from my friend.

Ronny turned to me. 'You must be Maggy. I'm Sarah's cousin, Ronny Eisvogel.'

I took his hand. 'Thanks so much for coming out here to meet with us. This can't be the easiest time for you.'

Ronny's face saddened. 'First Auntie Vi, who was so good to me, and then my father. He and I weren't close, but it's hard to have both your parents pass inside a week.'

'Probably means we're next.' Sarah, Plain-spoken and Tall.

I assumed it was a joke, but I thought I knew what she meant. Parents and grandparents are a buffer between death and us. Once they're all gone, Sarah's logic was unavoidable: We'd be next.

'It's a good thing nobody else got hurt,' Ronny was saying. 'My father shouldn't have been driving.'

'Could your dad have had car trouble?' I was thinking about the disconnected fuel line.

'Beyond it being crumpled by a train at ramming speed?' Sarah asked.

Ronny apparently knew Sarah too well to take offense. A lifetime of her might do that. 'The last time I checked, the Buick was running fine,' Ronny said. 'In fact, my father took, like, fanatical care of his car.'

'Better than he treated most people,' Sarah grumbled.

'Maybe.' Ronny let that lie. 'But he managed to keep the thing up and running for nearly thirty years.'

'I understand you're a contractor,' I said, hypocritically wanting to steer the conversation away from speculation on the subject I had broached. So on to my thing: The new Uncommon Grounds. 'Has Sarah explained the time crunch we're under?'

'Yeah, but it's very workable.'

'We already have a kitchen here.' I led him behind the ticket windows and through a door.

The kitchen looked to be fairly new, if renovated within the past twenty years qualified. It was arranged, though, for a short-order operation. Griddle for eggs and bacon in the morning. Burgers and grilled cheese at noon. Baskets to cook French fries and onion rings in hot oil.

67

A blender for shakes, and a soft-serve ice cream dispenser.

'You had a coffeehouse, right?' Ronny surveyed the room. 'You thinking of expanding, like maybe into a restaurant?'

'And actually *cook*?' He might as well have asked if I was going to leap feet first into the deep fryer. Sarah wasn't the only one who lived on carryout. 'No, we need to stay with what we know. Coffee and pastries. Maybe packaged sandwiches and soup down the line.'

'But we're not going to pull all this equipment out, are we?' Sarah picked up a fry-basket. 'What if we change our minds?'

'I don't see it.'

My partner bristled at my offhand rejection, so I tried to soften it. 'We'll have mostly commuter traffic. People heading to work in downtown Milwaukee. They're not going to be coming back here for hamburgers, fries and a shake at noon.'

'No,' Sarah said, rubbing her chin. 'But maybe they'd like a hot breakfast sandwich.'

'True.' I looked at the griddle. 'We'd have to find someone who can cook.'

'Anyone can cook eggs,' Sarah said. 'Even me.'

Before I could raise an objection (such as, 'what about your real estate business?'), she continued. 'And we shouldn't forget the evening rush. There must be *some*thing we can sell them.'

'A nice glass of red wine,' I said. 'But we'd need a liquor license.'

Sarah pursed her lips. 'Just a limited one, though. Beer-and-wine type.'

Against my will, I was getting sucked into the possibilities. Then, 'Wait! I've got it.'

'What?' an eager Ronny said. He seemed as excited about this as Sarah and I. I like that in a contractor.

'We could sell prepared foods,' I suggested.

Sarah and Ronny exchanged looks.

'As opposed to, like ... raw?' Ronny asked.

'No. No, I mean we could have a hot food and deli counter, where people could pick up something for dinner to take home. That way, they wouldn't have to stop at the store or cook themselves.'

Sarah cocked her head. 'Great idea, but if you're worried about grilling a couple of breakfast sandwiches, how are we going to "prepare" your food?'

I'd been thinking about that, too. 'Luc and Tien.' Luc Romano and his daughter Tien had owned a grocery store and deli in the same ill-fated mall that Uncommon Grounds had occupied. And I knew first-hand that Luc was a great cook.

Sarah's eyebrows rose. 'Not a bad idea. Though I thought Tien wanted to do something else.'

'Luc *wanted* Tien to do something else,' I said. 'And Tien wanted Luc to be free to do

69

whatever he chose. Last time I talked to them, they both had realized they liked things the way they are. Or were.'

'That girl's never going to get married.'

I looked at career bachelorette Sarah. 'So?'

She shrugged. 'Point taken.'

'Maggy?' This was from Ronny, now standing on a chair, looking at the ceiling tiles. 'Do you have a blueprint of your old place? It'd help me understand what should maybe be in this new one.'

'Not a blueprint, really, but a diagram.' I pulled a folded legal-size sheet of paper from my handbag as he climbed down off the chair. 'Will this do?'

'Perfect,' he said, then checked his watch and fluttered the paper. 'I'd love to go over this and talk to you more today, since time is short. But...'

'We're here,' Sarah said. 'Let's do it.'

'I have to go to Brookhills Manor.' Ronny seemed apologetic. 'Get Auntie Vi's things and make arrangements for Dad's.' Hope suddenly floodlit his face. 'Unless somebody else wants to do it?'

Sarah's face, on the other hand, darkened.

Ronny continued enthusiastically. 'That way, I'd have an hour or so to look at Maggy's plans and do some sketches before you get back.'

I grabbed Sarah's arm. 'C'mon, I'll go with you.'

She shook me off. 'I hate that place. All those

70

old people.'

'We'll be "those old people" some day.'

'Some day, but not yet, thank God,' Sarah muttered.

'It's sure up to you,' said Ronny. 'But we're cutting it close the way it is. I'm willing to work weekends, but even so—'

Sarah knew when she'd been out-leveraged. 'Fine,' she snarled at her cousin, 'but you call them about your father's things. I'm just getting Aunt Vi's.'

She turned back to me. 'C'mon, depot-freak. Next stop, Geezerville.'

Seven

Unlike Sarah, I was looking forward to the visit, mostly because I hadn't seen one of my favorite people, Henry Wested, for a while.

With Uncommon Grounds closed, there was no place for our regular customers to gather. I wanted to make sure Henry hadn't gone over to the dark side. Or 'Mickey D's', as in McDonald's.

We entered Brookhills Manor through the main entrance, labeled 'The Villas'.

'Villas, my ass,' Sarah said. 'They're tiny little apartments with two windows and a kitchen you can't even turn around in.'

'I don't know,' I said as we moved through the foyer. 'Henry seems to like it here.'

'I'm sure he does. Auntie Vi said Henry and Sophie have been banging each other like bass drums.' Sophie Daystrom had been another regular at Uncommon Grounds.

Sarah related her gossip loudly enough for the ten or so seniors, sitting in chairs and participating in a quasi-exercise class, to stop in the middle of their shoulder shrugs.

The instructor, a young, dark-haired man,

glared at us.

'Sorry,' I said, holding up my hand. 'My friend didn't mean it.'

'Well then, she's an idiot,' the second old lady from the right said. 'Sophie's been in that man's room so much she might as well just shack up.'

'Damn right,' said the only man in the class. He looked like an albino prune. 'And more power to 'em, I say.'

That started everyone chattering and arguing. I grabbed Sarah's arm and pulled her to the main desk while the instructor tried to control the roaring – if still seated – mob.

'We're here about Vi and Kornell Eisvogel,' I told the teenage girl behind the desk.

'Kingston,' Sarah corrected me. 'Violet Kingston. She never took Kornell's last name.'

'Gotcha.' The girl took a wad of gum out of her mouth and tossed it in the wastebasket before turning to her computer. 'Vi and – can you spell the Colonel's name for me?'

'Not "colonel",' Sarah said. 'Kornell: K-O-R-N-E-L-L.'

'Oh,' said the girl, 'like the Russian version of Cornell University.'

'Yeah,' I said before Sarah blew a gasket. 'Like that.'

'Sweet. We are the world, right?' She typed into her computer. 'Kingston and ... E-I-S-V-O-G-E-L.'

Through clenched teeth, Sarah said, 'You got it.'

The girl swiveled back to us. 'Sorry to tell you, but they're both, ah, no longer with us.'

'Yeah, like that'd be a novelty here,' Sarah snapped. 'We didn't come to visit them. We want their stuff.'

The girl's face almost relaxed. 'The old people have been dropping like flies around here. I just don't like to tell the...' She waved her fingers at us.

'Family?' I supplied.

'Yeah, that.' She unwrapped a new stick of gum and plopped it into her mouth.

'Did your chewing gum lose its flavor?' Sarah asked, quoting the old Lonnie Donnegan song.

Miss Information gave Sarah a curious look, like she recognized the line. 'Isn't that part of a legend or something?'

'Greek mythology,' Sarah said solemnly. 'I'm Goddess of the Juicy Fruit and she's my spearmint-carrier.'

I cleared my throat. 'Is there someone we can talk to about the property of the ... deceaseds?'

'Sure.' The girl wisely dropped the lesson in mythology gone awry and yanked a couple of lanyards with 'GUEST' passes dangling from them out of her drawer. 'Put these on and take that hallway.' She pointed to a sign that read 'Sunrise Wing'.

Plucking the second piece of gum from her mouth, she dropped it in the basket, too. 'When you get to the end of the hall, you'll see Mr Levitt's office. He's the social worker.'

74

'Thank you,' I said as we turned away. No wonder the kid was working so young. Had to support her gum habit.

I peered down the corridor. There was a window at the far end. 'I guess we should just walk to the light.' I slapped a hand over my mouth. 'Sorry. Didn't mean that.'

Sarah threw me her practiced, sidelong glance as we started down the hall. 'The hell you didn't.'

'I ... OK, maybe I did. But it wasn't nice of me.'

'C'mon, let's get this over with.' Sarah hustled me to the end of the corridor. There was nothing there but the window we'd seen and a right-angle turn.

'I guess we just keep going,' I said. Two more turns later, we were still walking.

'How in the hell do the old coots manage this?' Sarah said as we approached our fourth blind corner. 'Even *I'm* disoriented and exhausted.'

As she spoke, a leg encased in a pink plaster cast rounded the corner, coming fast. The leg was attached to a tiny woman projecting a scent of flowers and driving a candy-apple red motorized wheelchair with a joystick.

'Coming through!' she yelled, laying on her horn and glaring at us from under thick white bangs. She reminded me a little of Frank the sheepdog driving a bumper car.

The woman brandished her plaster cast like a

tank's cannon barrel. Sarah and I parted like the Red Sea, me ducking into the doorway of a stairwell and my friend seeking refuge behind a potted palm.

'Next time be more aware of your surroundings,' NASCAR Granny yelled as she left us behind in a floral-scented cloud.

Sarah brushed palm fronds out of her hair. 'I told you this place was—'

Just then, another plaster ankle swung around the corner.

'Take cover,' Sarah ordered. 'They must travel in packs.' She and I dove for our lives. Or, at least, our skeletal integrity.

'Hello?'

I stuck my head warily into the corridor. 'Sophie? Is that you?'

Sophie Daystrom sat in a wheelchair, cast on one elevated leg. Unlike the last chair, though, this one wasn't motorized. Instead, Henry Wested shuffled behind, propelling the chair onward.

Sarah emerged from behind her chosen palm and gestured at Sophie's leg. 'What happened to you?'

'I should ask you the same damn thing,' Sophie said. 'What are you doing to that plant?'

'Don't underestimate the allure of inter-species love.' I plucked a palm frond from Sarah's hair as she gave me a very sour look. 'We were hiding from a nasty woman in a wheelchair.'

'Must've been Clara Huseby,' Henry said, tipping his gray fedora to us. 'Was it a powered model?'

'Over-powered, more like it,' Sarah said, checking her hair for any other flora. 'The woman's a menace.'

'She lost her husband last year,' Henry said. As a long-time resident, he probably functioned as the place's archivist.

And, apparently, had shared the information with Sophie, who tended to be less charitable. 'That's no excuse,' Sophie said. 'My husband died, too, but I didn't turn into a kleptomaniac.'

'Kleptomaniac?' I asked. 'Doesn't that take finesse? How stealthy can a woman in a leg cast and wheelchair be?'

'Stealthy enough to ambush us at a blind corner,' Sarah said dryly.

She had me on that one. 'But where does Mrs Huseby shoplift? And how does she get there?'

I was imagining NASCAR Granny motoring across Poplar Creek Road to prey upon the drugstore down the block.

'Here at the Manor, I'm afraid,' Henry said. 'Rumor has it she glides silently into rooms when they're empty and pilfers toiletries and other sundries. Then she hides them in her lap-robe and backs right out.'

'Genius,' said Sophie, shaking her head in what seemed like reluctant appreciation.

'Sophie,' Henry warned.

'But wrong,' his main squeeze allowed. 'Very,

very wrong.'

Sophie rolled herself closer to Sarah. 'Your Aunt Vi was Clara's favorite mark. Vi was certain the woman was filching her silken petals.'

'Huseby stole my aunt's fake ... flowers?'

Since taking somebody's 'silken petals' sounded more like *de*-flowering to me, I just kept my mouth shut.

'No. No, even worse.' Sophie's voice dropped to a whisper. 'Her body powder, Silken Petals. I think that's just sick – don't you, Henry?'

He tugged at his collar, though he wore no necktie. 'Well, yes, I suppose so.'

That explained the blossom cloud enveloping NASCAR Granny, aka Klepto Clara. She was wearing her ill-gotten booty.

'The woman parades around, smelling of Silken Petals,' Sophie said. 'The real designer version, mind you. Not some knock-off. Clara has brass, you have to give her that.'

Again, that touch of grudging admiration in the voice.

Henry cleared his throat – theatrically so – and Sophie flushed.

I decided to change the subject. 'So you didn't explain, Sophie. What happened to you?'

'I fell out of bed,' she admitted. 'They have to make those damn things with rails if they're going to frickin' cater to the active senior.'

Four-foot-eleven Sophie had never been mistaken for Mother Teresa, but her language was bluer than her hair these days.

'The "active" senior?' I asked.

She threw back her shoulders and pushed out her breasts, which seemed to ride unnaturally high. 'Sexually, that is.'

No wonder they were the talk of the exercise class. I liked both Sophie and Henry, but I really didn't want to picture them being ... 'active'.

Sarah, on the other hand, appeared to be perking up. She pointed at Sophie's boobs. 'Are those new?'

'Nah,' Sophie said. 'I couldn't afford that, and neither could Henry, much as I'm sure he'd enjoy them.'

She twisted around in the chair to wink at Henry, who had a pained smile on his face. 'I just shortened my bra straps.' She pulled on the straps to illustrate, making her breasts dance like roly-poly marionettes.

'Smart thinking,' Sarah said in response to Sophie's preening. 'They look great.'

Sophie turned to me.

'Perky,' I managed.

Satisfied with our reaction, she settled back. 'So, what in blazes are you two doing in the Sunrise Wing? It's like that Hotel California. You can check out, but you can never leave.'

'Heh-heh.' The sound came from Henry. We all turned to look at him.

'Sorry,' he said, holding up his hand. 'She breaks me up sometimes.'

I loved that they both knew the Eagles.

'Then why are you here? Physical therapy?' I

asked. Despite the amount of time Sophie might spend at the Manor, I knew she had a home in Brookhills.

'Rehab,' she said. 'But Medicare won't pay anymore, so I have to get out of here.'

'To where, though?' I asked. 'Can you get around well enough to go back home?'

Sophie hooked a thumb at Henry. 'I'm selling my place and shacking up with him. We're going to follow our muse and live in sin.'

Henry blushed. Given the quiet, straight-arrow image he'd always projected at our coffeehouse, I was relieved the top of his skull hadn't blown off.

Time – no, *past* time – to go. 'We'd love to hear more,' I said quickly, 'but Sarah has to pick up her Aunt Vi's things.'

Henry threw me a grateful look.

'Such a blasted shame that was,' Sophie said. 'She was about as lively as they come. In my Red Hat group. Went out every day.'

'Which was her undoing,' Henry contributed ominously.

'Why?' I turned to Sarah. 'How did your aunt die?'

'I told you,' Sarah said. 'Kornell dropped her off at a store and pulled away too quickly. She had her hand on the door handle and fell.'

'Broke her hip,' Sophie said. 'A week later, she was worm food.'

'Pneumonia,' Henry pronounced. 'The enemy of the elderly.'

'Right,' said Sarah. 'Can we please get going?'

Having been reminded of our mission, she seemed impatient to get it done. And us out.

'Be nice,' I hissed at her under my breath.

'Nah, don't bother,' Sophie said as Henry started to push the chair again. 'Nobody here is nice. We live this long, we figure we can say whatever damn well comes into our heads.'

And with a wave of her hand, the lovebirds departed.

Contrary to Sophie Daystrom's assessment, Mr Levitt, the Manor's social worker, seemed nice.

'Please sit a bit,' he said, waving us into the two visitors' chairs across the desk from his own.

He took off horned-rimmed glasses and set them on the calendar that covered the small portion of his desk not piled high with file folders. 'I'm glad you found your way over here. This place is a labyrinth, especially since we added the Sunrise Wing. We prefer to have everything on one floor – for the wheelchairs, you know – but that means the building has to sprawl a scosh.'

'A scosh,' Sarah echoed with a straight face.

I elbowed her. 'We met one of the wheelchairs on the way here. Candy-apple-red, motorized model?'

'Ah, yes. Clara Huseby. A charming woman.'

Great, Mr Levitt was both nice *and* delu-

81

sional. I thought maybe I should set him straight before Klepto Clara added vehicular manslaughter to her Manor rap sheet.

'I'm certain she is,' I started. 'But with the speed of the wheelchair and that battering ram of a leg sticking out, she nearly flattened us coming around the corner.'

'Really?' Mr Levitt's face had changed from friendly to blank. That shade called 'wary of a lawsuit'.

'Really,' I said. 'I thought you'd want to know.' I considered telling him about the stealing, but I had that only via hearsay – and Sophie's hearsay, at that.

'She's a thief, too,' Sarah offered. 'Check her lap-robe sometime.'

'I'll do that,' Levitt said shortly. 'Now, though, back to *your* business?'

The placing of the emphasis on 'your' was nicely done, I thought. And fair as well.

'I'm so sorry about Mr Eisvogel,' Levitt continued. 'It's as if they couldn't live without each other. First, Vi went and then Kornell – what, a week later?'

'Let's call it a scosh,' Sarah said. This time I didn't elbow her. Let the social worker defend himself. 'My cousin Ronny said you had some of my Auntie Vi's things. He asked me to pick them up.'

'Yes. Yes, of course.' Levitt stood up and went to a closet behind his desk. When he opened the door, I saw that the shelves were lined with stuffed grocery bags, recycled from various area stores. Waste not, want not.

Levitt ran his finger along the top shelf, then the next, searching for just the right sack. On the third level, he found what he was looking for. An over-stuffed grocery bag from Schultz's Market.

'Ah, here it is.' Levitt set it on the desk.

I pointed at the closet. 'All personal effects?'

'Yes. Not everyone has a family member, or at least one who cares enough to claim them.' He shrugged.

'Lot of turnover, huh?' From Sarah, naturally.

Levitt shot her a questioning look. 'In the staff?'

'I think she means in the patients.' I was trying to be helpful again. 'You know, by dying?'

'*We* prefer to call the people living here at Brookhills Manor "residents". Even those who are in Sunrise, which is what we call the skilled nursing section, prefer not to be referred to as "patients".'

'*Or* coots,' I whispered to Sarah.

Unfortunately, Mr Levitt had especially good hearing, and sat up straighter. 'We would never call our residents "coots", Ms Thorsen, and I'd appreciate it if you didn't either. Or thieves, for that matter.'

'I wasn't,' I stammered, 'I mean, I didn't...'

Sarah stood up, grabbed the grocery bag and handed it to me to carry. 'Yeah, Maggy, keep your nasty thoughts to yourself.' She stuck out her hand to Mr Levitt. 'Thanks so much for everything. My cousin Ronny will be in touch to clean out his father's apartment.'

'Good, good,' Levitt said, following us to the door. 'We have a new resident eagerly awaiting it.'

'How did I turn into the bad guy?' I asked Sarah as we made our way down the long hall back to the Manor's front entrance.

'You shouldn't call people names,' Sarah said, sniffing the air. 'Ugh. This place reeks of disinfectant and dead flowers.'

I slowed as we approached the first blind corner. 'Lysol and bouquets are better than the alternative, don't you think?'

'If you're referring to stale urine,' Sarah said, wrinkling her nose, 'I can smell that, too.'

'I suppose the spray products and cleaners can mask only so much.' I rounded the corner and then stopped dead.

Sarah rear-ended me. 'Geez, what's the matter? The crazy coot in the motorized wheelchair is long gone.'

'Gone, yes,' I said. 'But I don't think all that long.'

On the floor in front of us was the motorized chair, one wheel still revolving. The other one was twenty feet down the hallway, as though the chair had hurled it like a horse throws a shoe.

Klepto Clara, though, was still in her saddle,

seat belt tight, eyes glazed open, hand on the reins – or, in this case, the throttle of her candy-apple-red wheelchair.

Eight

Add the vacant eyes to smells that even the cloud of pilfered body powder couldn't mask and what do you have?

Dead Clara 'Klepto' Huseby.

I stayed with the body while Sarah backtracked to Mr Levitt's office. As I waited, I noticed something wedged under one arm of the wheelchair, partially hidden by the lap-robe Henry had mentioned.

I stepped around the chair to get a better look, but I still couldn't make out what it was. Likely something else the woman had stolen. I moved the blanket a smidge.

Ah, yes. A crushed blue cardboard box, denture-cleaning tablets spilling out of it, and a used bar of Ivory soap. Proof of Klepto Clara's thievery. Now let Levitt deny—

'May I ask what you think you're doing?' Levitt had skidded to a stop around the corner, followed by Sarah.

'I "think" I'm confirming what we told you.' I pointed at the Efferdent and Ivory. 'The woman was a thief.'

'You mean the poor resident lying dead at

your feet?'

'Yes, the very one,' I said, feeling sheepish. Crowing over thievery seemed a little petty, given the mortal circumstances.

I stepped back, letting the lap-robe fall. 'You could be right. Maybe Mrs Huseby had just come from the bathroom.'

'Which is why she has a family portrait on her?' Sarah pointed at a plastic-framed photo I'd missed, half-hidden under the leg cast.

'Oh, dear,' said Mr Levitt, salvaging the picture. 'Mrs Chin has been looking for this.'

Sure enough, the posed portrait featured an elderly Asian woman surrounded by a family. Her *Asian* family.

'Are you accusing this "poor resident" lying dead "at your feet", of thievery?'

Levitt was saved from answering by the avalanche of nurses and aides in sherbet-colored scrubs descending on us.

Since this was an unattended death, I wasn't surprised when deputies arrived shortly thereafter, along with an ambulance crew. I *was* surprised, though, when the sheriff himself showed up twenty minutes later.

By this time, at the suggestion of Levitt, Sarah and I had retreated to the employee cafeteria.

The 'cafeteria' was more closet than room, with a concrete floor, folding tables and vending machines. Sarah had a two-pack of Pop-Tarts and I was drinking a Fresca. The bag containing Auntie Vi's things sat on top of a table.

'What do your deputies do?' I asked Pavlik when he tracked us down. 'Call you when they see me?'

I was a little irritated. A normal person could stumble over a body without having their 'other' – significant or not – know it.

Pavlik looked like he had intended to deny it, but changed his mind. 'Oh, what the hell. Yeah, they call me.'

He glanced at the can in my hand. 'I didn't know they still made Fresca.'

'It's probably been here since 1972,' Sarah said, proffering her snack. 'Pop-Tart?'

'No, thanks,' Pavlik started, then amended his answer. 'Wait a second. Is it the kind with the pink frosting?'

'Will you two stop?' I demanded. Then, turning to Pavlik. 'Are you having your deputies spy on me?'

'Of course not.' Pavlik had a mouthful of Sarah's Pop-Tart. Yes. I know it sounds dirty. 'They do it on their own.'

'Why?'

'It amuses them.' Pavlik gestured toward my hand. 'Can I have a swig of your Fresca?'

I handed him the thing. 'And you? Do you think it's funny?'

'Not so much.' Pavlik gave me back my Fresca. 'The social worker,' he took a pad from his jacket pocket and consulted his notes, 'one

Lloyd Levitt, says you had an earlier run-in with Mrs Huseby.'

'We both did,' Sarah offered from the vending machine, where she was going for seconds. 'That was the last Frosted Strawberry. How about Brown Sugar Cinnamon?'

'No Chocolate?' Pavlik joined her.

'Will you two pause long enough in your trip down Junk Food's Memory Lane to let me explain?' I stood. 'Klepto Clara ... I mean, Mrs Huseby came around the corner fast and nearly hit us on our way to see Levitt. I simply told him so he could slow her down before someone got hurt. Which they did.'

No reaction. I pointed to the vending machine. 'How about the Blueberry?'

'Ugh,' they said in unison.

'Fine.' I threw up my hands. 'If no one is listening to me on *any* topic, I'm heading home.'

'We're listening to you.' Sarah deposited coins in the slot. 'Just not about flavor options on Pop-Tarts.' She pushed a button and a foil packet slid down. Sarah pulled it out of the bin.

'You're saying Levitt should have done something?' Pavlik asked, watching her.

'To be fair,' I said, 'he wouldn't have had time to track Clara Huseby down before she took her spill and we found her.'

'Levitt's suggesting that you may have taken matters into your own hands.' Pavlik accepted a Tart from Sarah.

I couldn't believe it. 'Levitt thinks we tipped

over an old lady's wheelchair?'

'Nah. More like purposely ran her into the rail.' Pavlik gestured out the door at the wooden bar that was attached to the wall on both sides of the corridor, presumably to provide support for those unsteady on their feet. Or to protect the walls from wheelchairs gone wild.

'And you honestly buy that?'

'Nah.' The sheriff took a bite of Pop-Tart. 'He's just looking for someone to blame because he's worried about the liability issues. Maybe they didn't maintain the wheelchair properly.'

'Well,' I said, more relieved than I wanted to admit, 'I'm glad you know me better than that.'

'Yeah.' He was chewing. 'Besides, the surveillance video shows the wheel flew off the chair as Huseby took the corner.'

I smacked him lightly on the arm and the Pop-Tart flew out of his hand and across the room.

'My Pop-Tart,' Pavlik said, looking forlornly at his empty palm.

I'd actually assaulted the sheriff. 'I'm sorry. It's just that you were trying to scare me. On purpose.' I began scrabbling through my purse for spare change. 'Want me to buy you another?'

'Nah,' Pavlik said, tugging half a thin napkin out of the aluminum dispenser on one of the tables. 'I have to get going anyway.'

'So what did you come here for?' I asked. 'Just to haze me?'

'Exactly.' He kissed me on the lips. 'My guys do that to me. I figured I – and you – should see how it feels.'

'And how does it feel?' I said, running my fingers down his arm.

He took my hand and kissed the heel of it. 'Feels just fine.'

Then he hooked my Fresca and left.

We'd forgotten Auntie Vi's bag, so I ran back in to get it while Sarah went to start the car. I reached the cafeteria just in time to see Mrs Huseby's body rolled on a gurney toward the back door.

Demoralizing, to say the least, for members of the exercise class to see their inevitable fate wheeled past them and out the front door. The hell with the shoulder shrugs and arm circles – let's break out beer and potato chips.

When I returned to the Firebird, I stashed the Schultz's sack in the trunk, trying not to suck in a lungful of the exhaust that billowed out of the car's tail-pipe. Models as old as Sarah's didn't have to pass emissions checks like the ones built after 1995. More's the pity.

Still holding my breath, I slammed the trunk lid closed. The thing bounced back up at me. Like its owner, the Firebird had some eccentricities.

I stuck my head out of the exhaust cloud, took a cleanish breath and then went back in. This time, I lowered the trunk lid gently. When it reached the latch, I pressed down firmly. Success.

'Good car,' I said, patting its tail light.

As I climbed into the passenger seat, two seniors hobbled past. Sarah drummed her fingers impatiently on the steering wheel as she waited to back out. 'Talk about a wasted morning.'

I checked my cellphone for the time. 'Morning and early afternoon. It's nearly one thirty. Do you think your cousin will still be at the depot?'

'Sure. Ronny is dependable – too dependable, I always thought. Probably from living with Kornell and doing what he was told. I doubt Ronny would even think to leave.'

A back-hand compliment coming from anyone else. For Sarah, though, it was high praise. Hell, any praise escaping her was high praise.

'Well, we certainly have an excuse for being late.' I rolled down the window and stuck my elbow out into the fresh air. 'Who could expect to have someone die practically in front of us?'

I saw Sarah roll her eyes.

'What?' I asked.

'Please.' She looked sideways at me. 'That ... repository is God's Waiting Room, crammed with hundreds of people, just months, days or even hours away from the perpetual vacation. And I took you, Brookhills' own Angel of Death, there. I should have known better.' She jammed the transmission into reverse.

I thought that was unfair. I also thought a change of subject was in order. 'I'm confused. Levitt said that stuff I put in the trunk was from your aunt's room. Didn't your aunt and uncle live together there?'

'Sure,' Sarah said. The pair of seniors behind the Firebird had finally cleared the driver's side bumper, so she started to back out. Cautiously. 'Until Auntie Vi broke her hip and had to go to "Sunrise".' She laughed. 'Should have named it "Sunset". Or "Lights Out". Even Sophie's lucky to still be alive.'

'Oh, come on,' I said. 'I'm sure lots of people recover and go on to live productive "autumns".'

Sarah slammed on her brakes as a man walking a fat wiener dog crossed diagonally behind us. 'Recover?' she demanded. 'You don't recover from being old. You die. We all do.'

Sarah stared over the steering wheel. 'People leave us. It's just a question of when.'

'Geez. You talk about me being "Little Mary Sunshine",' I said. 'Are you OK?'

She finished backing out of the parking spot and barreled straight across the intersection to Junction Road.

'Sarah?' I tried again.

She slowed the Firebird as we approached the railroad tracks. After we rumbled over them, Sarah took a quick left and eased into an angle parking spot, nose-in to the depot.

It was only when we'd come to a complete

stop that she turned to me. 'Courtney and Sam want to visit their cousins for the summer.'

A little over a year ago, Sarah had become the guardian for our friend Patricia's two children after Patricia's death. Sam and Courtney were now both in high school and Sarah, who'd never so much as babysat, had turned out to be a much better 'mom' than anyone had ever expected.

However, a whole summer without them now? Sarah would go crazy.

'What cousins?' I asked. 'I thought Sam and Courtney didn't have family.'

'Not on their father's side, but Patricia's mother was married a bunch of times.'

'Only, as I recall, Grandma didn't want anything to do with her daughter's kids.'

'True.' Sarah took her foot off the brake in preparation for getting out of the Firebird and we started to roll toward the building.

'We're still moving,' I warned, opening my door and dragging a foot, like I was going to be able to stop the vehicle.

Sarah slammed on the brakes and I grabbed the buffering dashboard to keep from flying out with the door as it swung wildly. No passenger-side airbags on this baby.

Sarah set the parking brake, then looked at me like nothing had happened. 'You were saying?'

I had to think for a second before I realized we were talking about Courtney and Sam's family. Or lack of same. 'We agreed that Patricia's mother had no interest in the kids. Did something change?'

'Not with Patsy – that's Patricia's mother. But she has a second daughter.'

Wait a minute. 'The mother named Patricia after her*self*?'

Sarah shrugged. 'Men do it all the time and nobody thinks it's weird.'

She was right. I'd have to give that some thought another time.

'So Patricia had a sister?' I asked. 'And that means Sam and Courtney have a blood aunt?'

'And cousins. A boy and a girl, wouldn't you know it? The boy is a little younger than Courtney and the girl is a year older than Sam.'

Sam, by my calculations, was seventeen and Courtney, fourteen. 'So how did you find all this out?'

'I didn't.' Sarah climbed out of the Firebird. 'The kids found each other on Facebook. They've been e-mailing or twitting or whatever the hell they call—'

'Tweeting,' I offered as I hoisted myself out of the bucket seat. 'Eric keeps telling me I need to do it, but I don't see the point. If people want to know what I'm doing, they can just call me. I have a cellphone and text messaging. As far as I'm concerned, that already makes me far too accessible and—'

'Do you mind?' Sarah grew cranky. 'We were talking about me. For once.'

That was a little rude. True. But rude, none-theless.

'Sorry,' I said, biting my tongue. 'You were saying Courtney, Sam and their two cousins have been in touch by e-mail and Twit—'

'Yeah, yeah, that,' Sarah said impatiently. 'Anyway, they've been communicating about six months now and their Aunt Patrice—'

My turn to interrupt. 'Patsy bore two daughters, Patricia and Patrice?'

'And one son.'

'Don't tell me. She named him Patrick.'

'No. Bert.'

'After the father?' I asked.

'Who knows?' Sarah exploded. 'For all I care, they watched Sesame Street and he has a twin named Ernie. Now, can I continue?'

'Sure. Sorry.'

'Anyway, Patrice seems a nice enough woman, I guess, and they want Sam and Court-ney to spend the summer with them on Cape Cod.'

'Cape Cod? Well, that's ... unobjectionable, isn't it?'

'I suppose.'

I didn't respond right away because I had closed my car door and was looking at the depot. This side, the facade that faced the train tracks, had a large plate glass window, probably for train watching. The boarding platform was to the rear of the building – the left side as we faced it – with the wrap-around porch ending where the platform began.

I turned to my friend. 'You've checked them out, right? You're sure they are who they claim to be?'

I was thinking about online predators. Someone could pretend to be anybody. In a well-publicized case, a young girl thought she was applying for a nanny job, only to be greeted at the door of a nice house by a supremely *not* nice man with a gun. She never left.

'I'm sure of Patrice and her kids.' Sarah stepped back on to the tracks and pretended to survey the building.

'Be careful,' I said. 'We don't need another casualty.'

Sarah didn't answer.

I studied my friend. 'So what are you worried about? Sam and Courtney will have a nice summer with their cousins and be back with all sorts of stories to tell.'

'If they come back,' Sarah muttered, kicking at one of the rails.

Ah, that was it. 'You're afraid they'll like living on Cape Cod so much they won't want to return to Brookhills.'

But Sarah's face was stony. 'Sam has two more semesters of high school after this, then he'll leave for college. Courtney will take off three years after that. One way or the other, they'll both leave.'

Sarah shrugged. 'And I say good riddance.'

I smacked her one.

Nine

'Don't be a weenie.' I was leading the way around the depot building to the porch. 'When I used to play tag with my older brothers, I knew they would catch me eventually, so I'd just sit down. I let them tag me to get it over with.'

'Nice analogy.' Sarah stomped up the steps. 'But you're calling *me* the weenie?'

'I was *four* years old,' I said. 'You're forty—'

'—ish,' Sarah finished. She tried the door. Unlocked.

'Ronny?' she called from the threshold. 'Where are you?'

I said, 'Avoiding the subject isn't going to change the way you're feeling,' following her in. 'You're suffering empty-nest syndrome, but Courtney and Sam aren't even gone yet. In fact, you want to shove them out of the nest, so they won't have the satisfaction of flying away on their own.'

'Thanks, Dr Phil,' Sarah said, 'but that's ridiculous. I was fine before they came. In fact—'

'Here I am.' Ronny appeared from behind the ticket windows and looked back and forth between us. 'Is everything all right?'

'Sure,' Sarah said quickly.

Except for the fact his father was smashed by a train and we'd just come from the nursing home with his stepmother's meager personal effects. Oh, and then there was Klepto Clara, deceased as well.

'We were just talking about Sarah's wards,' I explained. 'Sorry to be late, but one of the ... residents at Brookhills Manor died. Everything was fine, though, with Mr Levitt.'

Besides him suspecting us of chair-hicular homicide.

'Just call Levitt and he'll let you into Kornell's apartment to clear it out,' Sarah said.

'No need. I have a key.' Ronny was looking at his cousin with concern. 'You said, "before they came". Is something wrong with Sam and Courtney?'

Of course Ronny would know them. Sarah and he might not share a blood parent, but the cousins were family after all.

'Nope,' Sarah said, holding up her hands as if to deflect any further conversation. 'They're just visiting mom's-side relatives for the summer.'

'That's great,' Ronny said, a smile lighting his face. He wasn't a bad-looking guy, despite his quirky taste in dress. 'Are they staying with their cousins on Cape Cod?'

Sarah scowled at him. 'How'd you know that?'

'Facebook.' Ronny shrugged. 'They're very excited about going and I'm glad you're letting them.'

'She doesn't want to,' I said, and Sarah threw me a dirty look. I didn't want to betray her, but I thought Ronny, who had lived with his father and stepmother, might be able to reassure her.

I proved right.

'They *will* come back,' he said. 'And they won't stop loving you because you're not "blood". Your aunt took me in, just like you did for Sam and Courtney.'

He turned to me. 'My mother remarried after the divorce. I was seven and not getting along with my new stepfather. Vi insisted that I come live with them when she and Kornell married. God knows where I'd be today without that woman.' He used the back of his hand to wipe his eyes. 'Sarah, it's the same for you, with Sam and Courtney.'

'Fine,' Sarah said, never one for sentimentality. 'They'll go. They'll come back. They'll still love me.'

She waved her hand at the ticket counter in front of us. 'Now can we talk about getting this place open by September?'

'Of course.' Ronny reached through the center ticket window and picked up a pad of yellow, lined paper lying on the counter beyond it. On top of his pad was the diagram of Uncommon Grounds I'd left with him.

'From what I can tell,' he said, 'you had

seating for twelve to fifteen people in your old store.'

'Between the cafe tables and counter, yes,' I answered, looking around me with a critical eye. 'I'm hoping, though, that we can get more in here.'

Ronny made a note. 'That shouldn't be a problem, if you're certain you need them. Are you planning on tables outside as well?'

I nodded. 'Yes, but those will only give us seating for the warmer months.' Which in Wisconsin, meant late May through early September. If we were lucky.

'But didn't you say most of our business will be takeout?' Sarah asked. 'Commuters buying something to have for lunch at work and, in the evening, picking up something for dinner at home? *That's* not seasonal.'

'Do you want counter seating?' Ronny asked.

I gestured toward the large window on the side facing the tracks. 'I'd love a counter running the entire length of that wall.' I turned to Sarah, remembering, finally, to include her. 'What do you think?'

Sarah flushed with pleasure. Under all that bluster and crust, she was still the kid who'd been picked last for volleyball in elementary school, so she was secretly thrilled to be included in anything.

And I could identify. I was picked second last. Unless Cyndi Luckwood was sick. Then *I* was dead last.

'What about the part of the wall with no window?' Sarah asked. Then she snapped her fingers. 'I know. We can put electrical sockets and a work area there, so people can plug in their computers and not be distracted by a changing view.'

'Perfect,' I said. 'And we'll have Wi-Fi!'

Sarah and I high-fived, like we'd just nosed-out Al Gore for 'inventing' the Internet. Her eyes narrowed. 'Wait a second. I thought you hated the cyber-cafes like HotWired. You said you wanted people to talk, not type.'

HotWired, a chain of Internet cafes, had been our chief competition in town until ... well, that's another story. Point is, though, HotWired was no more.

'That was because I hated the owner of Hot-Wired, Marvin LaRoche,' I added for Ronny's benefit. 'Besides, whether it's typing or texting or tweeting, people are going to be clacking away. Who are we to stop them?'

'And, better yet, why not profit from it?' Sarah added.

'Amen,' I said, wholeheartedly.

As if on cue, my cellphone rang. Pavlik.

'I'm looking for Sarah,' he said without preamble. 'Is she with you?'

'Sarah?' Call me silly, but I'd hoped he was calling my cellphone to talk to his principal *squeeze*. 'Why?'

'So she's there?'

Sarah mouthed, 'Who's that?'

102

'The sheriff,' I said aloud. 'He wants to know if you're here.'

'Maggy...' There was a warning tone in the voice coming from the phone.

I'd pushed Pavlik as far as I dared, so I handed the phone to Sarah.

'Hello?'

I couldn't hear Pavlik's voice anymore. Just my luck he didn't practice 'cell-yell'.

'No, she didn't tell me.' Sarah fixed on my eyes.

'Tell you what?' I whispered.

Sarah ignored me. Vocally, I mean. She was shooting darts out of *her* eyes, though. 'No, this is the first I've heard about someone messing with my uncle's car.'

Sarah listened again. Then, 'The clock? No, why would I touch—'

My mind was racing. The police must have decided the clock *had* been reset, despite Pavlik's skepticism. If they'd tested it and found Sarah's fingerprints...

'But you did touch it,' I burst out. 'You straightened the clock on the wall, remember?'

That got me another sour look and a hissed, 'Shut up!'

So I did.

'What's going on?' Ronny asked. I'd forgotten Sarah's cousin was still with us. I wanted to explain, but I wasn't sure how much I could or should tell him.

I was saved from my ethical dilemma by

Sarah, who handed me the phone. Evidently Pavlik had finished with her and it was my turn.

'Hello?'

'I'm surprised Sarah didn't know about her uncle's car.'

'I didn't know if you'd told me in confidence,' I protested. 'You know, pillow-talk?'

'More like porch-talk,' Pavlik said. 'But in this case, the information is public. It appeared in the paper this morning.'

So how was I supposed to know that?

Sarah was angry because I hadn't filled her in. On the other hand, if I'd blabbed about something Pavlik told me in private, he'd be upset. Result: Damned if I did, damned if I didn't.

'Maybe you should flag our conversations, private and not,' I said to the sheriff. 'Just so I know what to keep to myself?'

'I don't tell you anything that I'd regret getting around.'

Well, *that* was a little insulting. 'I do know how to keep a secret, you know.'

'I'm sure you do.' Pavlik's tone implied he didn't have enough personal anecdotal evidence to judge. 'But I wouldn't put you, or myself for that matter, in that position. Not about something that has to do with my job. I have a public responsibility, a duty.'

I took a moment to imagine what day-to-day life would be like with Pavlik. Our breakfast conversations. Soccer moms and coffee drinks could carry a couple only so far. And if Pavlik wasn't going to share, why should I keep him informed about Brookhills and its denizens?

I lowered my voice. 'So, you tell me only things I can repeat?'

'Sometimes I *want* you to spread the word.'

Maggy the pawn. He was using me as a cat's paw. A reverse snitch.

Not that I hadn't done the same thing, on occasion. Like when I informed Laurel Birmingham, our town clerk, that Ted and I had divorced. Seemed easier than telling people individually and Laurel could disseminate the word quicker than high-speed Internet. That very night three people brought over casseroles and wine. Lots of wine, God bless them.

I sighed. 'Fair enough, Pavlik. So, can you tell me, for public distribution, whether the clock had Sarah's fingerprints on it? Because if it does,' I added hastily as I saw her face contort, 'I can explain that.'

I held up my hand, palm-out, to Sarah as a 'Stop' sign. 'The clock was crooked when we came in and she straightened it.'

I declared it with a self-satisfied smile, but Sarah didn't look relieved.

'Good to know,' Pavlik's voice said. 'But we haven't fingerprinted it yet.'

'Why?' I asked. 'It's just metal and glass. Those surfaces tend to hold latents.' I know my forensics. I do watch TV, after all.

'And they would,' said Pavlik. 'If the clock

hadn't been missing when we went back to get it.'

I turned to look at the depot's wall.

Sure enough. Between Seattle and New York was a gaping hole where the Brookhills' time-piece had been.

Ten

'I noticed the clock was missing when I came in. I just figured you knew about it.' Ronny was trying to get a look at the hole in the wall, the cleats on his heels making tat-tat noises as he unsuccessfully tried to balance on his tiptoes.

I slid a chair over. 'Don't electrocute yourself,' I said.

'Better listen to her,' Sarah said. 'Maggy's lost a lot of partners that way.'

'No,' I said. 'Just the one.'

Ronny threw me a startled look and steadied himself.

'I was so busy imagining what the store would look like,' I continued, 'that I don't remember noticing the clocks at all. You?' I asked Sarah.

'Uh-unh. I didn't know the clock was gone until Pavlik asked me if I'd taken it down.' Sarah raised her eyes toward Ronny. 'What do you see up there?'

'Not much. Torn wires, mostly. Looks like someone was in a hurry and just yanked the clock off the wall.'

He climbed back down and pushed a lock of Brylcreemed hair out of his face. Then he looked around for some place to wipe his hand. Before he could go for his jeans, I dug a tissue out of my pocket and handed it to him. I guess one just never stops being a mother.

At least *this* one.

'So what's going on?' Ronny asked, ineffectively wiping at his hands.

I'd forgotten that, so far as he knew, his father had been killed in a bizarre but unfortunate accident. A convergence of seemingly unrelated circumstances that was starting not to seem so unrelated anymore.

Especially when you factored in the mystery of the missing clock.

I sighed. 'You want to tell him?' I asked Sarah.

'Nope.' She sat down on the chair Ronny had been standing on. 'I just heard about it, remember? And from the sheriff, rather than my dearest friend Maggy.'

Touché. 'It was on the news,' I protested weakly. Then I turned to Ronny. 'I wish I *knew* what's going on, but there's a possibility that your father's death was not an accident.'

'The train hit him on purpose?' Ronny looked back and forth between us. 'You were both here at the time. Did the engineer try to stop it?'

I was nodding as a knock came at our open door. Christy, the red-haired piano teacher with the germ fetish, stuck her head in. She smelled faintly of chlorine bleach.

'Oh, I'm sorry,' Christy said, obviously embarrassed. 'I didn't know anyone was here.'

'Then why are *you* here?' Sarah asked. Classic Sarah, but on point. If Christy didn't think anyone was in the depot, why did she come a-knocking?

'I mean, I saw the door open and thought the police had left it that way.' She flushed even more deeply. 'I was going to lock up.'

'That's awfully nice of you,' I said, trying to put the woman at ease, though I wasn't sure that was humanly possible. 'Have you met Kornell Eisvogel's son, Ronny?'

'Hello,' Ronny said, holding out his hand to shake.

Christy took it after a slight hesitation and got a load of hair goop for her trouble. She stared at it. 'How do you do?'

'Oh, sorry about that.' Ronny handed her the ragged tissue. Poor girl looked pale enough to pass out.

'We were just telling Ronny that Kornell might have been murdered,' Sarah told her, in what might have been an attempt to cut the Brylcreem tension. 'Now I have to boogy.'

Sarah was fishing through her bag for car keys, so it was left for me to explain. 'Kornell's Buick was tampered with and we believe someone reset the middle clock.'

'What clock?' Christy asked.

'The Brookhills one, that's missing. Somebody must have taken it to cover up something.'

'But they left a hole.' Christy pointed at the

far wall.

'I meant cover up ... oh, forget it.' I didn't want to be left behind by Sarah again and it would take too long to explain.

'The clock was wrong?' Ronny had turned as pale as Christy. 'Are you saying somebody wanted my father on the railroad tracks at a certain time? But what about the clock in the car?'

It was a good question, one that hadn't occurred to me. 'Do you know if it was working?' I asked Ronny.

'Like I told you, my father loved that car. If something wasn't working, I'd have heard about it.'

'Maybe,' Christy piped up, 'maybe the person who sabotaged the car changed the clock, too.'

'From the mouth of a babe,' Ronny said appreciatively. His outfit made it clear what meaning of babe he was thinking of. 'What did they do to the car?'

I shrugged. 'The sheriff said the fuel line was disconnected.'

Sarah had found her keys and was heading for the door. I scurried after her.

'But you'd have to be a genius to predict when the car was going to stop,' Ronny protested. 'The chances of being on the tracks at exactly the right moment ... Astronomical.'

Sarah stepped out on the porch, allowing me to pass before she answered. 'What can I say? *Some*body got lucky.'

* * *

'Geez,' I couldn't hold it in any longer as we drove home. 'Could you have been more insensitive? Kornell was Ronny's father.'

Sarah shook her head. 'Kornell was an asshole. Ronny knows that and, even more important, he knows I know. Besides, I wanted to get out of there and leave him with Christy. I sensed...' both hands splayed out '...love in the air.'

If love smelled like Brylcreem and bleach.

'How do you suppose Christy intended to lock the door?' I asked. 'Don't you need a key for that?'

Sarah's jaw dropped. 'Maybe she didn't know that.'

Reasonable. 'Maybe not.'

'Or I suppose Christy might have designs on Ronny and was looking for an excuse to stop over.'

'She's never even met Ronny,' I said.

'But she's seen him.'

'Right. Like greasy hair and tight jeans would entice a woman like Christy to cross the street.'

'Don't underestimate the maxim that opposites attract.'

Yeah, but hair oil and bleach water don't mix. 'So, Ronny is going to meet us at the depot tomorrow morning?' I asked as we slewed into Sarah's driveway.

The house she shared with Courtney and Sam was a pretty Victorian done up like a painted

111

lady. It was a big place and, if the two kids really did leave as Sarah feared, it would be an empty barn. Still, like Sarah said, she'd lived there without them before.

'Yup.' She turned off the car. 'Ten a.m. again.'

I climbed out and looked around. 'Where's my Escape?'

'At the depot.'

Damn. She was right. I'd driven to the depot this morning and left the Escape there when Sarah and I had driven to Brookhills Manor. With all the craziness since then, I'd completely forgotten.

Sarah was mounting the stairs of her porch. 'Sam and Courtney are out for the night. Want to stay for dinner?'

I started to ask her why she hadn't told me about my car, but I thought better of it. Sarah looked eager for me to stay. 'Sure,' I said. 'Vietnamese?'

'Only if it's delivered.' Sarah tossed her keys on to the hall table. 'I'm already going to have to drive you back to get your car.'

'Delivery it is, then,' I said, walking to the kitchen. 'I'll order and I'll pay.'

'Are we the Rockefeller Foundation all of a sudden?' Sarah groused, following me. 'You need the Yellow Pages?'

'No.' I picked up the phone. 'I know the number at Pho Vietnamese by heart.'

I was trying to be upbeat for Sarah, but I also was eager to call Pho and speak to Tien

Romano, who was working there. It was Tien and her father Luc I hoped might throw in with us.

Happily, she answered the phone. 'Tien,' I said. 'This is Maggy Thorsen.'

'Hi, Maggy.' I could practically hear the smile on her face, which combined her late Vietnamese mother's complexion and facial features with her Italian father's thick curly hair and hazel eyes. 'How's the hunt going?'

Tien knew that Caron and I had been searching for a successor location for Uncommon Grounds. What she didn't know was that Caron was likely opting out, resulting in Sarah and me partnering. I quickly filled her in on both that and the depot.

'Wow,' she said. 'That sounds wonderful. But when did all this happen? Didn't I talk to you just a couple of days ago?'

She had. The last time I ordered Vietnamese. Have I mentioned I like Vietnamese? And Thai? And delivery of both?

'It happened just...' I had to stop and think. 'Yesterday?' It was hard to imagine. So much water had gone under the bridge in the hours since Sarah and I drove to the station that first time.

'Hang on.' I heard Tien speaking to somebody, then she returned to the phone. 'And did you want rice with that?'

I got the point. 'Sorry to hold you up like this, but I would like to talk to you and your father

113

about working with us – maybe doing catering or takeout. We have a full kitchen.'

An intake of breath. 'That sounds great!' She caught herself. 'I think you'll love both the pho *and* the spring rolls. And you said the chicken with lemon grass and also the grilled beef and sesame on rice vermicelli?'

Tien knew I loved the chicken. The beef dish was a new one for me, but it sounded good. 'Perfect. And can you have it delivered to Sarah's house?'

'Of course. That's in Brookhills Estates, right?'

I gave her the exact address. 'Thanks, Tien. You and your dad call whenever you can, assuming you're interested.'

'Definitely. And you have a good night as well.'

I hung up the phone. 'All set.'

'Set?' Sarah was sitting at the kitchen table, looking not quite as out of place as a bull in a china shop. More like a bull in a flower garden, surrounded by floral wallpaper and delicate furniture. Everything was immaculate.

It was hard to imagine two teenagers living there. Either Sarah had a top-notch cleaning lady or she really had the kids whipped into shape. Which reminded me. 'You said Courtney and Sam were out for the night? Did you mean all night or should I have ordered extra?'

'Ordered extra? You didn't order anything.' Sarah was looking grumpy. And hungry.

'Of course I did.'

'Maggy, I may be getting old but I'm not deaf. You were on that phone for a full five minutes and not one menu item passed your lips.'

Tien had come up with the menu on her side of the conversation, so as not to get in trouble. Sarah wouldn't have heard any of it.

Now she got up and went to a wine rack on the counter and pulled out a bottle. 'Hell, if we're not going to eat, we at least can drink.'

Sounded good to me. 'Since when did you switch to wine with a meal?'

Sarah was holding the bottle by the neck like she wanted to slug me with it. 'For the third time, *what* meal?'

'Tien Romano was there and she knows what I like. Chicken with lemon grass, grilled beef, spring rolls and...' I was counting them off on my fingers and I wiggled my pinky. I knew there was one more. 'Oh, and pho – that's the beef rice noodle soup.'

'Not the one with beef balls in it, I hope.' Sarah seemed somewhat appeased but still borderline grouchy. 'I don't do testicles.'

There were *so* many ways to reply to that.

With the wine bottle still in Sarah's hand, though, I wasn't taking any chances. 'They're not that kind of "balls". They're made from ground beef.' I hesitated before adding, 'You can also get shrimp balls.'

'Must be microscopic.' But Sarah finally cracked a grin.

I sat down at the kitchen table as she opened the wine. 'Courtney and Sam?' I prompted.

'Don't remind me.' Sarah pulled wine glasses from the cupboard and brought them to the table along with the bottle. 'They're shopping.'

'Shopping.' I gave it a beat. 'I hope you didn't give them your credit card.'

'Do I look like an idiot?' She poured a glass and took a slug. 'Besides, they have their own.'

'Even worse.' Since Sarah looked like she had no intention of pouring a glass for me, I helped myself. 'What are they shopping for?'

'Clothes to wear on the Cape. They say a Wisconsin wardrobe won't be "suitable" for a Massachusetts summer.' Her fingers drummed the table, the way they had the steering wheel of her car. 'Then they're spending the night at a friend's house.'

'We do have summer, even in Wisconsin,' I pointed out. 'And swimsuits and shorts probably aren't a whole lot different here than they are there.'

Sarah didn't answer and I reached across the table and patted her hand. 'So it looks like they're going?'

'I told you that this morning,' she said, pulling back. 'Weren't you listening?'

'Yes, I was listening. But it sounded as if you hadn't made up your mind yet.'

'About what?' Sarah was acting intentionally obtuse.

'About the kids spending the summer in Cape

Cod, of course.'

She shrugged. 'It's their family. If Sam and Courtney want to go, I can't very well stop them.'

She took a sip of wine, then set the glass on the table and stared at it. 'I don't know why, Maggy, but I have a bad feeling about this, like something awful is going to happen. I'm afraid that if Sam and Courtney go to Cape Cod, I'll never see them again.'

When she raised her head, Sarah's eyes were filled with tears. 'Ever.'

Eleven

Sarah and I consumed a lot of wine that night and, when the delivery guy arrived, a lot of Vietnamese food, too. When we emptied the bottle of Pinot Noir, I suddenly realized Sarah needed to drive me back to the station to get my car.

And, I also suddenly realized, she was in no condition to do it.

Nor, in turn, should I be driving my car home from there.

'Stay over,' Sarah said, waving her wine glass at me. 'They're predicting thunderstorms, anyway.'

We had moved from the kitchen to the living room's sectional couch, the ends of which reclined like lounge chairs. Sarah was ensconced in one corner, me in the other. We faced the 42-inch flat screen. *The Big Chill* was playing. Life couldn't get much better.

'You can borrow whatever you need,' Sarah continued, 'and I'll take you to your car in the morning.'

'What time is it anyway?' I tried to sit up but the recline action kept defeating me. 'Oh, my

God, it's getting late. What about Frank?'

'There's a handle on the right side.' Sarah pointed. 'And it's only ten o'clock. How about Pavlik? He's Frank's buddy. Maybe he'll go let him out.'

'Or he could give me a lift home,' I said, trying to work the lever. 'Then I could walk to the depot tomorrow and pick up the Escape. It's less than a mile from my house.'

'Do you really want to admit you're too drunk to drive?' Sarah looked crestfallen. We hadn't talked further about Sam and Courtney, but I knew it was still bothering her.

'You're the one who said I should call Pavlik.' I eased myself out of the comfy chair and stood up. Outside the window, there was a flash of lightning.

'So I was wrong. Better to call a neighbor. What about that guy who just moved in?'

'Anthony.' I didn't relish telling my new neighbor why I wasn't coming home, either. Especially if he would have to go out into the storm to feed my dog. 'Maybe I'll just say I got hung up out of town.'

'Sure.' Sarah handed me the phone. 'Lie.'

As I took the phone, the thunder finally sounded. The storm was still far enough away that Anthony might be able to get to my house and back before it hit. 'Do you have the makings for fudge?' I asked.

'No, but Courtney made brownies today.'

'Sold.' I made the call.

119

* * *

Given the circumstances, it's not surprising that I was wearing the same clothes I'd had on the day before, when Sarah and I met Ronny at the depot.

Ronny, though, was always a surprise.

Instead of the greaser look, today he was sporting bright green polyester pants paired with a print shirt and long collar points.

I tried to imagine the man's closet, separated by fashion trends like a middle-schooler's notebook with subject tabs. 'Decade-of-the-day' instead of the day-of-the-week panties I'd worn as a little girl. If it's Wednesday, it must be the seventies.

Ronny pushed a pair of over-sized yellow plastic glasses up on his apparently once-broken nose. I wondered if his fashion sense had been the cause of that, too. The nose, not the glasses. If he'd dressed like this in high school, a bigger kid likely had beaten the crap out of him.

'Out of sight.' He looked me up and down. 'Bad trip last night? This looks like the walk of shame.'

I laughed. Sarah's cousin was obviously a student of pop culture and not just because he knew the expression 'walk of shame', which Eric had explained as heading home in the daylight after a night out drinking. But, 'Out of sight?' 'Bad trip?' Ronny chose his slang to match his outfits.

'Not really,' I said. 'I stayed over at Sarah's house last night because we had too much wine. We stopped by my place this morning to let the dog out, but since we were running late, I didn't take the time to change.'

Besides, the whole time I was inside Sarah sat in the Firebird revving the motor and honking.

I sniffed my underarm. 'I don't smell, do I?'

'No, but let's think about this.' Ronny ticked the points off on his fingers: 'You partied down, didn't make it home last night, and you're wearing the same threads you wore yesterday. That sounds to me like you are walking the walk.'

Well, sure, if you wanted to be literal.

Sarah's cellphone rang.

Ronny cocked his head to listen to the ringtone. '"Our House" by Crosby, Stills and Nash?'

'And Young,' I said as Sarah stepped away to answer the call. 'She tries to find real estate appropriate ringtones.'

'I'm not so sure it'll sell more places,' Ronny said.

'Probably not. But believe me, this is a big improvement over "Home on the Range".'

'How about "I Want To Go Home" by Michael Buble?'

'Nice. Suggest it to her.' I pointed at the clip-board in his hand. 'Do you have some ideas on the layout of Uncommon Grounds, Junior?'

'I do.' He looked at Sarah, who was still on

the phone. 'Should we wait for her?'

In truth? I wanted to see them now. But it was only right to accommodate her.

'Sure,' I said. 'She probably won't be lo—'

As I said it, Sarah closed her phone. 'I have to go.'

'But Ronny has a suggested layout.' I pointed at her cousin, spreading papers over one of the round tables. 'Can you take a quick peek?'

'Sorry.' She was already dragging car keys from her pocket. 'Sam and Courtney are at the house.'

I knew Sarah was worried about the situation with them, but the kids certainly were old enough to stay home alone for a while. 'They'll still be there when you get home, right?' I asked gently.

'Not necessarily. Sam said FedEx just delivered an envelope sent overnight from their aunt and uncle on Cape Cod. Two airline tickets to Boston.'

Sarah was heading for the door. 'Sam and Courtney are thrilled. And packing.'

'Packing? When does their flight leave?'

'This afternoon.' Sarah opened the door and stepped out. 'Sam says the tickets are a gift. For "all the birthdays missed".'

Sarah held up her hands in mock amazement. 'Surprise!'

Then she was gone.

I turned to Ronny, still bent over the table. 'Think I should go after her?'

He shook his head. 'This is something they need to settle themselves. What *you* have to do is make some decisions here, so the partnership can move ahead.'

'Just me?' I looked at the pages of drawings on the table. An office, a storeroom, the front facade. The floor-plan of the tables and chairs. So much to think about. 'What if I decide wrong?'

'All anyone can do is the best they can.' Ronny straightened and pushed up his glasses again. 'Then you step back and let things fall where they may.'

Wise words, even coming from a man wearing hot green polyester pants and yellow spectacles.

I said, 'I second-guess myself constantly. You have more guts than I do.'

'No, I don't.' Ronny hitched up his pants, which were already unnaturally high. 'You do what you have to do. I'm a coward in a lot of ways.'

I laughed. I couldn't help it. 'No coward would wear those pants.'

'What?' He did a turn. 'You didn't get down with the seventies?'

'I was eleven in seventy-seven, when *Saturday Night Fever* came out. A little young to hit the discos,' I said. 'And you were probably even younger.'

'True.' Ronny had a wicked grin on his face and he seemed to be loosening up. 'But you know what they say. If you wore the fashion the first time around, you are too old to wear it when it circles back.'

'Thank God.' I said. 'That means I won't have to revisit leg warmers, stirrup pants and mini-skirts.'

'Ah, but miniskirts are always boss.' He gave me the once-over.

A girl likes to be appreciated. Even by a guy who tomorrow would likely be wearing dayglo parachute pants.

'OK, OK,' I said. 'What do we have here?'

Ronny pulled the drawing from the center of the table toward us. It showed a bird's-eye view of the entire building, the driveway to our new back parking lot on the right, train tracks to the left.

Inside the square that represented the depot building itself, he'd used the original ticket windows as the service windows and plugged in (figuratively) our equipment, most of which we'd have to buy. Not much was salvageable from the original Uncommon Grounds.

'There are three ticket windows,' Ronny said, pointing. 'I'd suggest that you open up at least two of them, to form one big window.'

'I really like the train station feel of the three,' I protested.

'And we can keep it like that, if you want,' Ronny said, dropping the seventies jive. 'But I assume there will be days that you won't have three people working to staff all of the windows. And besides,' he gestured behind us, 'look at how narrow the openings are. You can't very well slide a latte through the ticket trough.'

He was right, of course. Both the ornate lattice-work that separated the ticket agent from the passenger and the shallow tin ditch under it were fine for slipping cash in exchange for tickets, but they wouldn't work for coffee.

The restaurant that last occupied the space had used the windows for looks only. Uncommon Grounds II needed them to be functional.

'OK,' I said, 'but let's leave this far right one as a separate window. We'll be using that as an Express Line for just regular coffee, so it should work.' I walked over to the window in question. 'Can we keep some of the lattice-work up top?'

'Sure.' Ronny joined me at the window and knocked on the wooden trim. 'And I can cut this back some to give you more width.'

'Did your layout show a counter there?' I asked, indicating a now blank wall.

'Yes, and a dishwasher and sink, too.'

'Isn't there already a dishwasher and sink?' The space had been a working kitchen and both were required by law.

'There are, but we need to switch things around, so we can build you a storeroom and office behind it.'

Just a couple of essential 'details' I'd forgotten about. 'Thank God you're thinking,' I said, patting Ronny on the arm. 'How could I forget we need an office?'

125

'The space will look out on the parking lot and you'll lose some square footage in the kitchen, but it should work for you.'

Which reminded me. I needed to call Luc and Tien later, if they hadn't already left me a message.

Ronny turned 180 degrees and swept his hand toward the dark, wooden tables and chairs now in front of the ticket/service windows. 'I'm picturing this area full of small, round tables. Mostly deuces, I think, but maybe a couple of four-tops.'

He was talking about tables for two and four people. 'Have you designed a lot of restaurants?' I asked.

'A few.' He cracked a grin. 'But I bussed tables in a lot more of them while I was in school.'

I got that. 'I did, too, and my son Eric is working in a Minneapolis restaurant right now.'

'Everyone should be on the serving side at least once,' Ronny said. He indicated the front corner closest to the tracks. 'We can put the condiment cart there.'

'Perfect,' I said, impressed. 'That will move people away from the service window, but keep them out of the boarding area.'

The boarding platform was at the far end of a long narrow space that, when combined with the seating in front of the service windows, formed an 'L'.

'I think we should use those tall stand-up

tables here,' I said, 'for people who just need someplace to lean or set down a coffee cup while they're getting out their tickets.'

'Great idea.' Ronny made a note. 'That way we won't be putting chairs where people are lining up for departures.'

'God, I hope they do.' I said, sinking into a chair myself.

A puzzled expression. 'You hope they'll queue up for the train?'

'I mean I hope there are enough of them to even *form* a line.' I was dying for a cup of coffee myself, head cottony from all the wine last night. Not to mention switching to white after we ran out of the Pinot Noir.

Never mix sugars, Sugar.

'Oh, I think there will be,' Ronny said. 'Enough customers, I mean. That's why Art Jenada is so upset about his lease not being renewed.'

'Somebody was thinking ahead,' I said. 'Was it your father or Vi?'

'My father, probably. The old man liked to make a buck and he was pretty certain the commuter line would be approved.'

'But then your aunt died and her half of the depot went to Sarah.'

'Did it? That must have corked the old man.' Ronny dropped into the chair across from me, looking tired. 'How do you think Sarah is doing?'

I patted his hand. 'Have you forgotten what

you told me?'

'I don't think so.'

'Then repeat it.'

'We can't help her with Sam and Courtney,' he parroted. 'All we can do for Sarah is to get things done here.'

He finally looked at me. 'Sorry. I guess I just identify with them.'

'Because of your own mom?' Ronny's mother hadn't died, but abandonment was abandonment, however imposed.

'That, and because we all were lucky. I got Vi and they got Sarah.' Ronny squeezed my hand and rose to retrieve two of the drawings he'd left on the other table.

'What are these?' I asked as he handed me the papers.

'Face-on drawings of the way I'm picturing the equipment set-up. Since I've never brewed coffee in a big urn – much less made a cappuccino – you should take them with you to be sure I got it right.'

'Of course.' I stood up. 'How quickly do you want to hear back? I'd like to run it past Amy, our head barista.' Our only barista. I wondered if Sarah was planning to work the counter.

It didn't bear thinking about.

'You think you could have it in a couple of days? I'd like to draw up plans for the electrician. To do that, I'll have to know where the urns, grinders and espresso machine should be.'

God, the guy was a quick study. Maybe I

should hire him as a barista. Unfortunately, the pay would be about a quarter of what I guessed he made.

Then again, I didn't know how much he charged. I started to ask him, but thought better of it. Sarah was his cousin. I'd leave the financial negotiations up to her.

'Thanks a lot, Ronny,' I said, sticking out my hand. 'It's a pleasure working with you.'

'Same here,' he said, taking it. 'It's good to be busy.'

I wasn't sure if he was talking about the recent deaths, the economy or both. Not that it mattered.

'Believe me, we'll keep you occupied.' I held up the drawings, then headed for the door. 'I'll get these back to you.'

'Maggy?' he called after me.

I turned back. 'Yes?'

'Day after tomorrow will be my fave: Fabulous Fifties Friday. Wouldn't want you to miss it.'

Twelve

Frank was understandably miffed when I got home.

'I'm sorry.' I was waiting for him to finish peeing on his favorite tree, a white – or 'paper' – birch in our front yard.

I feared Frank and his tree would soon be parted, so I didn't try to rush him. Birches are relatively short-lived anyway, but dry conditions had weakened the tree and I was seeing evidence of birch-borers, beetles that not only eat the leaves, but lay their eggs in the bark. The little buggers (read: the larvae) then burrow nice and cozy under the bark and proceed to eat the tree from the inside, while the adults are working on the outside. An industriously efficient family, but not the kind you'd want over for lunch.

I stepped back a bit to look at the trunk of the tree. The birch had apparently started out life as a triple-threat – three trunks springing from the ground like a stalk of broccoli. Two trunks had already been cut off by the time I bought the house after my divorce.

Something light in weight but with churning

legs dropped on my head. I jumped out from under the tree, swatting at my scalp.

'C'mon Frank. Pinch it off and let's get away from the tree.'

Frank glanced over his shoulder at me. A look that clearly conveyed 'slut'.

'I'm sorry I didn't come home last night.' I was still looking for the bug – or bugs – in my hair, 'but it's not like I was sleeping around.'

Frank grunted and dropped his leg. Then he scratched at the ground with his back paws like a cat trying to bury its handiwork in a litter box.

'For the last time, you're a dog. And besides, you didn't poop, you peed.'

If looks could kill.

Frank turned his back to me, assumed the position and let his turds fly.

I put my hand to my nose. 'Geez, Frank. What did Anthony next door feed you last night?'

Frank sniffed, a clear indication that our neighbor, at least, loved him enough to meet his needs.

What could I say? My pet was right. If Anthony gave him hot dogs and beans, I should be grateful.

Only, God: I hoped it wasn't hot dogs and beans. Frank would light up the night for days.

He finally finished and promptly sat down to clean himself.

'Shouldn't you let it dry or ... something?'

Getting no response, I went into the house, picked up the cellphone and settled on to the front stoop for the long haul. One hundred pounds of hairy sheepdog and one tongue. You do the math.

I punched in Sarah's number. She answered on the first ring. 'What?'

'How's it going?'

'Just peachy. You?'

'Frank's mad at me, but other than that,' my dog shifted and started work on the other side, 'everything is fine. Here and at the depot. Ronny and I made some decisions so he can get started. I hope that's all right.'

'Put the cups and saucers wherever you want. You're the expert.'

A hint of sarcasm, but I ignored it. 'Are the kids there?'

'You mean have they taken off yet?' Sarah said it in a tone that told me Courtney and Sam were still with her, probably in the same room.

'Listen,' I said, 'I know you're worried, but take it from someone who has had more experience raising kids than you have. Sniping at them isn't going to make things better.'

'Kid.'

'What?'

'You raised one kid. Singular. And you worked your way into it. A baby, a toddler, an adolescent. I got them practically full grown.'

'They're not puppies,' I said. 'And even if they were, it's like smacking them on the nose with a newspaper. Not the path to improvement.'

'I'd never hit them.' Sarah sounded subdued.

'Of course you wouldn't. Are they still there?'

'No, when they realized I wasn't talking to their aunt, they went back upstairs to finish packing. I'm driving them to the airport at three.'

'You talked to the aunt ... is it Patrice or Patsy?'

'Patrice. She apologized for not clearing it with me.'

'She should.' It really was inexcusable to plan a trip like this and not get the permission of Sam and Courtney's guardian. Then, again, Patrice might feel her niece and nephew were old enough to be the ones making the decision.

'Patrice said she thought the kids had talked to me. And they had.' Sarah sighed. 'I just didn't think it would happen so soon.'

'Want me to come with you to the airport?'

'You kidding? With both kids and their luggage, I'd have to strap you on the roof.'

'Then why don't you come over here for dinner afterwards?'

'Afterward? At three?'

'You're going to stay with them until they go through security, right?'

'I suppose.' Sarah sounded like she'd contemplated dropping them off at the curb. Without stopping.

'You know you are. And then blubber. By the time you leave the airport and drive all the way out here, it'll be nearly five. Cocktail hour.'

'I don't blubber.'

'Good,' I said. I'd never seen Sarah cry and I didn't want to. It would be like watching hell freeze over in high-def.

On the other hand, I wasn't exactly the poster-girl for easy goodbyes. I had, according to Eric, 'totally embarrassed' him, when Ted and I had left our son at the university. Then, less than twenty-four hours later, Ted up and left me.

'We'll order pizza,' I offered. Hey, it always cheered me up.

'Would it kill you to cook?' Sarah asked, sounding more like herself.

'You're a fine one to talk,' I said. 'No, it wouldn't kill me, but it might kill you.'

I rang off just as Frank was getting back on to his four feet.

'Have a nice bath?' I asked as he walked past me to get to the door.

As I opened it, the phone rang. Pavlik.

'I swear,' I said. 'I don't know what happened to the clock.'

'That's not why I was calling, but it's good to know. Did you happen to notice if anything else was missing?'

'I don't think so, but then I'd never been in the place until that day. Sarah or her cousin might know.' I had a thought. 'Or maybe Art Jenada.'

'Jenada? The guy who looks like a frog?'

Great minds think nearly alike.

'A toad. Granted, a real hairy one. But, yeah.

134

Jenada was the last tenant in the depot, so he might know what belongs there.'

'I'll have somebody check with him. I have to tell you, though, pretty much everyone is signing off on this as an accident. DOT, NTSB, FRA.'

'The whole alphabet, huh?'

A pause, just to let me know Pavlik didn't approve of my making light of the law enforcement acronyms.

Then, 'So what are you doing tonight? I thought we could get some dinner and go listen to a little music.'

Damn, damn, damn. The one night I have plans, Pavlik wants to go out. On a real date.

Good thing I'm not the kind of woman who ditches her girlfriends for the guy of her dreams.

Not that I wasn't tempted. It even occurred to me to suggest a late dinner, like ten. If Sarah was here by five, she'd probably be sick of me by nine. At least that was the old Sarah. The new Sarah seemed, surprisingly, a little needier.

And a friend in need, is a friend ... oh, hell, in need.

'I'd love to do dinner and music,' I said to Pavlik, 'but I can't. Sam and Courtney – you remember Patricia's kids, who live with Sarah now? They're going to visit relatives. Sarah's pretty upset about it and I suggested she come over here to eat after dropping them off at the airport.'

'I'm surprised Sarah is upset about the kids leaving for a few days.'

'Not just a few days, Pavlik. All summer. Besides, what she's really afraid of is that Sam and Courtney will decide to stay on with their cousins.'

'You realize that if they do want that, and their cousins agree, it'll happen. Sarah's their guardian, but older kids plus family will trump that court-created tie any day.'

'I know. And I'm sure Sarah does, too. She's also just plain worried about them.'

'My recollection is that Sam and Courtney's family wasn't exactly stable.'

That was putting it mildly. 'I think Patricia's side was OK, though.' If you ignored her mother's multiple marriages and the fact she didn't want anything to do with her orphaned grandchildren.

Pavlik said, 'From what I've been told, Patricia had a co-dependent personality. There's usually a reason for that.'

All of a sudden, the sheriff's become a psychologist. 'Are you saying Sarah should try to stop them from going?'

I checked the kitchen clock. Just after one p.m. – still time to get hold of Sarah before they started for the airport. I bet she'd love a legitimate excuse to keep Sam and Courtney home.

Unfortunately, Pavlik dashed my hopes. 'No, I'm not saying that. To be honest, I'm not sure she would have a legal leg to stand on if she

136

tried. I can just understand why she's a little anxious.'

A little. If I told her what Pavlik said, I'd have to peel her off the ceiling. 'What should she do?'

I heard Pavlik speak to someone on the other end. Then he came back. 'Sorry, what was that again?'

'I was asking if you had any advice for Sarah.'

'Only to suggest she stay in touch with them. Do they have cellphones?'

Earth to Pavlik. 'Is there a child in our solar system who doesn't?' Hell, Eric had a better cellphone than I did.

'Good. Listen, I've got to go. You two have a good time together.'

'We will. I'm just sorry that the one night you *are* available, I'm not.'

'Don't be sorry. Something came up here anyway. Besides,' his voice lowered, 'We'll have lots of nights.'

'I...' My hand clamped over my mouth.

'I, what?' Pavlik asked.

Between trembling fingers, I managed, 'Call you tomorrow.'

'Great, talk to you then.'

We hung up and I turned to my dog. 'Holy shit, Frank. I almost told Pavlik I loved him.'

The sheepdog farted, then joyously sniffed his butt.

Thirteen

I got pretty much the same reaction from Sarah, sans fart, thanks be to God.

'Why would I do that?' I asked her as we settled in the living room with glasses of wine. She'd arrived just shy of five p.m. 'There's no way that I can love him. I don't know him well enough to love him.' Lust after him, maybe. No, understatement: definitely a green light on the lust front.

'Societal expectations,' Sarah posited.

Geez, was there a free Psych 101 class going on at the Community Center? First Pavlik and now Sarah.

'Humans grow fond of each other,' she continued philosophically, 'and we call the next step "love". Whatever that is.'

'Where do you get this crap?'

'I make it up. Now, let's talk about me.'

Great. 'How did it go at the airport?'

'Fine.' Sarah searched absently through her pockets for even one long-departed cigarette. 'Damn, I wish I still indulged.'

'Fine,' I repeated. 'So, you drove them there on time, they got their boarding passes and off they went?'

'Yup.' A sip of wine.

I felt frustrated. 'You wanted to talk about this, right? So, give.'

'I said I wanted to talk about *me*. My plans, my hopes, my fears.'

My ass. 'So what about Courtney and Sam? You *are* going to keep in touch with them?' I was thinking about Pavlik's advice.

'Of course. They're my responsibility.'

'But...'

'But,' Sarah put her fingers to her mouth like she was taking a last hit on a coffin-nail and blew her legendary, if phantom, smoke ring into the air. 'I need to get on with my life, Maggy. Me. Sarah Kingston. Real estate agent, partner in a coffeehouse.'

She leaned forward. 'I'm not just somebody's parent, or to be precise, two kids' guardian.'

I understood Sarah's declaration of independence. I'd done the same. It was a defense mechanism and not necessarily a bad one, assuming she didn't take it too far.

Example of 'too far'?: I quit my salaried PR job and opened a coffeehouse.

Even so, 'That's the attitude,' I told her. 'But I do think you should call Sam and Courtney every day. Either that or ask them to check in with you.'

'Why?' Sarah was looking at me suspiciously. 'Do you know something?'

I squirmed. I didn't want to worry her unnecessarily. She'd be a basket-case all summer with the information she did have, and we needed to open a coffeehouse by September first.

'I don't know anything,' phrasing it carefully, 'except that children need to know you are still there and care about them. That you're interested in their daily lives, even when you can't be with them in person.'

That look of the unpersuaded. 'You call or text Eric every day?'

'Yes,' I said solemnly. Starting tomorrow.

'OK.' Sarah shrugged. 'Sometimes I just don't intuit this stuff. I thought constant contact would make them crazy.'

'They'll say it does,' I said, 'but in their hearts? They'll be secretly, even heartwarmingly, grateful.'

Right. As would my son Eric. I could imagine his text message reply: 'Y do u keep calling'

Though now I could reply: 'Solidarity with Sarah.' Including proper punctuation and spelling.

'So do you want to know what Ronny and I talked about after you left?'

'Not necessary. I called him on the way back from the airport. He filled me in.'

'You shouldn't talk on the cellphone while you drive,' I said automatically.

'Yes, Mom,' Sarah said, equally as automatic. We'd tanked to this tune before, especially when she had both smoked and talked on the cell while driving. 'Ronny said you were figuring out where all the equipment should go. The coffee-makers and such.'

'Brewers,' I supplied. 'Do you want to see the plans? I have them right here.'

I got up to get the papers, but she waved me off. 'I don't know anything about where the stuff should go. Just show me when you've figured it out.'

Worked for me. 'So you said you're getting on with your life. How are things going with the agency?'

As I spoke, Frank wandered in. He passed me, still not deigning to recognize my existence. Then he saw Sarah and his stump of a tail started to wag.

Sarah wasn't much of a dog person, which was why Frank showered affection on her. Not to mention drool. I think it contributed to his amusement.

Tonight, though, Sarah came alive when she saw Frank. 'That's my good boy,' she crooned, as he shamelessly hula-danced in front of her. 'You love your Sarah, don't you. Don't you? What a sweetheart you are. Yes, you are.'

Wow. I present, for your edification, a woman with abandonment issues.

Frank wound himself around and leaned against Sarah's leg. Then he slid down to the floor, landing with a 'huff' and laying his head on her foot. He gave me a self-satisfied smirk.

Traitor.

Sarah leaned down to scratch him. My sheepdog flipped over on his back, legs waving like four hairy flagpoles.

'And *I'm* a slut?' I asked him.

'You're obviously not giving this creature enough affection.' Sarah bent like a pretzel to put her head down next to Frank's. 'Isn't that right, Frankie? She just left you last night.'

'Watch yourself,' I warned, 'or I may let him follow you home.'

'A hundred pounds of love, aren't you, boy? Aren't you?'

Frank licked her face.

Sarah looked at me, startled, a string of drool trailing off her chin. 'He's really ... hydrated.' She sniffed. 'And his breath...'

Just the tip of the iceberg. 'Wait until he farts.'

The power of suggestion. Frank stood up and poisoned the atmosphere. Then he gave me a little grin and padded out.

'Jesus,' Sarah said, fanning the air, 'what did he eat?'

'My guess? Beans and wieners.' I got up. 'Ready to order pizza?'

Sarah followed me into the kitchen. 'Can we get anchovies?'

'Sure, on your half.' I picked up the phone. 'But you'll have to share. Frank just loves the little fishies.'

'Wait. Forget the anchovies. On top of the beans and wieners you'd have to get the house fumigated, then the dog laminated. I don't want to be here when that happens.'

'Good call.' I didn't want anchovies in the vicinity of my pizza, anyway. They manage to migrate from their half of the pie to mine, and they stink worse than Frank.

I punched in the phone number for Pizza Palace, which had recently been taken over by a chain.

'Pizza Palace,' the canned voice on the other end said.

I opened my mouth, but was put on hold without getting a chance to speak.

'No answer?' Sarah asked.

'I'm on hold. A Pavarotti sound-alike is waxing eloquent about pizza toppings.'

'Classy. Well, while you're waiting, let's talk about our building schedule. I don't think the accident will delay anything, though it's a damn good thing nobody was hurt.'

I disengaged the receiver from my ear. 'Accident? What accident?'

'Ronny didn't tell you?'

'No. I haven't spoken to him since I left the depot this morning, and everything was fine then.'

There was a click on my phone, so I put the thing back to my ear. Pavarotti-Lite was still filling my ear, now singing 'O Sausage Pizza' to the tune of 'O Sole Mio'.

What had happened to my country? And my pizza place? 'Was Ronny in a car accident, too?'

'No, a fall. He leaned on some deck railing and the wood broke away.'

I held up my hand as there was another click on the line. I was concerned about Ronny, but I didn't want to lose my place in the phone queue.

'Pizza Palace. Can you hold please?'

'I've *been* holding,' I screamed into the receiver. No use, the music started up again. I held it out so Sarah could hear.

'"Funiculi, Funicula"?' she asked.

'A Calzoni, A Calzona,' I said. 'So, is Ronny all right?'

'Fine. Except that he landed in the bushes so he's a little scratched up.'

'Are you talking about our railing at the depot?' I asked.

'Yup. Just to the right of the stairs.'

That didn't compute. 'But I tested that railing and it was solid as a rock. There's no way someone as slight as Ronny could have gone through it.'

The overture to *A Chorus Line* struck up into my ear. Then, click. 'Pizza Palace, can—'

I didn't let him finish. 'No, I can't hold,' I snapped. 'I've *been* holding for ten minutes. Your canned music is now moving on to Broadway show tunes, and in my current emotional state, I can't take that.'

'I was just—'

'I don't care what else you were doing. You need to answer your phone. And all your songs are stupid,' I added for good measure. 'Now, will you take my order? Please?'

'Certainly, ma'am,' the young voice said. 'Umm, I was just going to say "Can I take your order?".'

'oh.' Lower case.

'Can I interest you in...'

Sarah looked at the writing on the third of three flat cardboard boxes. 'Dessert pizza? What the hell's that?' She opened a bag. 'And wings? Garlic sticks? Did you order everything on the menu?'

'I felt terrible about yelling at the kid,' I admitted. 'I couldn't say no to him.'

'To the tune of a hundred-dollar pizza order? They should be paying you for listening to their tacky advertising jingles. Just be glad they took our order before they reached Rodgers and Hammerstein or Lerner and Loewe.'

I picked up a garlic stick. 'If ever I would leave you,' I sang to it, 'it would be a bummer. Leaving you's a bummer I ... never ... could *do*. Your—'

Sarah took the relay baton. 'Your dough streaked with butter ... my hips big as *Mame*'s.' She grabbed a stick for her own microphone. 'Your breath full of garlic ... that puts Frank...' Right on cue, the sheepdog came padding through, '...to shame.'

Frank stood in the center of the room in front of the fireplace as Sarah and I collapsed in laughter.

'*Mame*?' I said, when I could finally form words again.

'Maybe it was a stretch, but remember her quote? "Life is a banquet and most poor suckers are starving to death".'

'Not us.' I said, surveying the spread of food. 'This is ridiculous.'

Frank trotted up and sniffed one of the pizza boxes.

'Sorry, no anchovies,' I told him. 'Do you like artichokes? Same first letter.'

He turned tail.

'Suit yourself,' I called after him. 'But you'll thank me in the morning.'

'Unlike me,' Sarah said, holding her stomach. 'Don't let me eat too much of this crap.'

'I won't. But back to Ronny's fall. That railing – if we're talking about the same one – was not flimsy. I pushed on it. I leaned on it. Sturdy, absolutely solid.'

'Yeah,' said with a poker face. 'And you probably weigh more than he does.'

'I do not,' I said indignantly. Though, admittedly, Ronny was a skinny little guy. Not that skinny, though.

I hoped.

'Then what's your point?' Sarah, after considering all three pizzas: pepperoni, mushroom and banana peppers; smoked chicken and artichokes; and the aforementioned 'dessert pizza', chose a slice of each and topped them off with

146

a buffalo wing.

'No bleu cheese dressing for the wings?' I asked.

'I'm watching my weight.' She poured herself a glass of Zinfandel. 'Besides, I try not to eat anything that's started to mold.'

'Please. I've seen the contents of your refrigerator. You're probably top-ten nationally in the cultivation of penicillin.' I considered the pizzas and opted for 'dessert', which turned out to be a chocolate chip cookie the size of a hubcap and covered in whipped cream.

Selecting a garlic stick as a sensible side dish, I checked out the wines. Two were open – the Zin and a Cabernet Sauvignon. I chose the Cab – a perfect accompaniment to chocolate chips. And God knows, everything goes with garlic.

'So?' Sarah asked. She was ensconced on the couch, feet on a hassock, facing the fireplace that took up one full wall of my sky-blue stucco living room. Not my color choice, but I had been there just two years. And I was lazy.

Not to mention poor as well. Like my grandmother said, you get used to hanging if you hang long enough, which I thought was akin to 'prisoners fall in love with their jailers'.

These days, though, even the green toilet was looking good to me and I was falling in love with my baby-blue stucco walls. Tomorrow we'd be picking out drapes together.

Struggling back to the context of our conversation, I said, 'So what?'

My favorite chair, a big overstuffed floral number that didn't fit in the room, enveloped me. But then again, Frank was too big for the room and I didn't toss him in the dumpster, either. He was splayed out on the hearth of the unlit fireplace.

'God, you're getting old,' Sarah took a bite of the pepperoni slice. 'Short-term memory loss. My question is, so what are your thoughts on the railing?'

I set my Cabernet on the end table. 'Honestly? I don't know what I'm thinking.'

Sarah looked like she had waited a long time for a non-answer. I tried to give her something: 'It just seems like there have been a lot of inexplicable accidents at the depot over the last two or three days. Your uncle and the train, your cousin Ronny and the deck, the missing clock—'

'Not exactly an accident.' Sarah put her hand up to shield the fact that she was talking with a mouthful of pizza.

'But inexplicable, you have to admit.'

'Uh-huh.' Sarah was still chewing. She'd once told me her mother had taught her to masticate every bite fifty times. Given the size of Sarah's choppers, the food must experience the equivalent of five minutes in a Cuisinart. 'So my question is, again, what's your point?'

'And, again, I say, I don't know what my point is.' I started to toss the end of my dessert pizza to Frank and then thought better of it.

Chocolate – chips or otherwise – and dogs don't mix.

The sheepdog, however, alerted by my aborted movement, was sitting up and looking plaintive. Full-blown begging at his size would be overkill. 'Give Frank your crust.'

Sarah seemed offended. 'I want the crust. It's my favorite part.'

'You have two of them,' I pointed out. She'd already finished most of both the pepperoni and the smoked chicken slices, leaving only the end portions.

'I save them for last.' Her jaw jutted out.

'Fine.' I climbed out of my cushy chair. 'Be selfish.'

'You bought enough pizza to give him a whole pie. Or maybe he'd like a wing.' She held said chicken part up and Frank came running.

'No, Frank! Sit.'

The sheepdog put on the brakes, but the polished wood floor of the living room didn't give him much traction. He went sailing past Sarah and into the wall. Sitting back up, Frank looked dazed.

'Good boy,' I said, bringing him a slice of smoked chicken and artichoke. I patted him on the head. 'You OK?'

He wobbled a bit, burped, and then scarfed down the pizza.

Sarah frowned. 'He can have pizza, but not wings? What kind of diet is he on?'

'He should be on a diet, but in this case it's

the chicken *bones* he can't have.' I pointed at the wing in Sarah's hand. 'If he swallows them they can splinter and get stuck in his stomach or intestines.'

'Why would he eat the bones?' Sarah was stripping the meat off the wing as she spoke, with Frank looking on plaintively. I tossed him another piece of pizza.

He caught it and swallowed it whole.

Sarah looked at me. 'Got it.'

Fourteen

The next morning was pretty much a repeat of the one before, except that I was clean, changed and piloting my own vehicle.

As I rounded the corner from the parking lot, I saw Christy standing in the window of her studio, presumably watching for a student. I waved and she waved back. I couldn't see the yellow rubber gloves, but maybe she changed into transparent latex for work.

The front railing of the depot porch already had been replaced with fresh, unfinished wood spindles and handrail. 'Quick work,' I said to Ronny as I entered. 'It looks great.'

He was wearing khaki shorts, a polo shirt with the collar flipped up, and a sweater tied around his shoulders.

'Nineties?' I guessed.

'Yes.' He shrugged, hands splayed. 'It's not my favorite decade.'

'You do look pretty normal.' At least in comparison to yesterday. 'The sweater's a nice touch.'

'You think?' Ronny petted the V-neck. 'Cashmere.'

'Timeless,' I agreed. 'But wearing it with the collar on the polo shirt flipped up is what projects Nineties.'

He tugged on the sleeves tied at his throat. 'Thank you.'

'And tomorrow?' I asked. 'The Fabulous Fifties?'

'I think so. The twenty-first century is a wasteland so far and, though I enjoy the forties, I'm too short for double-breasted.'

'No twenties or thirties either?'

'Poverty, war – even more depressing than the rise of the double-breasted suit.'

'Well, at least you look very cheery today,' I said. 'Not to mention comfortable.'

'Pleated-front khakis.' He put his hands in the front pockets of his shorts and rocked back on his heels. 'Comfort *and* style. A good breather after the polyester pants of yesterday.'

Both literally and metaphorically.

'Speaking of yesterday,' I touched a scratch that ran from his temple to his lower cheek. 'Is that from your fall? I'm so sorry you got hurt.'

He turned red. 'It's nothing. I should have looked before I leaned.'

I laughed at his turn of phrase. 'I'm not so sure it would have mattered. I tested that part of the porch railing when Sarah and I arrived the first day to look at the place.' I was trying to avoid saying it was also the day his father was killed.

'The day my father was killed?' Ronny asked.

'Was the railing loose then? I have to say I never noticed it. And I should have, being a contractor and all.'

'But that's my point. No movement at all when I pushed on the railing.'

'Did you wiggle it forward and back?' Ronny seemed puzzled.

'Absolutely. From the porch side.'

'That's odd.' He was chewing on the inside of his cheek.

I followed him outside. 'I pushed right about here.' I pointed at the center of the new handrail that spanned the four-feet from the stairs to the first post on the right.

'That's where I went through,' Ronny admitted. 'But there was no rigidity or resistance at all.' He rubbed his chin. 'I have to admit, it seemed wrong.'

'Wrong how?' I asked.

'Well, like I said, there wasn't even any resistance. The top railing,' he pointed at the horizontal cross-piece, 'just slipped from the box post.'

The box post was apparently the four-inch by four-inch piece of wood that connected the railing running up the front steps with its sister spanning the veranda.

'Once that happened,' Ronny continued. 'There was nothing to hold the spindles in and the whole section came down.' He laughed. 'Not that it mattered, I was already swimming through the air.'

'How is this attached?' I said, pointing at the box post.

'Sometimes with angle brackets, but this one seemed to be toe-nailed in.' I could tell that he saw the blank look on my face. 'You drive long nails through the railing at an angle so they also go into the post. Only it's not as sturdy as brackets or using long screws.'

Evidently not. But I was looking at the railing. 'This has brackets.'

'Sure. I used them when I rebuilt it.'

I gestured at the section in front of me. 'No, I mean here. The old part.'

Ronny came over and looked. When he bent down his tied sweater did a 180, so it looked like a cashmere bib. 'Huh? Sure enough.'

He rearranged the sweater. 'Maybe part of the deck had already been replaced.'

'And not very well,' I said, eyeing the shrubs where Ronny had landed. A pile of spindles and railings were stacked to one side. 'Good thing the juniper bushes were here.'

'You're telling me.' Ronny went down the steps and examined the pile. Holding up the top rail, he asked, 'See anything?'

'Nails,' I said. 'On both ends.'

'Anything else?'

'They're bent,' I tried.

'Nothing else?'

Risking redundancy, I'm not one for twenty questions or guessing games. I hate it when somebody knows something I don't and won't tell me. Still, Ronny seemed a good guy, so I went along.

'They're silver?'

'Bingo!' He looked very proud. I just wasn't sure why.

'Aren't most nails silver?' I asked. 'I mean in color. I know they're not really the good stuff.'

'Yes, but these are shiny, which means they're not mechanically galvanized.'

'OK, I'll bite.' If he teased me anymore with this, I might actually do it. 'What does that mean?'

'Mechanically galvanized nails are used in treated lumber and they have a dull gray coating, so you can tell the difference.'

I was following him: I just wasn't sure where we were going. 'So these aren't mechanically galvanized.'

'Correct.'

'And therefore...'

'If they're not, the same chemicals that treat the lumber would have eaten away at the coating of the nails. They would have started to rust.'

'Sarah said the deck was rebuilt a few years back, when the antique store was here.'

'But understand, that's exactly my point. The whole porch is fairly new, and it's constructed – properly – with treated wood and galvanized nails. We know that because otherwise the chemicals that preserve the wood would have eaten away at the coating of the non-galvanized nails and caused them to rust.'

That didn't compute. 'But you said the nail in your hand isn't galvanized and it hasn't rusted.'

'Correct.' Ronny nodded and held up the nail triumphantly. 'Because this is new. Brand new.'

'So you two are saying someone intentionally sabotaged the porch rail?' Sarah asked.

She'd arrived late looking a little ragged, but the moment she parked her car, Ronny and I had fallen on the poor woman/realtor/partner, talking over each other about what we'd found.

'Somebody must have taken off the...' I turned to Ronny. 'What did you call them? The little L-shaped braces?'

'Angle brackets.' He tugged at the collar of his polo shirt, clearly proud of what he'd deduced. 'That same somebody must have removed them on both ends of the top rail and then replaced them with a couple of nails. So when I leaned on it—'

'The rest is history,' I said, indicating the long scratch on his face.

Sarah, though, was always one to rain on another's parade. 'Great work, Spin and Marty. But have you asked yourselves the question ... why?'

'Why?' Ronny and I echoed.

'Yes, why. As in, what would anybody gain by booby-trapping our porch?'

I said, 'Destroying our business, of course. I mean, think about it. First your uncle's car has its fuel line disconnected. Whether the perpetrator expected it to go any further or not, it's still vandalism.'

'Perpetrator?' Sarah asked. 'Will you lay off the TV and movie jargon?'

'Impossible,' I said. 'But that's beside the point. May I continue?'

'Sure. So Lieutenant, do we have a profile of the perp?' She said it in her best James Earl Jones voice.

'Very funny.' Actually, it was. Yet I was having none of it. 'Next, the clock was torn off the wall and now this.' I gestured toward the rebuilt portion of railing.

'Seems kind of petty, don't you think?' Sarah said. 'We certainly aren't going to change our plans because of a little vandalism or thievery.'

'Your uncle's death wasn't exactly petty,' I pointed out.

'True.' Sarah blushed. 'But as you've already said, tinkering with his fuel line may have been simple vandalism that just happened to result in something worse.'

'Far worse,' I said, cocking my head toward Ronny.

'Right,' Sarah said, rolling her eyes. *'Far* worse. Or maybe Kornell just didn't tighten the line and the thing slipped off on its own.'

'I doubt that,' Ronny said. 'My father didn't make mistakes. At least, with his car.'

'Which is why it's still running,' I said.

'Or was,' from Sarah.

A moment of silence.

Ronny and I were getting nowhere with Sarah. I didn't have anything beyond intuition to support my suspicion that someone was targeting us in particular. Or the Junction in general.

Not unlike that 'uneasy feeling' Sarah had about Courtney and Sam.

Which reminded my dim self. 'Have you called the kids?' I asked Sarah as we followed Ronny into the depot.

'They called last night after I got home,' she said.

'But you didn't leave my house until after eleven – that makes it midnight, eastern time.'

'You would have been a pain-in-the-ass mother.' Sarah said. 'The kids are on vacation. Besides, their bodies are still dialed to central time.'

'That's not such a good idea,' Ronny said, beckoning us over to the ticket counter. 'When you travel you should start living according to the local time immediately.'

'I think that's when you're going abroad, not just one time zone away,' Sarah said.

'The principle still applies.'

Sarah squinted at Ronny. 'Have you ever visited another country?'

'Of course,' Ronny said defensively. 'Niagara Falls.'

'Niagara Falls is half in the US, isn't it?' I pulled the diagrams Ronny had given me yesterday out of an old Priority Mail envelope.

'We crossed the rainbow bridge,' Ronny said.

'More than once, I'll wager,' Sarah mumbled under her breath.

I stepped hard on her foot. As a mother of a proud gay man, I figured I was entitled. Besides, I was fairly certain Ronny was *not* a gay man. Despite the fact he played one. To the hilt.

'Why'd you do that?' Sarah was standing on one shoe, rubbing the other one.

'Sorry,' I said.

'No, you're not.'

I shrugged. 'You're right.'

Ronny was looking back and forth between us. 'Did you want to talk about the electrical?'

'Yes,' I said. 'But I invited Luc and Tien Roman—' I was interrupted by an uncertain knock on the door.

'Come in,' Sarah and I called in unison. Ronny had already been heading over to open it. Probably why he was so skinny. Wasted calories.

Tien Romano stepped in. 'Am I late?'

'Not at all,' I said, waving her over. I introduced Ronny and Tien. If infatuation was a physical force, I thought Ronny would have fallen over. Good thing he wasn't wearing his platform shoes.

'Where's your father?' I asked after the pleasantries.

'He's not coming.' Tien had her head down, a curtain of dark hair covering her delicate

159

features. She looked up. 'I hope it's all right, but he said he wanted me to do this alone. He's enjoying retirement.'

'Of course,' I said. 'I don't blame Luc for wanting to take time off. He's earned it.'

Tien's mother, An, and Luc met when he was stationed in Saigon during the Vietnamese War. The two married in the United States, but An died when Tien was just a year old.

The baby became a fixture in the family delicatessen – full-grown adults making fools of themselves trying to entertain the beautiful little girl in the playpen behind the counter. Later, practically as soon as she could walk, Tien became an indispensable partner in the store.

When the business went under with Uncommon Grounds and the rest of the strip mall, Luc told me Tien should strike out on her own – that he'd held her back all these years. Tien had said the same thing, but about Luc.

I thought neither of them had meant it, but now it looked like Luc was doing his best to push his daughter out of the nest.

And what better transition for Tien than to land at Uncommon Grounds?

'Wow,' she said, looking around. 'I'd forgotten how big this place is.'

'You've been here before?' I asked, surprised.

'When Art Jenada had the cafe. We sold soups and bread to him, so I delivered here a couple times every week.'

The woman was amazing. She probably baked the bread herself before hopping into the truck toward delivering it.

'How did he do here?' I figured a supplier might have the inside line on the *bottom* line of their customers. Our vendors – especially our bean roaster – were as close to us as family. Closer.

'I think he was just making it,' Tien said, sticking her head around the corner to check out the area behind the ticket counter. 'I know he was hoping the commuter line would more than bail him out. He said it could be a "goldmine".' The light in Tien's eyes as she toured the place indicated she thought the same.

'But then his lease wasn't renewed.' As I said it, I glanced toward the door where Sarah and Ronny stood talking. I wanted Tien to be able to be honest, without worrying about insulting the family.

I already had gotten Art Jenada's side: Kornell had talked Sarah's Auntie Vi into not renewing Jenada's lease, figuring that if anyone was going to make big bucks at Brookhills Junction, it was going to be Kornell.

And then Kornell died.

'Leases, what a racket.' Tien shook her head. 'The tenant pays upfront to build out the space and outfit it, and then pays back-end again to rent it.'

A bit of a sore spot for both of us. In fact, for anyone who had been a tenant of our former

161

landlord, the late and unlamented Way Benson.

'Until the owners decide they want you out,' I agreed.

'You can take your equipment and all.' Tien was in the kitchen now, opening the cupboard doors, checking out the cooler. 'But sometimes it's more expensive to move the stuff and retrofit your new space to accommodate it, than to simply start all over.'

She was at the stove now. 'Gas, that's good.' She colored up. 'I'm sorry. Here I'm acting like this is my kitchen and I don't even know what you have in mind.'

'That makes three of us,' I admitted. 'But Sarah and I certainly have no use for the kitchen, other than as a place to store pastries and milk and such.'

I showed her Ronny's plan with the long counter and office added.

'So you have no interest in a full-service restaurant?' she asked, after looking it over.

As enticing as the idea was, I had known too many wannabe restaurateurs who had embraced that siren song. Owning a restaurant meant getting up early and working late. And then doing it all over again the next day. And the next, and the – you get the drill.

Coffeehouse ownership was no picnic, but when I finished at six or seven p.m., I was done. Might even have time for a date. Oh, rapturous day.

'A full-service restaurant? None,' I affirmed.

'But I would be interested in having packaged takeout meals that people could reheat at home.'

'Sure,' Tien said. 'Like Jacque at Schultz's Market. I picked up their turkey meatloaf the other day.' She made a little face.

'Not good?' I was surprised. Schultz's had a terrific reputation.

'Not as good as mine,' Tien said, her smile lighting up the room. 'I think we could give Jacque a real run for it.'

Even more reason to make the effort. Jacque Oui, owner of Schultz's, would benefit from being taken down a few notches.

'I could even make pastries for you.' Tien had pulled out her checkbook and was making notes on the deposit slips at the back.

Her enthusiasm was contagious. 'That would be great,' I said, thinking about our customers' reaction to getting baked goods still warm from the oven. 'And everything at night should be packaged and ready-to-go,' I said, 'so people can get off the trains—'

'Disembark,' Tien offered.

'Yes, *disembark*, grab what they want and head out.'

'Convenience is everything!' Tien dropped her checkbook, practically clapping her hands.

I held up my own, palms toward her. 'Now we need to take this one step at a time. I don't know how much we'll sell or how long it will take to catch on.'

Tien didn't even slow down. 'We can have sandwiches, too, that people can take with them in the morning toward lunch at their desks. I'll make the bread and Kaiser rolls for the sandwiches and the soup, too. Maybe we can find cups that can go straight into the microwave at work.'

She retrieved the checkbook and made another note, then skipped to the next deposit slip. Like me, she probably didn't have that much use for them these days, anyway.

'Can you really do all this?' I asked. 'You're only one person.'

A grin. 'Something tells me my dad might change his mind down the road.'

'How far down the road?'

'About half a block,' Tien said. 'He's going to love this idea.'

'I thought he wanted to retire?'

'He wants me to be in charge of my life.' She shrugged. 'I'll tell him I'm the boss and he works for me.'

A laugh came from behind us. 'You've been the boss from the moment you were born, at least with that father of yours,' Sarah said, joining us in the kitchen.

Tien put her finger up to her lips. 'Shh. He hasn't figured it out yet.'

'Where did Ronny go?' I asked, peeking around the corner.

'He ran over to Brookhills Manor to pick up the rest of Kornell and Auntie Vi's things. So,

164

did you two come up with a plan?'

Tien and I looked at each other.

'Perhaps too many plans,' Tien said. 'But don't worry, I'll scale down what we talked about,' she patted her checkbook, 'and put together a "starter menu". Then we'll go from there.'

'Do more of what works and less of what doesn't,' I said.

Tien laughed. 'Got it.'

From what I'd been able to tell, there was no rhyme or reason to the gourmet coffee business. Assume you'll sell hot coffee on a winter's day and you can be sure you'll run out of ice for the cold drinks.

I was looking at the revised kitchen plan in my hands. 'Hmm.'

'What?' Sarah asked.

I stood in the center of the room and stretched my arms out wide. 'This is a pretty big room, but once we take out space for the office and a storeroom, it might get a little tight for all of us.'

I nodded at Tien. 'We won't be in the kitchen for long periods, but we will need to be in and out. Is that a problem?'

Tien tapped her pen on her makeshift pad as she surveyed the kitchen.

'I've got it!' she said. 'You close at six, right?'

'Well, we did.' I looked at Sarah apologetically. 'You and I haven't talked about this yet, but we may have to stay open later for the last train if we plan to sell the commuters an easy dinner.'

'The last train is scheduled to arrive here at six thirty,' Sarah said. 'We could close at seven.'

'Makes sense.' I turned to Tien. 'Why do you ask?'

'I'll work nights. That way I'll have the kitchen to myself and all the food cooked and packaged when you get in the next morning.'

Beautiful. In fact, everything was coming together perfectly. Even as I had the thought, though, I knew I was daring fate to, as Sarah put it so pithily, smack me in the ass.

Fifteen

The crash came not ten minutes later.

Sarah was the first one to the front door. She stopped dead at the threshold. Tien piled into her and I piled into Tien.

'What...'' I struggled to peer over Tien's shoulder and around Sarah.

And then I saw it. A car. Not just any car, but a Firebird. A 1975, lemon-yellow Firebird.

It was nose-up on what was left of the porch steps, winged insignia not eight inches from where its owner was standing.

Sarah cried like someone who didn't know how.

The sobs were more like strangling noises. In fact, at first I thought she was having a heart attack as Tien and I edged around her to the side of the deck Ronny had repaired.

He'd have to do it again.

'Are you OK? I asked.

'Call nine-one-one,' Sarah gasped.

'What is it, chest pains?'

'Not for me, you idiot. For him.' She nodded to the car. A little string of snot dangled from

Sarah's nose like a syrupy icicle.

'Sniff,' I said.

'Sniff?'

'You've got ... mucus coming out of your nose.'

'I've got "mucus" coming out of my nose?' She advanced on me. 'My Firebird, the love of my life, is permanently planted in the depot.' She had me backed up against the wall and we were toe-to-toe. 'And you're worried about my nose running?'

'I'll call nine-one-one,' I said, and slipped away, climbing over the rail and dropping to the ground four feet below.

Abject terror makes fools of all of us.

I landed hard on my hands and knees. I hadn't gone inside to call, partly because Sarah stood between me and the door, but mainly because the depot didn't have a working landline. And I had no idea where my handbag and cellphone were.

I tried the florist shop next door.

The 'Closed' sign was still up and when I peered through the window, the place looked deserted. Only a counter and, in the center of that counter, a planter shaped like a cow. The orange and green plants in it were still bright, the arrangement obviously artificial. And just plug ugly.

'No wonder they went out of business,' I muttered.

It wasn't good news that we had an empty

storefront next to us, but I had a hunch it wouldn't lie fallow for long.

But that didn't help me now.

On the other side of the street was Party-People. I stepped out to cross, and almost became the hood ornament for a Lexus SUV. I would have asked the soccer mom driving it to call for help on her cell, but she was already busy texting. She did a double-take as she passed the Firebird on the steps to the station, but drove on.

Art Jenada didn't answer the door when I pounded. No hours were posted, but I assumed his work as a caterer didn't require regular 'open' hours for the public.

As I stepped off his front stoop, Rebecca Penn jogged across the road from the direction of the florist shop. She was wearing shorts and a T-shirt and had a bottle of water in her hand. Despite that, the woman didn't seem to have broken a sweat.

Disgusting.

'What happened?' she called, dark ponytail bobbing as she pulled up in front of Penn and Ink. 'Is everyone OK?'

As I opened my mouth to explain, Jenada pulled open his door, finally. 'I'm in the middle of baking one-hundred-fifty dinner biscuits,' he said, smacking flour off his hands. 'What do you want?'

I pointed to the depot and Jenada stepped out. 'Whoa. What happened?'

'The parking brake on Sarah's car must have given out.' I said. 'Our phone isn't working. Can somebody call nine-one-one?'

'I will,' Rebecca volunteered and disappeared into her studio.

'Don't you need to get back to your baking?' I asked Jenada, who hadn't budged.

'Hell, no,' he said. 'The biscuits'll keep. I've got to see this.'

We crossed back to the depot. Sarah and Tien were nowhere in sight.

'Jesus,' Jenada said, surveying the damage. 'Where did she have the thing parked, on the tracks?'

'Got me.'

But I saw what Jenada meant. To fit the trajectory the car had taken, it would have had to come from the artificial rise supporting the train rails on the other side of the street.

Craning my neck, I could see that there was a gravel apron on the crest between Christy's piano studio and the railroad bed. I wouldn't put it past Sarah to have snugged her beloved car up there rather than risk parking it on the street.

As Art and I approached the porch, he took off his flour-covered apron and hung it over the rail. Then he stepped back to survey the scene, hands on hips. 'Holy shit, you're going to have to repair this whole section of porch. That's after you get a tow truck in here to pull the car out. It'll cost a fortune.'

He said it with a little more delight than I'd have liked.

I left him there and carefully climbed the stairs on the side where they were still somewhat intact. Inside the depot, I found Sarah sitting on a chair, breathing into a bag.

Tien was standing over her. 'She started to hyperventilate, poor thing.'

'Isn't that supposed to be a paper bag?' I indicated the plastic grocery bag, which was going in and out each time Sarah breathed like an ICU prop from a TV medical show.

Sarah pulled it away from her mouth. 'Give me a twist tie and I'll finish the job,' she snarled.

'Don't tempt me,' Tien muttered as Sarah returned to the bag.

Then, more loudly. 'You have to relax, Sarah. It was just a car.'

A long inhalation, that sucked the bag up against Sarah's face like she'd been laminated.

I snatched it away. 'Stop it! The police are on their way and you have to talk to them.'

It wasn't true so far as I knew, but as soon as I said it, sirens started to wail in the distance. First I'd anticipated the crash and now this. I should be a fortune-teller. Or the Prophet of Doom.

Sarah stood up, but grabbed the back of her chair as she wobbled a bit.

Art chose that moment to finally come in, followed by Ronny, back from Brookhills

Manor with his father and Vi's things.

'What happened?' Ronny asked, setting the two Schultz's bags down to steady Sarah. 'Are you hurt, Cuz?'

'Hurt?' Sarah snapped. 'Of course, I'm hurt. Deeply. Did you see my car?'

'She wasn't in it,' I told Ronny. 'We were in the kitchen with Tien when we heard the crash. The parking brake must have given out.'

'All his brakes were fine,' Sarah said, tearing up again. '*He* was fine. We both were.' She collapsed into the chair again, sobbing.

'He?' Jenada asked.

'The Firebird,' Ronny told him as he awkwardly patted Sarah's shoulder.

'They were very close,' I added.

'Right.' Jenada cleared his throat uncomfortably. 'Well, umm, I'm going to go. The police will take care of things from here.'

Like he had been such a big help up to this point, gawking and exclaiming. Nonetheless, I stuck my hand out to him. 'Thanks for your help, Art. I'm looking forward to being neighbors.'

'Yeah. Me, too.' Art shook my hand and took his leave.

'He didn't sound like he meant that,' Tien said. She was jotting more notes on her checkbook's surplus deposit slips.

'He doesn't.' The handshake had transferred flour from Art's hand to mine and I was looking around for something to wipe it on. I didn't find anything, but I did spot the handbag I must have dumped in the corner of the room. Since the bag cost more than my denims, I wiped the flour on my jeans and retrieved it.

As I reached through the ticket window to set the bag down out of sight, I saw the plans I'd worked on after Sarah had left the night before.

I beckoned Ronny over, just as the sirens cut off outside. 'Can you and Tien take a look at these? I made a couple of changes and maybe she'll have some more ideas.'

I nodded toward Sarah, who was standing at the door, looking out. 'Your cousin and I should talk to the police.'

The two of them obediently took the papers and went off to the kitchen. I joined Sarah.

'Two fire trucks, an ambulance and two squad cars.' She turned back to look at me. 'You're in luck – they're town.'

Both the municipal police and the county sheriff's department had jurisdiction in Brookhills. Manpower, the type of call and exactly where it was located all had a bearing on which entity responded.

If the Brookhills Police were here, that meant I didn't have to worry about Pavlik showing up.

'Good,' I said, hustling Sarah out. 'Let's get this over with.'

'Hellooo.' I waved at the two uniformed officers. 'Car owner? Right here.' I pointed at Sarah.

'Thanks, friend,' she muttered, but picked her

173

way down the steps to speak to them.

I remained on the porch to one side of the Firebird, trying to stay out of the way of the firefighters, who were charged with figuring out how to extricate Sarah's car from the superstructure of the depot. The discussion, though, seemed to center more on how it had gotten there.

'You're telling me nobody was driving this buggy?' A firefighter, dark shaggy hair streaked with gray, thumped the fender.

'Hands off,' Sarah snapped from down below. She'd been in deep conversation with the police officers, so I could only assume she had a telepathic link to the Firebird. Maybe *she* was the Prophet of Doom.

'Hey, lady,' the firefighter said, holding up his arms. 'I'll be happy to, but I hope you have decorating ideas for this baby, because it's not coming out without some help.'

'Let them look,' I heard one of the cops advise Sarah. 'If there's a way to get your car out without damage to the structure, they're your best bet.'

'Structural damage?' I chirped from my perch.

Startled, the cop looked up. 'Right. If there's damage to the building, no one will be going in or out until it's repaired and you get a new permit.'

'Touch it all you want,' I called to the shaggy firefighter. 'Do you need help? A crowbar maybe?'

The firefighter waved me off, but I did get a grin out of him. I sidled over. 'Is this something you guys can really do?'

My thinking: *Is this something that won't cost Uncommon Grounds II anything?* In other words, our tax dollars at work.

But he shook his head. 'We just advise. A tow-truck will do the actual work.'

He looked at the hole in the deck the Firebird's front wheel had made. 'And it'll have to be the Godzilla of all tow-trucks.'

'Hey, Brady,' a younger firefighter called. 'Check this out.'

My guy – Brady, presumably – joined his colleague at the driver's side door. The younger firefighter was pointing at something. Then he licked his index finger and ducked into the Firebird. When he came out he sniffed his finger and waved it in front of Brady.

Before the junior G-man could taste it, Brady grabbed his hand. 'Heckleman!'

The police officer I'd spoken to looked up.

'Got something here,' Brady said.

I exchanged looks with Sarah as Heckleman climbed the stairs. He leaned into the car, then beckoned for his fellow officer to join him.

I was on the far side of the Firebird and since the car was sitting at an angle – one tire lodged into the aforementioned hole in the deck – I couldn't see what they were looking at.

Finally, the officers conferred and then made their way down the steps to Sarah. Heckleman took out his handcuffs. 'I'm sorry, Ms Kingston, we're going to have to take you in.'

'Whoa.' I came off the porch as I had earlier. I landed the same way, too, and by the time I got to my feet, they were already snapping the shackles on Sarah.

'What are you arresting her for?' I demanded, trailing them. 'Forgetting to set her parking brake?'

Heckleman turned, his hand resting lightly on the butt of his gun in its holster. 'Funny.'

My relationship with Pavlik had taught me a few things. Like when to back off.

I held up both hands. 'I'm sorry. Just trying to understand why you're detaining my friend.' I'd learned some cop words, too.

'We're "detaining" her,' Heckleman sounded like he was making fun of my vocabulary, 'on suspicion of drug possession.'

Oh.

Sixteen

It was *Cops*, come to life in our own town of Brookhills.

Heckleman opened the squad car's rear door and put his hand on the top of Sarah's head to ease her into the backseat.

Through the driver's side window I could see what looked like a ticket book – the kind for traffic citations, not police raffles – on the passenger seat and, on top of that, a radar gun. Apparently Heckleman had been lying in ambush for speeders when our call reached headquarters. An empty McDonald's coffee cup and balled-up Egg McMuffin wrapper lay on the floor in front of the seat, alongside a covered kettle that I suspected was used as a porta-potty.

'Don't be ridiculous,' Sarah was squawking. 'I can't leave my car. Look at it.' She tried to gesture toward the Firebird, but her hands were cuffed behind her back.

'Look at it?' Brady hitched his thumbs in his belt and rocked forward on his toes. 'Oh, believe me, we'll look at it. With a fine-tooth comb.'

177

Heckleman ignored the mangled metaphor, but not the sentiment. 'Like hell you will,' he said, straightening up. 'Don't touch that car, Brady. Understand? Crime Scene is coming out.'

Brady's face reddened, but he kept on rocking. 'Sure, sure. Heckleman. We'll do our job and the techies will do theirs. We know the drill.'

'I swear, if you so much as—'

'—touch my car,' Sarah took over from inside the squad. 'I'll have your badge.'

'He's a firefighter,' I pointed out.

'Then I'll have his hose.' Sarah looked like she meant it.

Brady, however, seemed uncertain. 'My ... hose?'

'You heard me,' Sarah snarled. 'Sleep with one eye open.'

Shades of Lorena Bobbitt. 'Shut up before they add threatening an officer to the charges,' I hissed.

'But he's not a cop. You said so. Is there a law against threatening firefighters?'

Before I could make something up, she broke into tears. 'I need you to help me, Maggy.'

'Of course.' I went to pat Sarah's shoulder, but pulled back as Heckleman moved toward us. 'Tell me what I can do.'

'Please,' she managed between sobs, 'call Mario.'

Sarah's attorney, presumably. 'Which firm is

178

he with?'

'He's on his own.' She swung her legs out of the squad as Heckleman started to close the door.

'OK, then how will I find him? What's his last name?'

The officer stuffed Sarah's feet back in and tried again.

'Look in the *Yellow Pages*,' she managed before the door slammed shut between us.

'Under "attorneys"?' I yelled at the closed window. How many pages of lawyers' listings would I have to wade through if Sarah couldn't tell me the guy's last name?

As Heckleman circled around to the driver's side and started the car, Sarah shook her head emphatically. 'What the hell are you talking about?' came through clearly, albeit muffled.

It was as the squad began to pull away, though, that I nearly missed Sarah's Kingston's touching final words to me:

'I said Mario, you idiot. He's my mechanic.'

As far as I was concerned, finding St Mario of the Oil Stain could wait. Getting the car-owner out of the slammer was a whole lot more important to me than getting the car itself repaired.

The first thing I did was alert Ronny and Tien to what was going on.

'I don't understand,' Ronny said, stepping to the door of the depot to look out. 'What did they find?'

'I don't know.' I pointed at Brady and the other firefighter, who were talking to a guy with an auto club logo on his shirt. Something told me the American Automobile Association's Basic Coverage wasn't going to cover this. 'But I'll bet they do.'

Ronny nodded. 'Maybe you should go ask them.'

I started moving toward the klatch, but Brady lifted his head. His look wasn't exactly welcoming.

I retreated. 'Maybe *you* should go talk to them, Ronny. You know, man-to-man?'

He nodded, folding down the collar on his shirt. Thank God the green polyester pants had been yesterday's muse. 'I'm on it.'

As Ronny crossed to the other men, Tien asked, 'Think they'll tell him anything?'

'Probably not, but I've grown tired of rejection. Let somebody else share the dream.'

As we watched, Ronny exchanged a few words with Brady before the other man stuck his hand out to shake. Then the firefighter must have introduced Ronny to his younger co-worker because the two of them also shook and, finally, the AAA man joined in.

'What? No secret male rituals?' Tien asked in a stage whisper. 'No primal screams?'

I snickered and Brady threw *me* the dirty look.

Not one to be a tattler, I simply slewed my eyes toward Tien.

Brady didn't take the hint, turning back to the group. The four men spoke, one or the other of them gesturing toward various parts of Sarah's car. When the AAA man descended the steps to look at the rear, Ronny took the opportunity to point to the driver's side.

Another exchange and, when the fourth man rejoined the group, Ronny shook hands all around and returned to us.

Except he passed by and continued on into the depot.

'Where's he going?' Tien asked.

'Shh. It's his cover. We'll wait a couple of minutes and then go in.'

I counted to five in my head. 'Oh, hell, let's go.'

We found Ronny behind the ticket counter waiting for us.

'So what did you say?' Tien asked. 'Did they tell you anything?'

Ronny puffed out his chest. 'Well, first I introduced myself.'

'As Sarah's cousin?' This from me.

'Of course not. I told them I was the contractor and was concerned about the stability of the building and how soon I could start repairs.'

'Brilliant,' Tien breathed.

Ronny blushed. 'Not really.'

'Really,' I confirmed. 'Now, what did they say?'

'About what they found?'

'That, too. But first, when can you begin

181

work?' OK, so it was a little self-centered of me. But I was certain Sarah would concur when I bailed her out.

'They said if the Firebird was towed away later this afternoon, the building inspector could check the depot out as soon as tomorrow. I have to pull permits anyway, so I'll run over and see him this afternoon. Take the bull by the horns.' Ronny was looking mighty pleased with himself.

'Why are they waiting to remove it?' I hooked my finger toward the window, where we could see the big AAA wrecker with a winch on it. Who needed Mario anyway? 'The tow-truck is here, why don't they do it right now?'

'They have to examine the Firebird.' Ronny nodded to a van that was pulling up in front. The vehicle was unmarked, but I recognized it as the county crime scene investigators' wheels.

'Oh, God. Not the sheriff's office,' I said as a man climbed out of the van on the driver's side. I remembered him as one of the people who responded to Kornell's train wreck. A photographer popped out from the passenger's side.

Oh well, one way or the other, Pavlik was going to hear about this. 'Examining it for what? What did they find? And where?'

'The "where",' Ronny said, milking it, 'is the driver's seat. Oh, and I think the gas pedal.' He put his index finger to his chin and tapped like he was trying to remember.

'And the "what"?' I was getting impatient. I

could see flashes of light as the county photographer took photos on the shady porch.

'The "what"?' Ronny repeated.

I glared at him. 'Don't play with me.'

He flushed and snuck a peek to see if Tien was listening.

She had been, but now she gazed off at the ceiling, walls – anything but us. In a second, she'd start whistling.

Could there be something brewing between these two? I looked from Ronny to Tien and back again. 'Give.'

Ronny cleared his throat and, as Tien turned to him, puffed out his chest. 'Oh, you mean what did they *find*?'

Before I could smack him upside the head, he moved hastily on. 'Cocaine.'

'What?' I knew we were dangerously close to a 'Who's on first' moment, but I honestly couldn't believe it.

'Cocaine. You know: Coke. Snow. Nose ... umm, nose...'

'Candy,' Tien supplied.

We both looked at her.

This time *she* blushed. 'I do watch TV.'

'*Law & Order*.' Ronny positively glowed. 'I love that show. Watch each episode, over and over.'

'Me, too,' Tien said, moving a little closer. 'I know it's not real life, but...' She trailed off.

'No, but Pavlik tells me it's very accurate as far as...' I caught myself. 'Enough television

183

talk. Are you serious? They found cocaine in Sarah's car?'

Ronny shrugged. 'That's what they told me. Of course, until they get it to the county lab, they can't be sure—'

The county – I should have guessed. Our cops were outfitted to ticket out-of-town speeders and direct traffic after church, not bust a drug ring.

'Listen,' I said, digging out my car keys, 'I'm going to see what I can do for Sarah. Would you,' I pointed at Ronny, 'take care of things here?'

'Of course.' He pulled on his collar. 'You can count on me.'

'I know I can.' I glanced around. 'Is there a rear exit? I'm parked in the lot.'

Good thing. If I'd parked on the street in front, Sarah's car would have T-boned mine. Of course, then the porch might have been saved.

'Use the boarding platform door.' Ronny hooked a thumb around the corner of the ticket counter.

I took his advice and exited at the back corner of the building. I was not only close to my car, but also had avoided the men on the porch.

That didn't stop Brady, though, from glaring at me as I pulled past him in the Escape.

'I can't understand why that man doesn't like me,' I said to Pavlik after I'd filled him in. I was sitting in the guest chair in the sheriff's office,

184

my handbag next to his brass nameplate. 'Sarah was the one who threatened to lop off his weenie.'

'Brady doesn't like you because Heckleman doesn't,' Pavlik said mildly.

'Heckleman? The cop who arrested Sarah?'

'Yup.' Pavlik steepled his fingers. 'They're ... tight.'

'Are you saying they're gay?' I asked bluntly. 'Because if they are, it's no one's—'

'I know, I know. But they're not. And you are the proud mother of a gay son.' Pavlik cracked a grin. 'Rightfully. Eric's a good kid.'

Pavlik and Eric are ... well, tight.

'So what *did* you mean,' I said, ashamed of myself, 'about Heckleman and Brady. They're friends?'

'More mentor and mentee,' Pavlik said. 'Brady wants to move into law enforcement. He haunted me for a while after I arrived in Brookhills. Now he's turned his attention from the county sheriff's department to town police force. Hangs around any cop who'll let him.' Pavlik shrugged. 'I think Heckleman realizes now that he shouldn't have encouraged the guy, but he doesn't see how to shake him.'

'Why would he want to go from fire department to law enforcement?'

'The Brookhills Fire Department is volunteer. The guys don't work full-time and are paid peanuts in comparison to the risks.'

'What's the "volunteer" part, if they're paid?'

'It's different in each town or city. In Brook-hills they have salaried firefighters and supple-ment the force with guys,' he looked at me, 'and gals, who have other jobs. They're paid, but only for the hours they work.'

'And they don't have benefits, I'll wager.'

'Not health insurance, disability. Nothing.'

I could see why Brady would want to change professions. And why he might follow Heckle-man's lead. The guy was sucking up. However, what I didn't get: 'So what does Heckleman have against me?'

Understand, I'm the kind of person who needs to be liked. Even by people I detest.

'Nothing,' Pavlik said. 'Heckleman doesn't like anyone.'

I'd make it my mission to change that. If I ever ran into him again.

Which made me wonder whether I'd ever see Sarah again.

After leaving the depot, I'd called Pavlik. He said Sarah would likely be brought to the build-ing we were sitting in. The Brookhills Police Department was so tiny they used the county's jail and booking facilities.

I gestured toward the phone on his desk. 'Can you call and see what's happening?'

Pavlik shook his head. 'I confirmed that Sarah is in the building and I asked to be kept up to date. I can't interfere, even if she is a friend. *Especially* if she's a friend.'

'This is ridiculous,' I said, repeating what I'd

told Pavlik earlier. 'Sarah does not do cocaine.'

'I'm sure you're right. If so, the drug test will confirm that.'

Pavlik didn't seem to notice the inconsistency. If he was so 'sure', why the 'if'?

'You can't blame the officers for suspecting, though,' Pavlik continued. 'According to Heckleman, Sarah's nose was red and she was sniffing. Classic symptoms of recently snorting cocaine.'

'Or of crying,' I said, exasperated. 'You know how much Sarah loved that car. The woman was sobbing like someone had killed her dog.'

'Sarah Kingston?' Pavlik looked surprised. 'Crying?'

'You'd believe Sarah did drugs before you believed she was capable of crying?'

Pavlik cocked his head. 'Well, yeah. Pretty much. You?'

Maybe if I hadn't seen it with my own eyes...

I didn't answer the question. 'Sarah's nose was running because she cried. First, Courtney and Sam left her and now it's the Firebird.'

As I said that, I realized that everything Sarah loved was indeed gone. Though I hoped she liked me. Sort of.

'I'd forgotten about the kids,' Pavlik said, leaning back in his chair. 'How's it going?'

'Sam and Courtney were in touch every day,' I said. 'Until you put Sarah in the slammer. Now, what happens to them?'

'I didn't put Sarah in jail,' Pavlik reminded

me. 'She'll be tested for drugs. If the results come back clean, they'll likely let her out.'

'Likely?'

'Probably.' Pavlik looked uncomfortable. 'It depends on what they find in the car.'

'But if Sarah doesn't use cocaine—'

'It doesn't mean she doesn't sell it.'

'A dealer?' I couldn't believe my ears. 'You think Sarah's a ... pusher?'

He held up his hands. 'Again, I don't think anything. The car is being checked. If they find the substance is cocaine, then they'll check for amounts. If it's more than simple possession, I'm afraid—'

This time, I interrupted. 'Wait a second. You don't even know if it *is* cocaine?'

'Like I said, I don't—'

'I know, I know, you don't know anything. Yet. Including that there actually *was* a drug in the car? That's ridiculous.'

I warmed into my rant: 'How can you arrest someone for being caught with something, when you don't even know what that "something" is?'

A character trait of Pavlik: the crazier I get, the calmer he is. Until we reach his boiling point. Then he blows. I feared I was edging close to the top of his thermometer now.

His eyes became a stormy gray. 'I *assume* that the officers detained her on suspicion of possessing a controlled substance.'

'Heckleman made fun of me when I said

"detained",' I muttered. More proof he didn't like me. 'So what if that "controlled substance" turns out to be baking soda, or baby powder, or, or...'

I stopped.

Then took a deep breath and let the piece fall perfectly into the puzzle.

Seventeen

Pavlik gave me an odd look. 'So we'll apologize and release her. You have to understand what's at stake with all the drugs on the streets. Sure, mistakes are made, but we can't—'

'Wait, wait.' I waved my hands for him to stop.

He did.

I said, 'Flour.'

Pavlik seemed confused. 'Flower? The kind you plant?'

'No, the kind you bake with.' I leaned forward. 'Art Jenada is the caterer across from the train station. He was making biscuits when I rousted him for help after Sarah's car crashed into the depot.'

'And?'

'I know Jenada had flour on his hands when he was nosing around the car, because when I shook hands with him afterwards, I got it all over me.'

'At least your jeans.' Pavlik pointed to where I'd wiped my palms. 'I was wondering where that came from.'

Guess I should be grateful that *I* wasn't being

drug-tested.

'Anyway,' I continued, 'I think he got flour in the car when he was looking at it.'

'But on the seat?'

'Sure, if he leaned in.'

Pavlik looked doubtful now, but almost immediately his phone rang. He picked up.

The sheriff listened for a while and pulled a pad toward him. Said, 'uh-unh,' 'uh-huh,' and a couple of two-syllable sounds that could have been either positive or negative. He jotted down a few words, then asked the person on the other side of the conversation to repeat something. Which he wrote on a corner of the page.

Finally he hung up. 'Sarah is being released.'

I nearly leapt from my chair. 'See? I told you she wasn't a druggie.'

'And you were absolutely right,' Pavlik said. 'Sarah tested negative for cocaine and any other illegal substance.'

I thought the sheriff was tempted to say more. Instead, though, he slid my handbag toward me. 'You might want to meet her. She should be downstairs in a couple of minutes.'

'Sounds good.'

When Pavlik came around the desk, I flung my arm around his neck and kissed him lightly on the lips. 'Want to come over for dinner tonight?'

He hesitated. 'Maybe you should have dinner with Sarah. As you say, she's having a rough time.'

191

'That's very considerate of you.' I studied Pavlik's face. 'Is everything OK?'

'Sure.' He gave me a peck back. 'Just got a lot on my mind. I'll call you tomorrow.'

'How about dinner then?'

Another hesitation. 'I'll let you know.'

'Great.' I wound my hand through the strap on my bag, not sure what to do.

There had been a distinct change in the atmosphere of the room. Had I done something to push the sheriff over the cliff? Asked one too many questions? Tripped over one too many bodies?

Or was Pavlik just, like the old joke goes, 'sick of my shit'.

I didn't want to ask, but I knew I'd drive myself crazy if I didn't. 'You said everything was OK. Did you mean with you, or did you mean with us?'

'Both.' He took a step toward me and drew me into his arms. This time when we kissed, it felt like we meant it.

Pavlik moved me back, hands on my shoulders so we could be face to face. Or as near as possible. Pavlik is considerably taller than I am. My head fits perfectly on his chest for slow-dancing.

I looked up at him. 'We're fine?'

He smiled and his eyes flared blue. 'We're better than fine.'

'So what happened?' I knew I hadn't imagined it. God knows I'd imagined enough things to appreciate the difference.

Pavlik sighed. 'I can't go into specifics, but I think you should keep an eye on Sarah. I said no to our having dinner because it would free you up to see her.'

'So I guess I should have asked if *Sarah* is OK.'

'You told me yourself that she's not, remember?' He gave me a playful shake. 'She *cried* today.'

He was right. Sarah was not herself and I knew it, no matter how much she tried to hide it. And the really worrisome thing was that she *wasn't* trying to hide it anymore.

'A cry for help,' I said and then felt myself blush. 'Sorry, a little dramatic.'

'But maybe not inaccurate.' He squeezed me again and then released me. 'Go get Sarah. She shouldn't be alone.'

'She won't be.' I turned around at the door. 'She'll have yours truly.'

'Leave me alone,' Sarah growled as she stomped past me, her shoes making slapping noises on the marble floor of the chair-lined lobby where I'd been waiting

I trailed after her. 'I'm just trying to help.'

Sarah turned to face me. 'Help? All I asked you to do is call Mario and you couldn't even pull that off. I don't need your help, Maggy. I need my car. Or whatever's left of it.'

'Triple-A was there,' I said. 'The tow-truck is

193

probably pulling the Firebird off the porch as we speak. I didn't think Mario—'

'That's right,' Sarah snapped. 'You didn't think. Nobody touches my car but Mario.'

Assuming no psychic link, I didn't quite see how Sarah could know I hadn't called her mechanic. I didn't bother to ask, though, since we were already drawing the attention of everybody waiting in the lobby as well as the uniformed and armed sheriff's deputy behind the desk. I put my hand on Sarah's back in an attempt to guide her outside.

'Don't touch me,' she said, smacking my hand away and, thankfully, heading for the door. 'I've had enough of that to last a lifetime.'

'You mean when you were searched?' I was just following her now, trying not to say the wrong thing. At least until we were safely off the premises.

'Searched? Yes, searched. Twice. And ordered to stand here, sit there, turn right, then left, face the camera, get fingerprinted.' She stopped just outside the door and held up a shaky hand to show me her blackened pads. 'I have to get this ink off.'

Poor Sarah. The invasion of her personal space – the radius of which was already twice that required by most people – seemed to freak her out more than the accusation of drug possession.

I started to put my hand on her shoulder again, but caught myself. Instead, I dug through my bag and handed her a small bottle.

'Waterless hand-cleanser?' She unscrewed the cap and worked the liquid into her hands. Didn't do much for the ink, but the process seemed to make her feel better. 'Where did you get this? Steal it from Christy?'

'Hey, she's not the only one who's hygienic.'

Sarah recapped the bottle and squinted at the label. 'Good until October ... ninety-nine?'

I snatched the cleanser away from her. 'This stuff doesn't go bad.'

'Says you,' Sarah said, thankfully sounding less shaky. 'It's probably "Bacterial Cleanser" now.'

'Instead of *anti*-bacterial? Cute.'

Truth was, the stuff had probably been in my handbag since I worked in the health room of Eric's grade school. Not the *same* handbag, you understand. The contents of the old got dumped into its successor, with the bags getting progressively larger to accommodate. Finding stuff was akin to an archeological dig. I didn't delve too deep, lest I stumble on the primordial ooze at the bottom.

We had reached the parking lot and Sarah looked around.

'My Escape is next to the tree over there,' I said, indicating the vehicle.

'I don't need a ride. Ronny's across the way getting our building permits.' Sarah cocked her head. 'And why are you being so nice?'

'*Trying* to be nice,' I corrected. 'You're not

exactly making it easy. And how do you know Ronny's here?'

'He told me when I telephoned him. The accused does get to make one call, you know.'

I was hurt. 'And you didn't think of me?'

'Just the opposite. No answer. There should be a profane message on your voicemail. I'm just lucky they let me contact Ronny after you couldn't be bothered. He was still with the Firebird and *he*,' her eyes were shooting darts, 'didn't even know anything about Mario.'

Stoolie. Deciding that pretense was the best defense, I dropped the cleanser back into my handbag and unearthed my cellphone. 'I don't know why I wouldn't have answered.' I pushed the volume button on one side of the flip-phone. 'Damn, I forgot. I set the thing on "vibrate" when I went to see Pavlik. I don't know why I didn't feel it, though.'

Sarah gestured at my tote-sized accessory. 'In Santa's sack of toys? You should put the phone somewhere you'll notice, like a clothes pocket.'

'My jeans are too tight,' I said. 'It'd ruin the lines.'

'Then your bra. That's what a lot of women do.'

I looked down at my breasts. 'Within ten steps, the thing would fall through, hit the ground and shatter into—'

'Fine.' Sarah turned away. 'I told you where to stick it.'

And right back at you, dear friend and business partner.

Something in motion caught my eye. 'Look. It's Ronny.' I pointed across the parking lot.

Sarah's cousin was just coming out of the county administration building. Sarah hailed him and he came over to us.

'They sprung you, huh?' He gave Sarah a hug. Sure. *Him,* she didn't hit.

'Had to,' Sarah said. 'They didn't find cocaine in my system.'

'How about biscuit flour?' I asked.

'Biscuit flour?' Ronny seemed lost.

'Yes,' I said. 'That's what I think was in the Firebird. Biscuit flour from Art Jenada's hands or clothes.'

I turned to Sarah. 'Don't you remember he was covered with it?'

'I don't remember much after seeing my baby...' Her voice cracked and she cleared her throat, 'the Firebird on the porch.'

Ronny unlocked his car. 'What I can't figure out is how it landed where it did.' He stopped. 'Unless somebody drove it?'

'You think this was done on purpose?' I asked.

He looked uncomfortable. 'Sorry to pile-on, ladies. It just seems like there've been a bunch of accidents. Don't you wonder if they're related?'

'Somebody murdered my car on *purpose*?' Sarah's eyes were saucers. Hell, make that dinner plates.

'Let's not jump to conclusions.' I couldn't believe I was the voice of reason here. It showed you what a low bar had been set for me.

'But Ronny's right,' Sarah said. 'We talked about this, Maggy. First Kornell is hit by a train. Then the clock's ripped off the station wall, followed by the front railing failing. Now, now,' a sob rose in her throat, 'this.'

She sniffled.

I didn't dare tease her about the 'railing failing' rhyme. And I couldn't stand to see Sarah cry again. It was like the hundred-year storm. Once in a lifetime is more than enough.

Besides, commiserating wouldn't help. But maybe action could. 'Fine. Say you two are right. Then maybe we should find out who's targeting us and why.'

Ronny looked surprised. 'We should find out? What about the police?'

'Aww, we don't need them.' Sarah was getting into the spirit. 'Maggy and I have gotten good at this.'

'We have.' I felt like a young Judy Garland encouraging a little Mickey Rooney to 'Put on a show!' 'Besides, the police will just slow us down.'

'They're too stodgy,' Sarah agreed, 'what with evidence and all.'

From Ronny, 'We don't need evidence?'

'Gut feeling is more important.' Sarah said. 'Intuition. We know the people involved. We can do this. Someone wants to stop us and we're not going to let them.'

It was the most enthusiastic I'd seen Sarah in a long time. Actually, it was the most enthusiastic I'd *ever* seen her.

Which in itself was cause for worry.

Still, if the thought of tracking down the vandals buoyed Sarah as she dealt with the Firebird, I was all for it.

'I'm in,' I said, turning to Ronny. 'But what about you? Still willing to continue with the work?'

'You betcha.' Ronny was nodding.

Well, what do you know? We *were* going to put on a show.

Fifteen minutes later, we were back at the train station, staring at Sarah's car.

The Firebird had been lifted off the porch and left sitting cockeyed in the driveway between the depot and the florist shop next door.

The poor vehicle faced us, one front tire blown, hood crumpled, paint crackled. The Firebird's black bumper, minimal in the first place, was hanging lopsided like a glued-on mustache that had half come loose. The right headlight was popped out, hanging by its wiring.

Sarah and I observed a moment of silence before she heaved a sigh. 'It's a metaphor for life, isn't it? We start out a sports car and end up a cross between Bride of Chucky and

Groucho Marx.'

'Amen,' I agreed. 'Though I'm hoping to avoid the mustache.'

'You saw the coots back in the nursing home.' Sarah was still staring at the Firebird. 'You live long enough, hair grows everywhere.'

'We both have a few years before needing to worry about that.' Not that the thought wouldn't wake me up at three a.m. screaming in terror. 'I'm surprised they didn't tow the car away to the jun—.' I stopped, but not fast enough.

Sarah glared at me. 'You were going to say "junkyard".'

'I was not,' I lied. 'I'm sure the Firebird can be repaired.'

The dangling headlight picked that moment to fall. It hit the ground and rolled, ending up near our feet.

Sarah looked down at it. 'I think not.'

'Really?' It was unlike her to give up. 'What about Mario?'

'Even Mario can't work miracles. Besides, we had a good run. It's time for him to help others.'

'Mario?' Geez, did she have this guy on personal retainer?

Sarah looked at me like I was crazy. 'No, of course not. The Firebird.'

Now she was spooking me. 'How can it ... he do that?'

'As a donor.' She picked up the headlight and cradled it in the crook of her arm.

I was almost afraid to ask. 'Umm, you mean like an organ donor?'

'Don't be stupid.' Sarah gestured at the car and, as if on cue, the bumper fell completely off. 'It's a car, Maggy. It doesn't *have* organs.'

The Sarah I knew and feared was back. Be careful what you wish for. 'So you're going to donate the car to a charity?'

'Of course not,' she said, looking offended. 'Don't you know they would just junk him?'

'All right. So what *are* you going to do?'

'You'll see.' Sarah held up one finger and then proceeded to dig out her cellphone.

As she punched in a number – as in single digit, so whoever she was calling must be on speed-dial – I wandered over to the porch where Ronny was surveying the damage left in the wake of the car.

'How bad is it?' I asked as I picked my way up the steps.

He was on his hands and knees, face through the hole created by the tire. At the sound of my voice he jumped and banged his head on one of the ragged boards.

'I'm so sorry,' I said, 'I didn't mean to startle you.'

'That's OK,' Ronny said, rubbing the spot ruefully. 'I'm pretty tough, despite the way I dress.' He straightened his sweater, which had swung around again.

I had a hunch he was tough *because* of the way he dressed. 'Are you sure you're not

201

bleeding? Those boards were sharp enough to blow a tire.'

'Nope, no blood.' He held up his hand to show me. 'Besides, the tire wasn't punctured. The tow-truck driver deflated it. Easier to pull the car off that way.'

I guessed it made sense, as in easier to draw a limp balloon out of a hole than an inflated one.

'Did you find any structural damage?' I asked. I was hoping the answer would be no. If there were problems with the integrity of the building, the project was in trouble, given the September first deadline looming.

'That's what I was checking out.' Ronny motioned toward the hole. 'The car just took out some planks. It didn't damage the building, or even the deck posts.'

I let my breath out. 'Well, that's good news.' I turned to summon Sarah and found her right behind me.

'No, no,' she was saying into the phone. 'I won't hear of it. You've been so kind to us all these years.'

She listened for a moment. Then, 'I'm just glad that something good can come of this. We'll be here waiting for you.'

Sarah flipped the phone closed. 'His passenger-side door is going to a sixty-year-old man with a blue Firebird. They'll have to paint him to match, of course.'

I was going to ask if she was talking about painting the man or the Firebird, but that would be petty. Besides, Sarah was getting misty.

She swiped at her eyes and pushed on: 'Both rear tail lights are going to a Milwaukee family for their son's car. It's a birthday surprise.' She smiled through the tears. 'I'm so glad they won't be split up.'

I heard Ronny say something that sounded suspiciously like 'parts is parts'.

'Me, too,' I draped my arm over Sarah's shoulder and gave Ronny a warning look. 'Who's ... making the arrangements?'

A choking noise from Ronny. 'Sorry,' he said. 'Frog in my throat. I'd better get some water.'

As he ducked into the station's doorway, Sarah answered my question. 'Mario.' She sniffed. 'It will be his last duty for us.'

'Don't be silly,' I said. 'You'll have other cars. And Mario will take care of them, too.'

'You think?' Sarah asked wistfully.

What I thought was that she was going off the deep end and I wasn't far from following her. 'I don't think, I know. What we have to do now, though, is to look forward. One, get the depot ready for opening. And two, make sure that whoever is doing this to us is stopped.'

'You're right.' Sarah balled her hand into a fist and shook it over her head in defiance. 'As God is my witness, I'll never—'

'That's enough of the dramatics, Cuz,' Ronny said from the doorway. 'Snap out of it.' He handed her the glass of water he was carry-ing.

She drank half of it and set the glass down. 'OK.'

I looked at her quizzically. 'OK?' I turned to Ronny. 'That's all I had to do?'

'Pretty much.'

'We Kingstons weren't molly-coddled,' Sarah admitted. '"Straighten up and fly right," my father used to say.'

My friend might be selling her family mantra, but I wasn't sure even she herself was buying it.

No matter, though. At least Sarah wasn't channeling Scarlett O'Hara anymore.

Ronny leaned out on the deck to get a better view of the Firebird. 'Did you ever tell us where you parked?'

'Up there.' The raised area Sarah indicated was the high, gravel-covered spot I'd noticed earlier. It was directly across the street from us.

'I won't ask you why.' Ronny looked back and forth, forth and back. 'I guess the Firebird could have simply rolled down the hill and across the street.'

'But would the car gain enough speed coasting to land on the deck?' I asked. 'We're four feet up.'

Ronny nodded to the street in front of us. 'If the tires hit the curb just right, I guess the vehicle could have gone airborne.'

'Did you set the parking brake?' I asked Sarah.

'Of course I did,' she said indignantly.

'I'm just asking because usually I don't.'

South-eastern Wisconsin is pretty flat. Then again, Sarah's car hadn't needed a San Francisco-style hill to ski-jump on to the porch.

She folded her arms. 'Well, I always do.'

'Maybe a better question,' Ronny said. 'Did the parking brake work?'

I could practically see Sarah's hackles rise. 'Mario kept my baby in perfect condition. I set the brake. This is not our fault.' She said it like she was trying to reassure not only herself, but the mortally wounded car squatting in the driveway.

'Of course it isn't,' I was quick to reassure her. 'Now when you backed the Firebird in, did you see anyone hanging around?'

'I didn't—'

'No one, huh?' I mused. 'Not Christy or Art or anybody.'

Sarah just about shouted. 'Look, I didn't—'

'You don't have to get mad,' I said, feeling a little dig. Here I was trying to help and—

Sarah clamped both hands on my shoulders, shaking me. 'Will you let me finish? I did *not* back the car in.'

En masse, we turned to look at the magic Firebird.

Ronny voiced what I believed everybody was thinking. 'Then how in the hell did it turn itself around?'

Eighteen

The answer, of course, was that it hadn't.

'Someone must have started the car, pulled it out and then backed in,' I said.

'First of all,' Ronny said, 'how could they start the car?'

I turned to Sarah. 'You didn't leave the keys in the car, did you?'

'Of course not.'

Ronny frowned. 'You have a spare key anywhere?'

She matched his frown, line for line. 'Yes, but I put it in one of those little magnetic cases.'

'Like the infomercial where the pitchman hides the thing inside the wheel-well?' I turned to Ronny. 'They show this bumbling thief looking everywhere and not finding it. What a joke.'

'Uh, Sarah,' Ronny asked, 'where did you put yours?'

'The wheel-well,' Sarah said.

Ronny and I both looked at her.

Sarah bristled. 'I'm not an idiot. I stuck it inside the rear one on the passenger side, not the front driver's side like in that commercial.'

'Smart,' I said. 'No one would think of looking there.'

'Hey,' she protested. 'There's a lot of fiberglass on my baby. Hiding places that are metal aren't easy to find.'

Ronny was rubbing his chin. 'Maggy, this might answer the question you originally asked. If the car was, in fact, running as it came off the hill, the jump on to the porch seems a little more likely.'

'Geez, we're lucky the unguided missile didn't go through the door.' I was shaking my head. 'Think of all the added expense. Not to mention the time we'd lose.'

Ronny seemed like he was about to say something and thought better of it.

'What?' I asked.

He looked uncomfortable. 'I need to talk numbers, but not just now. You have enough to worry about.'

'Great, so now we can worry about what you're not telling us.' Sarah said sourly. 'Give.'

Even as she said it, a pristine white tow truck pulled up in front. Sarah broke off and picked her way down the steps to meet the driver, who was wearing equally pristine white coveralls.

I would have known this was Mario, even if he didn't have his name embroidered on his shirt pocket, or 'Mario's Repair and Restoration' tastefully stenciled on his truck.

Sarah fell on the man like he was the father of her children. Or child, in this case. He listened as she spoke, wagging his head sadly. Then, together, they walked over to the Firebird.

'We should give them some time alone,' Ronny said.

He was right. 'Why don't we grab a table inside and go over the numbers?'

I had a feeling Ronny was harboring bad news for us. I preferred to be sitting down when I heard the details.

'Is this about the deck repair costs?' I asked as we settled into chairs. 'I thought you said there was no major damage.'

'There isn't,' he assured me. 'Repairing the decking, stairs and railing should be easy enough and covered by insurance.'

'After the deductible,' I said.

'True, and we'll have to check the insurance policy.'

'Maybe Sarah knows.'

We turned in tandem to look out the window to where Sarah and Mario were standing, heads bowed.

'Probably not a good time to ask her,' Ronny said.

'Agreed. But, if you're not terribly worried about the recent damage, what's the problem?'

Why-oh-why do I ask questions no rational person would want answers to?

'Wiring.'

I was relieved. I knew electrical work was expensive, but I was expecting to hear that the station had been built on a cemetery or something. 'Oh, well—'

'And pipes.'

Plumbers were really costly, but you had to expect that with—

'Only the sewer is what really worries me.'

That was it. The triumvirate of unexpected costs.

'What's wrong with the sewer?'

'Nothing now,' Ronny said, 'but there's an old lift pump system. Tomorrow, next week, a year from now, the thing is going to have to be replaced. And it'll be expensive.'

Brookhills had put in city sewers about fifteen years back, but didn't set them deep enough for the properties below street level to connect to them.

That meant that some businesses and homes were forced to install pumps to 'lift' the sewage up to the sewer pipes.

Apparently, shit really *does* run downhill.

Why do I know all this, you ask? Because the home Ted and I owned had a lift pump. Our house, though, was below street level, with a steep driveway that gave us fits in the winter. The depot, on the other hand, was elevated from ... 'But doesn't the sewer line run down Junction Road here?'

'That's what I thought, too,' Ronny said, getting up and approaching the window by the boarding platform. I followed him.

'When I met with the building inspector,' Ronny continued, 'he told me that because Junction is a two-block, angle road—'

'The only one in Brookhills—'

'—they didn't bother running the pipes down Junction. Instead, the buildings connect through the backyards to the sewer on Civic.'

I followed his pointing finger past the parking lot to the not-so-gently rolling hill beyond, leading to Civic.

And one hell of a long way up.

'But our lift pump is OK for now, right?'

'Right,' Ronny assured me. 'On the other hand, similar ones started failing about five years ago and owners are finding it tough to get replacements.'

'How tough?' Ted and I had managed to keep our residential entry limping along.

'About ten thousand dollars tough,' Ronny said, pulling his sweater sleeves tight, like he'd prefer to strangle himself rather than give me this news.

I appreciated his effort. 'That's ridiculous. A lift pump doesn't even have that many moving parts.'

'Right, but somebody has to go down into the holding basin to install it.'

'Ugh.'

'And that person is required to wear a hazmat suit, because—'

I held up my hands. 'Please, no more poop. What other good news do you have?'

Ronny sighed and I followed him into the kitchen. 'We'll need to put a door there,' he pointed at a blank wall, 'so anyone working in here doesn't have to exit through the service area.'

'Makes sense.'

'The electrical is in this wall and when I punched a hole,' Ronny opened a storage cabinet and showed me the opening he'd made. 'I found ... this.'

He pulled out a mess of wires, some capped with little plastic tops, others exposed and still more held together with duct tape.

'Not code?' I asked, dreading the answer.

A headshake. 'Not even when this place was built.'

'So, how much?'

'No way of knowing until I get an electrician out here. And...' Ronny swung open the cupboard door below the sink, '...a plumber.'

I peered in. 'A *garden* hose?'

'Yup.'

'As the drainpipe?'

'Ditto.'

'Great.' I walked through the area behind the ticket counters, past the swinging half door and took my seat at the table.

'What are you thinking?' Ronny said, joining me there.

'Thinking?' I lifted my head from its burial place in my hands. 'I'm thinking we can't do this. I don't have the money and I doubt Sarah does, either.'

Ronny heard the catch in my voice and patted my forearm. 'Don't jump to conclusions. Maybe—'

'What are you guys talking about?'

Sarah joined us, flipping around a chair and straddling it. With the Firebird evidently in Mario's reverent control, she seemed calmer.

'Not much,' I said. 'Just ... talking.'

'The wiring and plumbing are below code,' Ronny said, even as I shook my head at him, trying to warn him off.

'How below?' Sarah asked.

Ronny looked at me apologetically before he answered. 'Sorry, Maggy. But she's the owner. Sarah has to know.'

Back to her. 'Duct tape and garden hoses.'

'Shit.'

'Yeah,' I agreed.

The three of us sat silently, staring out the window. As we did, Mario's truck passed by, Sarah's Firebird hooked by its nose like a wall-eyed pike on a fisherman's stringer.

Sarah groaned, then came back to life.

'This is it.' She spread out her arms. 'I've got this place and have to pay taxes and maintenance. I rent the space the office is in and that rent's going up. The house...' She laid her head on the back of her chair.

I patted Sarah's shoulder. 'That's OK. We tried. Maybe instead we rent that industrial-park place you showed me.'

Sarah lifted her head. 'The one you hated?'

'The price was right.'

'Yup. So much for being partners, huh?'

'What do you mean?' I asked. 'Just because

we can't open here, doesn't mean we won't open somewhere.'

'We?' Sarah asked. 'You mean you and me?'

'Of course.' I wasn't sure what she was getting at. 'Unless you don't want—'

Sarah cut me off. 'I just figured if I was not contributing the building, you would not want—'

This time I interrupted her. 'The building?' I looked around. 'It's great. But...' I punched her in the arm, 'you're better.'

For the third time since I'd known her – hell, for the third time in less than twenty-four hours – Sarah burst into tears.

'Holy shit,' Ronny said, as he brought a mug of water back from the kitchen. 'What did you say to her?'

'You were there. I didn't say anything.' I tried to hand the water to Sarah, who had gone from sobbing to a glassy, fugue-state stare. She didn't take the mug.

And I *hadn't* said anything beyond the fact that I wanted Sarah to be my partner. Despite the fact that, even without the expense of updating the depot, we probably couldn't generate enough funds to get started and pay rent.

'C'mon Sarah,' I said, sitting back down. 'We're going to do fine. We'll get financing or, or...'

Sarah showed the first signs of life in about ten minutes. 'I'll sell my house.'

'The hell you will,' I said. 'It's beautiful *and* paid off. Where else would you find a place that's big enough for the three of you?'

Sarah's face puckered up again and she scrabbled through her right pocket until a folded piece of paper saw the light of day. She shoved it across the table to me. 'There is no three of us.'

With that, she lapsed into hysteria again.

Ronny patted Sarah, while I unfolded the paper.

Maybe you *can* go home again, but from the printed-out e-mail message, apparently Sam and Courtney didn't want to. At least not Sarah's home.

Nineteen

'So what does this mean?' I asked Sarah when she finally returned to coherence. The bottle of Jim Beam Black that Ronny dug up probably helped.

'It means they don't want to live with me anymore.' The words came out mush-mouthed, but at least Sarah was talking again.

I studied the e-mail, which had been sent that morning. 'The kids just say they want to look at schools out east. Maybe—'

Sarah slammed her hand on the table and even Jim Beam jumped. 'Patrice followed up that e-mail with a phone call. Wanted me to know that if Sam and Courtney stayed on the coast, she thought it would be best that hubby and her – as "family" – take over legal custody of both kids.'

To quote Ronny's earlier words, holy shit.

No wonder Sarah had been late this morning. She'd been dealing with Patrice and then, when she had finally arrived, we'd bombarded her with theories about the relatively insignificant porch railing.

Worse, Sarah had been carrying the e-mail

215

around all day with her, not showing it to us, not telling us. The Firebird's demise must have seemed like the final blow.

'You know what I think?' Sarah continued. 'I think they had the whole thing planned. No way this just occurred to people last night.'

Much as I hated to think it, she might be right. Sam and Courtney had been with their cousins for less than a day. 'We should talk to Caron's husband, Bernie. He's a lawyer.'

'I'm trying to adopt them, Maggy, not copyright them.'

Even tipsy, Sarah could be clever, if not crystal clear. 'You want to adopt Sam and Courtney?'

'No, but I damn well don't want Patricia and "hubby" to.' She slammed her hand again and Ronny, anticipating, grabbed the bottle of bourbon just as it achieved lift-off.

'Have you talked to Sam and Courtney?' he asked. 'Is this really what they want?'

'I left voicemail messages. They didn't call back.'

'Text them,' I suggested. 'It's less confrontational.'

Sarah didn't answer at first.

Then, finally: 'I guess I don't want to confront them, Maggy. I want them to be happy and if this makes them happy, I ought to be content.'

She didn't sound content, much less happy. Sarah took the Jimmy Black from Ronny and

216

downed a swig. Then she set it on the next table. 'Now, let's talk about Uncommon Grounds.'

It was a cue to move on, so I did. 'Ronny, do you have any idea how much it will cost to bring this place up to code?'

He played along. 'Maybe it won't be too bad. I haven't looked into most of the walls. A lot of times people mess with what's easily accessible and leave the rest the way it should be.'

'That's true,' I said, trying to be equally upbeat. 'When I bought my house, there were all sorts of quirky little things about it. The stuff in the walls, though, was in pretty good shape.'

'Right,' Ronny said, 'and I'm sure the lift pump—'

'Lift pump?' Sarah's head snapped to attention. 'Don't tell me there's a lift pump here, too?'

'Well, yes,' I said, uncomfortably. 'But it's working just fine.'

'Now, sure.' Sarah got to her feet, a trifle unsteadily. 'I'm a real estate agent, Maggy. I've sold houses to people who didn't realize there was routine maintenance required on these things. I'd try to tell them, but they'd ignore me. Until, of course, it broke.'

'The pump at my old house is OK,' I said. As far as I knew.

'Yeah, because *you* listened.' Sarah sagged back down as though the prospect of both standing and walking lay a bit beyond her current horizons. 'Most people don't. The motor falls off and suddenly somebody in a spacesuit has to go diving. Then it's *my* fault.'

'Hazmat suit,' Ronny corrected. I thought Sarah was going to smack him one.

'It doesn't matter.' Maggy Thorsen, Voice of Reason. 'We'll take care of the pump and, if it fails, deal with it then. For now, let's figure out how we can pay for the repairs that need to be done in order to open.'

'How in the hell did that frog guy get away with this?' Sarah grumbled.

'Not a frogman, Sarah,' I said, gently. 'Hazmat, as in "hazardous material".'

'No, no, no. I'm talking about Jenada, the guy who looks like a frog and ran the restaurant here. How did he get a license if this building wasn't up to code?'

'Beats me,' Ronny said. 'But the current inspector is new. And he did say that the last one had some ... dubious dealings?'

That was putting it mildly. 'We had some personal experience with Roger Karsten. I wouldn't be surprised if he looked the other way for a price.'

'God,' Sarah said, hitching herself up to grab the bourbon she'd set on the next table. 'So Ronny, without bribing officials, how much will it cost to get us up and running?'

'It's hard to say, but, maybe ... seventy-five?'

'Seventy-five thousand?' I grabbed the bottle from Sarah.

'That includes the equipment,' Ronny said,

looking a little hurt. 'Espresso maker, coffee urns, stove, refrigerator.'

'There's no way,' I said to Sarah.

She snatched the bottle back. 'You're being negative.'

'No. I'm positive. We don't have the money. And Ronny is absolutely right. Nearly all that stuff has to be replaced.'

Ronny raised his hand.

Sarah ignored him and drained the rest of the bourbon. 'Well, I guess that's it, then. The end of a dream.' She tipped the bottle over and pounded the back end of it. 'The end of all dreams.'

Ronny and I looked at each other. His hand was still up.

'Yes, Ronny?' I said.

'If you wouldn't mind having a silent partner, I think I know where you can get the money.'

Sarah blinked rapidly. 'Where?'

Ronny's hand was still in the air. Now he took it down and shrugged, both hands palm out. 'Me.'

'You? Where would you get the money?' The question came from Sarah, though I have to admit I was thinking the same thing.

Of course a contractor probably makes a whole lot more than a coffeehouse owner. Which begged the question: 'And why would you want to invest it with us?'

Ronny looked back and forth between his

potential new partners. 'Who do you want me to answer first?'

I pointed at Sarah.

He turned to her. 'My father left me some money and property, believe it or not.'

Then he swiveled over to me. 'I like you, Maggy, and I love this old hulk of a place. I think having a business here would be great, especially with the new commuter train coming through.'

'Kornell left you money?' Again Sarah had posed the question that was on my mind, but was better asked by a family member of sorts. Or, here, out of sorts. 'He didn't even like you.'

'Now, Sarah,' I started. 'I'm sure that's not—'

'No, she's right,' Ronny said. 'My father never forgave me for my little brother's accident.'

'I'm so sorry.' I didn't know what else to say.

'Don't be. I had Vi. Like I said, the one good thing that miserable man did for me was to marry her.'

'And the inheritance?' Sarah reminded him. Amazing how sentimental she could be one moment, admittedly about her own car and her own foster kids, and how callous the next.

Ronny said, 'The way I understand it, I'll get the inheritance more by negligence than benevolence.'

'Your father died intestate?' I guessed.

'Correct. He kept putting off making a will

and...' Ronny shrugged.

Kornell *had* been hit by a train. Made sense that he hadn't seen it coming.

'I can't think of a more fitting place to invest the money than in the family business.' Ronny gave a sheepish grin, now, like he was worried that Sarah was going to remind him that he wasn't really family.

But Sarah seemed genuinely touched.

'That's really nice of you.' She sniffled. 'Family is so important.'

'And I can stretch the inheritance dollars,' Ronny continued, 'save the three of us real money. I mean between sub-contractors who owe me favors and my own sweat equity...'

Before Sarah could break down again, I interrupted him. 'We do need to be practical here, though. The shop may not produce a return on your investment for years.'

I spoke, sadly, from personal experience.

But Ronny was shaking his head. 'I think you may be wrong on that, Maggy. This place, done right, could be a huge success. I just want to help you do it right. Be a part of it.' Now *he* sniffled.

Oh, for God's sake. Two days ago I had no partners. Now I had two weepy step-cousins and a 'family' business.

I looked around the depot. The kitschy ticket windows. The space. The potential.

'Works for me,' I said, standing up. 'Let's shake on it.'

* * *

Of course, nothing is that easy. Nor should it be, in business.

We needed to have a real partnership, with legally proper documents. Sarah and Ronny readily agreed that I should be the one to talk to Caron and get a concrete answer on whether she was in or out.

By the time we left the station, the sun was slanting through the windows toward sunset. To me, it was eerily reminiscent of the night Kornell was killed.

'Want to grab something to eat?' I asked the other two. Pavlik had suggested I keep an eye on Sarah. Especially since the Sam/Courtney e-mail – and the subsequent bourbon – that initially good idea had grown in importance.

But Sarah shook her head. 'Nah. I've got too much to do.'

'That's right,' I said, glad Sarah was thinking about her business again. 'The realty agency doesn't run itself. I'll give you a ride.'

Another shake of the head. 'I'm packing up Sam and Courtney's things.'

'Don't you think that's jumping the gun a little?' Ronny asked as we circled the building to our cars.

Sarah straightened her shoulders. 'Maybe. But it's what I have to do.'

I said, 'There aren't *other* things you "have to do"? Beautiful houses to list, eager buyers to—'

'I'm going to close down for a while.' Sarah walked right past my Escape.

'Close down the realty?' I followed her. 'Why?'

She turned and shrugged, arms hanging at her side like they were too heavy to lift. Whether it was from the Jim Beam or the events of the last two days, I didn't know.

Either way, I needed an ally. And I had one.

'Up to you, Cuz,' Ronny said smoothly. 'Something tells me we're all going to be mighty busy over the next few months. Now Maggy, you're going to talk to your former partner, correct?'

'Correct,' I said. Talking business had helped lift Sarah's spirits earlier, so we'd give it another try.

'What about the partnership agreement?' Sarah asked.

'If things go well with Caron,' I said, encouraged, 'maybe Bernie could draw up the partnership papers. He did ours. I mean Caron's and mine.' Patricia's name had been on the agreement, too, though I didn't necessarily want to remind Ronny what had happened to the last person who'd been my 'third partner'.

'That'll be awkward.' Sarah shivered. Apparently the bourbon wasn't enough to keep her warm in the cool night air of spring.

'Want me to look into having it drawn up?' Ronny asked while untying his sweater and placing it over Sarah's shoulders.

'I'd love it,' I said. 'The conversation may be difficult enough as it is.'

'Done,' Ronny said. 'Sarah, are you riding with me?'

She looked around like her mind still hadn't registered the plight of her Firebird. 'Oh, yeah. I guess so.'

'Good,' Ronny said, opening the passenger-side door for her. 'We can talk about the layout Maggy and I put together.'

Ronny gave me a little wink as he closed the door.

'Good thinking,' I said, then lowered my voice. 'You'll make sure she's OK before you leave?'

'Of course.' He stuck out his hand. 'Happy to have you as a partner, Maggy.'

'Same here, Ronny.' I paused as I tried to remember his wardrobe rotation. 'Fifties to-morrow, right?'

'I changed my mind,' he said, opening his car door. 'I think all these good vibes cry out for the Psychedelic Sixties.'

'I'll look forward to it.' As I waved and turned back toward my car, I realized I meant it.

Me. Ronny. Sarah. This was going to be one hell of a trip.

Twenty

As it turned out, the conversation with Caron the next morning was easier than expected. In fact, I sensed she might be relieved.

'Oh, thank God.' Caron threw her arms around me.

'So, you're certain you want out?' I managed from inside the clinch.

'Want out?' She released me and collapsed on to her flowered couch. 'Of course, I'm going to miss it, but...'

Caron burst out laughing. 'I can't do it. I can't pretend I'm sad. I'm happy, happy, happy!'

I collapsed even more than my friend had, though into a matching chair-and-a-half. Had everyone around me gone nuts? Next thing you knew she'd be dancing a jig in her designer yoga outfit.

'I can see that,' I said evenly. 'And I certainly understand if this takes financial pressure off you. The economy has been tough on all of us.'

Caron hunched forward. 'I suppose, but that's not why I'm feeling good.'

'Drugs?' I wondered if Ronny's Psychedelic Sixties came complete with marijuana. Was it wrong to hope so?

'Well, that too,' she said. 'For the seasonal affective disorder, you know.'

'Seasonal ... Caron, it's mid-May.'

She looked hurt. 'I didn't say which season affected me.'

For myself, I was feeling a little *dis*affected. I rose from the chair. 'Well, I should be going. Lots of work to do.'

Caron followed me to the door. 'Don't forget there's that stuff from the old store in my garage.'

'I'll clear it out as soon as I can,' I assured her.

'I hope you've thought this through.'

I turned, my hand on the knob. 'Sarah and me? I think we'll do just fine.'

And I did believe that, despite Sarah's current problems and the 'accidents'. Plus, Ronny's presence should have a balancing effect – and not just on our bottom line.

'I didn't mean so much with Sarah and you, specifically,' Caron said. 'I'm talking more about staying in the coffee business, period.'

She moved closer. 'The first morning that I didn't have to get up at five? I slept in till noon.'

'We took turns opening,' I protested. 'And if that was a problem, we could have asked Amy to take opening. She wouldn't have minded.' Amy certainly would have, but I preferred to ignore facts that didn't support my point.

'But Maggy,' Caron continued, voice hushed

in wonder, 'I realized that I didn't *ever* need to get up at dawn again. Not ever. Not if I didn't want to.'

What *I* wanted to do was smack her one. 'Some of us have to work, Caron. It's not just a frolic. We can't take yoga classes at ten a.m.—'

'Ten thirty,' Caron corrected.

'—because we have to support ourselves.'

'That's not fair, Maggy. Before you and Ted divorced, you could have quit.'

'First of all, it wasn't that Ted and I "divorced". We split because he fell in love with somebody else.'

'Ted was a fool.'

'As it turned out,' I said. 'My point, though, is that the failure of our marriage was not my choice.'

'Until you found out what a cheating manwhore he was,' Caron said.

'Yes.' I wasn't going to let her get me off-topic. 'Thing is, I enjoyed working – both at the bank and at Uncommon Grounds.' Though truth be told, I wasn't so fond of the five a.m. starts, either.

'But even if I hadn't enjoyed jobs, I needed to work. Ted never made much money as a dentist.' At least that he didn't spend on drilling his hygienist.

'I'm sorry, Maggy. I didn't know.' A tear ran down Caron's freckled cheek.

This time I was the one who gave *her* a hug.

'No, it's me that's sorry. For myself.'

'You don't even like yoga,' Caron said with a timid grin.

I laughed. 'They'd have to pay *me* to put my foot behind my head.'

'I understand there are places that are willing to do that.' Now she was laughing, too.

'Heavens,' I said in mock horror. 'Not in Brookhills.'

Caron raised her eyebrows. 'Don't tell the town chairman.'

'Our secret.'

We stood staring at each other.

'I'm going to miss you, you know,' I finally said.

'Me, too,' she sniffed.

'Do not do that,' I warned. 'It's tough enough dealing with Sarah's tears.'

'Sarah? Tears?'

'Long story, but her car was pretty much totaled yesterday, and Sam and Courtney want to move in with relatives on the east coast.'

'Relatives?' Caron echoed. 'I didn't think any existed. At least, who wanted them.'

'Things have changed. Patricia's sister Patrice—'

'Her sister is named Patrice?' Caron interrupted.

'And mother, Patsy. You didn't know?'

'Patricia didn't talk about her family much.'

'Well Sam and Courtney connected online with their cousins – Patrice's son and daughter.

The cousins invited the two of them to visit on Cape Cod and just a day into the stay they both have decided they don't want to come back.'

'Oh, God,' Caron said. 'That's not good.'

'Sarah's absolutely despondent.'

'I'm sure, but that's not what I mean. Patricia once told me her family was about as dysfunctional as they come.'

'In what way?' I asked, a new worry growing in my gut. 'I mean besides Patricia's mother's multiple marriages.'

'And lovers,' Caron said. 'Apparently there was a parade of them coming through. A legion of "daddies".'

God. 'Meaning, abuse?'

'Patricia wasn't specific, but ... well, that was my impression.'

'But let's be fair here,' I said, not wanting to jump to conclusions. 'Even if it's true, Patricia came through all right. Maybe her sister did, too.'

'Patricia survived it, but she spent her life doing what men told her to do. Does that sound normal?'

Not to me, it didn't. And, in truth, it was probably what got Patricia killed.

'Tell you what,' I said. 'I'll talk to Pavlik and see what he can find out about the family.'

'Good, and I'll talk to Bernie and see what Sarah's legal options are.' She caught the doubtful look on my face. 'Hey, copyright attorneys know the law, too. And they also know other attorneys who might be able to help.'

She was right. It was like Ronny being able to call in favors from his subcontractors.

'What should we tell Sarah in the meantime?' I asked. I didn't want to keep anything from her, but I also didn't want to alarm Sarah through mere speculation. Especially given her current state of mind.

'Nothing,' Caron said. 'All we have to go on is my memory of what Patricia told me.'

'Hearsay,' I agreed. 'You know what I don't understand, though? Sarah and Patricia were best friends. Wouldn't Patricia have told her?'

I didn't add 'if she told you'.

'If she told me, you mean?' Caron didn't take offense. 'I honestly believe she didn't mean to tell me. We went to a Hitchcock film festival and *Marnie* was the feature.'

'Oh.'

Not Hitchcock's best film, but I could see that it could spark memories for Patricia. 'I'm going to call Pavlik. You talk to Bernie. Is he at his office?'

'His office here,' she nodded over her shoulder toward the back of the house.

'I didn't know he had a home office,' I said.

Caron's face reddened. 'He gave up the outside office. Didn't really need it.'

'And Flora?' She'd been in Bernie's office for years.

'We couldn't...' Caron's face was nearly

burgundy, the freckles gone. 'I mean, Flora retired.'

I took my friend by the shoulders. 'It's me, Caron. Not your yoga friends. Everyone has to cut back.'

She swiped at the tears and tried to smile. 'The new measure of stature in Brookhills is how much you've lost in the market.'

'Hell,' I said, smiling back. 'It's easy to lose it in the market. You've got to really *try* to have the roof literally fall in on you.'

'So you're not mad at me?' Caron asked tearfully. 'I mean about bailing on you with Uncommon Grounds?'

'No. Like I said, we're going to be fine. Maybe even better than fine if everything works out with the commuter train line.' I looked at her. 'Sure you don't want in?'

'Absolutely sure. We can't afford it.'

I punched her in the shoulder lightly. 'See? Doesn't it feel good to admit it? It's nothing to be ashamed of these days. Being broke is the new black.'

Now Caron laughed outright. 'Glad I'm keeping up with the trends. And I wasn't lying when I said it felt good to sleep past five.'

'Don't I know it.' I tugged on the door handle. 'I'm going to make the most of these weeks before we reopen.'

I stepped out on the porch and turned back to her. 'Friends?'

'Always,' Caron said. 'Now you go see Pavlik

and I'll trek to the back bedroom and consult with Bernie. We have another friend who needs our help.'

I drove to the depot and parked. Then I called Pavlik and relayed what Caron had told me.

'Even if Patricia meant what Caron thought she did, any abuse was a long time ago.'

'Would there be records?' I asked.

'We'll see. Do you have any idea when this Hitchcock film festival was?'

'Caron didn't say,' I said. 'Is it important?'

'Probably not,' Pavlik said. 'I'm just curious. Patricia Harper decided to take control of her life in Brookhills. I wonder whether seeing *Marnie* triggered that.'

'And opening up to Caron,' I said. 'Maybe it freed Patricia in some way.'

'I'll see what I can find out about her early life and anything current on the sister. Do you know what Patrice's last name is? She's married, right?'

'Right. And I don't know if she took her husband's surname or not.'

'I'll be able to find out easily enough,' Pavlik said, and I could hear his pen scratching across the paper as he made a note. 'You do know that even if a child is abused, it doesn't naturally follow that he or she will become abusive later on.'

'But the statistics—'

'Most statistics cite the percentage of abusers

and child molesters who were abused as kids themselves. That's not the same as the percentage of victims who eventually victimize others. And we don't even know how many children are abused. It's vastly under-reported.'

'That's not exactly reassuring.'

'I know. What have you said to Sarah?'

'Nothing. I wanted to talk to you first.'

'Good. We don't want her going off half-cocked.' I could hear him tapping his pen on the pad now. 'I was going to suggest that I come over tonight, but maybe you should be with Sarah.'

Again the concern over Sarah. I was worried, too, but I had a feeling Pavlik had more basis for it than I did. I'd wring it out of him tonight. Maybe even make him go off half-cocked.

'Sarah's cousin Ronny – or step-cousin, really – is watching over her.'

'You mean Kornell Eisvogel's son? I saw his name as next-of-kin in the reports.'

'Right. He's going into partnership with Sarah and me in the new place.'

'Really?' Pavlik's voice got playful. 'I think I'm jealous. What does he have that I don't?'

'Money,' I said, matching his tone, 'and neon green polyester pants. How do you measure up?'

'Negative on the first two, but I think otherwise I measure up pretty well.'

'That you do,' I said, getting twinges – and I don't mean of guilt. 'Why don't you come over about seven? We'll have dinner and a sleep-over.'

'Is Frank going to be there?'

Since I knew Pavlik loved Frank, I wasn't sure how to answer that. Sheepdog as nuisance or sheepdog as incentive. But I hadn't been in public relations for all those years and learned nothing. 'He will be, at the appropriate moments.'

'But not the inappropriate, huh?' Pavlik's voice was low. 'Sounds perfect.'

'To me, too,' I said. 'See you at seven.'

'Yes, you will.' He hung up.

I held the flip phone to my heart for a moment before I hung up, too.

Thud-thud. Thud-thud.

I jumped.

'You OK?' Ronny asked from outside the car. 'You've been sitting out here for a while.'

Sarah's cousin was wearing a purple and white striped long-sleeved T-shirt, flowered suspenders and jeans. The jeans had a peace sign embroidered on the front pocket and a double strand of beads as a belt.

Who knew Ronny was a beads-and-suspenders type of person?

'I just stopped by to see how things were going,' I said, getting out of the Escape. 'Wow, you look—'

'Like Ronald McDonald after a bender.' Sarah was waiting for us in the recliner on the porch.

I sized up the outfit from his platform shoes to ... 'The orange Afro might be a bit much,' I told him.

'You think?' He pulled it off and patted down his brown hair. 'I don't want overdo it.'

'Heaven forbid,' Sarah said dryly. She seemed more herself today. Bitter, cynical, sarcastic. In other words, reassuringly normal.

'So did you two go over the plans last night?' I asked as we reached the front of the building.

Before they could answer, I stopped short. 'Ronny, you fixed the steps.'

'It didn't take long,' he said, modestly. 'I replaced the planking on the deck, too.'

'We can walk to the door without edging around the hole,' I said appreciatively. 'Thank you so much.'

'You don't have to thank him,' Sarah said. 'Ronny's one of us now. We can treat him like crap.'

Yes. Definitely the Return of the Emotionally Prodigal Sarah.

'We cannot,' I said, taking Ronny's arm. 'He is contributing seventy-five thousand dollars plus his expertise. We will treat him like a king.'

'I only do the twentieth century,' Ronny said with a straight face. 'Royalty isn't my thing.'

Good to know.

Having found Ronny impervious to insult, Sarah turned on me. 'He's contributing money and his contracting work. I'm contributing the building. What do you bring to the table?'

'The tables themselves, for one thing, plus whatever else we salvaged from Uncommon Grounds. Caron doesn't want any of it.'

'So you talked to her?' Ronny asked eagerly. 'What did she say?'

'Caron's happy to be free and clear,' I said with a shrug. 'She wishes us well, but is absolutely thrilled to be able to sleep in and take her yoga classes at reasonable hours.'

It was true, as far as it went. And I didn't intend to go any further, either with Caron's confidences about their financial state or with what she'd told me about Patricia's family.

'Great,' Ronny said with a huge smile. Then he tried to temper it. 'I mean, I'm sorry she's not going to be working with us and all.'

'Even if she had,' I assured him, 'we wouldn't be jettisoning you. We're very, very lucky to have you.'

The smile got bigger.

'Can we stop this love-fest and talk business?' Sarah said sourly. 'Ronny, did you tell me you're having an agreement drawn up?'

'I did.'

'Oh, good,' I said. 'I didn't even see Bernie.'

'No worry. I called a lawyer friend and he's putting a partnership contract together. We should have it to read over on Monday.'

This being Friday, that sounded just right.

'Oh,' Ronny continued. 'You asked earlier

whether Sarah and I went over the plans.'

I'd forgotten. 'And did you?'

'We did. They're fine,' Sarah said. 'What do I know about this stuff anyway?'

'Which is the other thing that I'm contributing,' I said, sticking out my chest. 'My expertise.'

'Right. Like you knew anything about coffee eighteen months ago. Have Tien and Amy looked at the layout?'

'Tien has, but not Amy. I can drop off a copy to her.' I looked around. 'What's the agenda for today?'

'I'm meeting with the electrician and plumber to get an estimate,' Ronny said. 'Depending on what they come up with, we may want to change our thinking.'

'In what way?'

'If some electrical and plumbing can be salvaged, then it's going to be a lot cheaper to keep the appliances and sinks in the same area, rather than moving them.'

'And if not?'

'Then we can put things wherever we want.'

Well, that didn't sound so bad.

'Because,' Ronny said, 'it's going to cost a fortune anyway to rewire and replumb the place. Might as well do things the way we want them.'

'Good thing it's your fortune,' Sarah said.

'Maybe I'll hold off on taking the plans over to Amy until we see what the electrician and plumber say.' I fished my car keys out of a pocket. 'Is there anything else I can do here that's helpful?'

I was hoping to clean the house this afternoon and do a little shopping toward Pavlik's visit. Oh, and change the sheets.

Also, on a more serious note, I wanted to call Caron and find out what advice Bernie had given her.

'Nope,' Sarah said.

'I can't think of anything either,' Ronny said. 'Except maybe make a list of what you've been able to save from the old place. And the lawyer wants the deed in order to draw up the papers, along with proof of the seventy-five thousand dollars from me.'

'Gotcha on the inventory,' I said. 'Most of the stuff is in Caron's garage.'

'I'll get the deed today,' Sarah said. 'And you should do likewise on your proof of funds, Ronny. The banks are closed tomorrow.'

She turned to me. 'Maggy, why don't you have Tien and Amy meet us here Monday afternoon. That way, if we need to make changes, we can all brainstorm them together.'

'Great idea,' Ronny said. 'They are our team, after all.'

'Which means they should come to us, rather than us going to them,' Sarah said pointedly.

Admittedly I was a lousy boss. With Caron gone, I'd have to do better. Or best yet, I could let Sarah play bad-boss. I was a classic wimpy-boss.

'What are you doing today?' I asked Sarah, glad that she seemed to be taking charge of her life, and ours, again. 'Going to the office?'

'Nope,' she said, standing up. 'I'm looking at cars, then to the bank and, finally, to see a lawyer.'

'That's terrific.' I was genuinely delighted. 'But isn't Ronny handling the agreement?'

'Not that kind of lawyer,' Sarah said. 'A family law attorney. I'm not letting that Cape Cod woman take my kids without a fight.'

Twenty-One

Buoyed by Sarah's current attitude, I practically skipped down the sidewalk.

'Good news?' a male voice asked. Writer Michael Inkel was standing to the side of the driveway, nearest the florist. 'You guys sure deserve it. What a stretch of tough luck you've had.'

'I think things are starting to look up.' I certainly was, the guy being a foot taller than me. And probably fifteen years younger. I tried not to let the latter depress me. 'What are you doing on the wrong side of the street?'

'Sometimes I venture over here,' he said. His eyes were hazel, I thought. A golden green. Or a greeny gold. Whatever, they were mighty fine to look at. 'I've even been known to stray to the other side of the tracks.'

I hesitated, not sure if he was hitting on me or looking to buy drugs.

Michael pointed to the railroad crossing. 'Joke bad, brain hurt.'

I laughed. 'Sorry to be obtuse.'

'Hey, you're entitled. You've had a tough few days. Let's hope it's all downhill from here.'

'That expression has always confused me,' I admitted to the writer. 'When people "go downhill", it means they're getting worse.'

'True,' Michael said, thinking about it. 'But in this case it means the worst is over. You've reached the top and now you can coast.'

'Coasting down, because things are looking up. Crazy.' I shook my head, which was starting to hurt. 'We're having the plumbing and electrical checked out today.'

'Good luck with that. Our building was built just after yours. Every time we turn around there's another expense.'

'Please don't tell me that.' I didn't want to lose my high.

'Don't get me wrong,' Michael said. 'They're great buildings and once the commuter train starts running, we'll all have plenty of money to do repairs and maintenance.' He pointed toward the florist shop behind him. 'I just wish they would have been able to hold out.'

'How long ago did they close?' I asked.

'Maybe a year now?' he said. 'A damn shame.'

'Were they good?' I asked. Given what they'd left behind, my implied compliment was hard to imagine.

'Some people thought so.' Rebecca Penn came up behind Michael and linked arms with him possessively.

An apologetic smile from Michael. 'We did their advertising. They left us with a bunch of media bills.'

'*Some*body,' Rebecca said, 'was too trusting.'

From her intonation, I was pretty sure the 'somebody' wasn't Rebecca. 'Who ran the shop?' I asked.

'A woman from Madison.' Rebecca was tugging Michael away.

'Any idea what will go in there?'

'Anybody's guess,' Michael said. 'It's not a great time to rent out space, but I think things in the Junction will do all right.' He crossed his fingers. 'Or at least I hope so.'

'Me, too.' I watched them walk back toward their studio, a big smile on my face.

If a babe like Rebecca was worried about her significant other talking to me, I was feeling mighty good. And, therefore, it was time to get ready for my own date.

But, duty call before booty call. I telephoned Caron.

'I'm so relieved Sarah is taking charge of the situation,' she said.

'Me, too. She was acting so unlike herself. Just letting things happen and not hitting back. Now she's back to female wolverine.'

'Maybe the drugs kicked in,' Caron said.

I laughed. 'Not to worry. She tested clean and the police released her. Oh, and I think the white powder they found in the car was baking flour, anyway.'

Silence at the other end. Then, 'What are you

talking about?'

I'd forgotten Caron had no way of knowing about either the white powder in the Firebird or Sarah's subsequent arrest.

I filled her in quickly.

'Interesting,' she said, 'and a little bizarre. But I was talking about her meds.'

'Meds? What is she taking?' I knew Sarah seemed depressed, but I didn't realize she'd seen a doctor. It was uncharacteristically wise of her.

'I don't know exactly, but we go to the same doctor. I ran into her a couple of weeks ago and she had a bag of samples.'

'If you didn't see them, how do you know they were drugs?'

'The nurses always put a few samples in a brown bag, like the kind you pack kids' lunches in? They do it to tide you over until you can fill the real prescription.'

'Maybe Sarah has an infection and they were antibiotics.'

'Maggy, you don't go to a psychiatrist for antibiotics.'

Had me there. 'What did Bernie say about Sam and Courtney?' I asked.

Caron tsk-tsked. 'Let's just say I'm glad Sarah is getting legal advice.'

'Let's just say you're going to be more explicit.' Caron tended to the cryptic side at times. I didn't have the patience for it today.

She sighed. 'Fine. Essentially, Bernie knows

243

squat about custody. He gave me a couple of names of family law specialists to give her. Do you know who Sarah's seeing?'

'She didn't say, and I was so happy to hear it, I didn't think to ask. Did Bernie tell you anything else?'

'Only that if the kids, at their ages, want to go,' I could hear a veneer of regret in Caron's voice, 'Sarah's going to lose them.'

I stopped at Schultz's Market and picked up a couple of nice rib-eyes for the grill. Before Luc and Tien's store closed, I had gone to Schultz's only for fish and seafood.

The owner of the store was Jacque Oui. Despite his name, he wasn't all that agreeable, but he did know quality in his raw materials.

'What do you buy, Maggy?' The fishmonger extraordinaire demanded when he caught me turning away from the butcher's counter, steaks in hand. 'You eat the red meat?'

He checked the label on the butcher-wrapped steaks. 'More than one pound? This feeds a family of six in my homeland. You eat this? You and your bear, perhaps?'

Somehow he'd gotten it into his head that Frank, admittedly big and furry, though also white, was a bear.

'First off, Frank is a sheepdog, not a bear, Jacque. Secondly, I'm having company.'

'Ah, the sheriff,' Jacque said smoothly. 'A good man, but you feed him this?' He held up the prime beef. 'You will kill him. And the death? She will be an ugly one.'

I grabbed for my meat. 'We are having rib-eyes, mushrooms and onions and French fries. With ketchup. Not exactly your idea of a gourmet meal, but it's comfort food and once a month or so it won't kill us. Next time Pavlik comes over, I'll buy some nice fish and cook it.'

'You will cook?' Jacque said, holding the steaks out beyond my reach. 'That, too, will kill him.'

Why were people trying my patience? I snatched away my thirty-two dollars a pound, dry-aged, grass-fed instruments of mass destruction and dropped the packet into my basket.

'Thanks, Jacque,' I said, moving away. 'I'll keep it in mind.'

Not exactly a stinging reprimand, but I'd found taking the high road worked best with him.

True to form, he politely wished me a good evening and went off to torment other customers. Scary thing was, they seemed to like it. Indeed, I thought as the cashier toted up my bill, we all paid a premium for the privilege, whether we relished it or not.

Frank was waiting at the door when I arrived. He started out to relieve himself and then pulled up short.

He sniffed the air.

Then he sniffed his hindquarters.

Then he came back and sniffed my grocery bag.

'I'll try not to be offended that you're confusing my platinum rib-eyes with your hairy butt,' I told the sheepdog.

Frank padded down the porch steps. Once on the grass, he immediately squared up to poop. Guess that explained the butt-sniffing. Probably seeing if he had time to investigate the steaks before his situation became dire.

I was still being punished. Frank didn't so much as look at me as he finished, instead stalking away to water the trees.

Geez, everybody was touchy these days.

Shrugging, I left the door open so the ungrateful lout could come in when he was done and went to the kitchen to start my preparations for dinner.

I was starving. I didn't want to ruin my dinner, though, so I poured myself a glass of cabernet and started to unload the groceries. Simultaneously, I was trying to organize my thoughts, which were as *dis*organized as my refrigerator, but without the moldy bacon.

As far as I could see, things were moving along nicely toward the new coffeehouse. I still had to put together the list Ronny needed, but other than that – assuming the plumber or electrician didn't throw us a curve – I thought we had a good chance of opening by September first.

I slid the rib-eyes into the fridge and took a slug of my wine.

Sarah's situation, too, seemed to have stabilized. If Caron was right, our friend was under a doctor's care, presumably for depression. Her new, more positive attitude made it clear that, whatever the treatment, it seemed to be working.

A celebratory sip.

Then there was Courtney and Sam. Again, some progress had been made. Sarah was seeing a family law attorney, who should be able to help her far more than any of us, including Pavlik, could.

As for the 'accidents', I intended to tell the sheriff tonight that Sarah had parked her car nose-in. That meant that the Firebird should have landed on the deck back-end first. Sort of a breach berth. Tee-hee.

Uh-oh. Empty stomach and red wine – not a good mix. I slid my glass down the counter, out of arm's reach and harm's way.

It was just after seven – house clean, mushrooms and onions ready to sauté, frozen French fries placed on the baking sheet, me sober, showered and dressed – when I realized the door was still open and there was no sign of Frank inside.

The sheepdog didn't usually wander off, but since he was miffed at me, I couldn't rule out the possibility that he had taken a walkabout.

I started out the door and nearly tripped over Pavlik sitting on the porch steps.

As I steadied myself on the railing, Frank came bounding back with a tennis ball in his mouth.

So much for being the center of either creature's universe.

'Hi.' I dropped down on the step next to Pavlik. 'I didn't know you were here.'

'Just arrived,' he said, turning and planting a light kiss on my lips. He was wearing a gray-blue shirt that matched his eyes and his dark hair was tousled. I wanted to do unimaginable things with him.

Frank dropped the ball between my feet. When I reached for the already slimy thing, he reclaimed it and placed it square in front of Pavlik.

Maybe I'd do better with the sheriff. 'Can I get you something to drink?' I said, getting up.

'Oops.' Pavlik threw Frank's ball and then pulled a tall brown bag from under the bush next to him. He handed it to me. 'I brought this.'

I unsheathed a nice bottle of ancient-vine Zinfandel. 'Thank you. This will be perfect with the rib-eyes.'

'Rib-eyes?' Pavlik got up to follow me in, Frank trailing us.

Figured. The mention of meat drew males of any species like flies.

I gestured at the steaks I'd set out to gain

room temperature before cooking. 'I thought we'd grill them.'

'I'll do it,' Pavlik volunteered. 'I'm great at grilling.'

Having been a subject of his grilling techniques, I couldn't disagree. 'They're all yours, then. Do you want them marinated?'

Pavlik was eyeing the steaks like I wished he'd eye me. 'These babies? They're too beautiful to marinate. They'll be perfect just the way they are.'

Like I said.

Still. Once the rib-eyes and Frank were put to bed, I planned to have *my* way with Pavlik.

After the steaks, which were perfectly cooked, and the French fries, which were not, Pavlik and I settled down on my couch with the remains of his wine, while we waited for our coffee to brew.

Much as I wanted to canoodle, work before pleasure. 'Were you able to find anything on Patricia's sister?' I asked.

Pavlik whipped out his notebook, flipped it open and scanned his notes. Then he closed it. 'Nothing.'

'You're kidding, right?'

'See for yourself,' Pavlik handed me the notebook.

I looked at the first page. Patricia's name. Her mother's name (Patsy) and current address in Buffalo, New York. Patrice's married name

(Fontana). Her husband's name was Harry. Patrice's brother, Bert. No Ernie.

Next to each name was a colon. Next to that was a check mark.

'What's the check mark mean?' I asked.

'That they checked out,' Pavlik said, reaching for the pad.

'Cute,' I said, moving it away from him. I flipped the page. Empty, except for the words 'wheat flour' and, under that, 'talcum'. In the bottom right corner, something that started with an 'L' was scribbled.

'What's this?' I asked, pointing. 'Lithuania?'

Pavlik took the notepad away from me and slapped it closed. 'As I said. None of the family seems to have a record. Not for abuse or anything else.'

'Police reports?' I figured we should close this subject before I interrogated the sheriff on page two.

'A couple of noise complaints dating back to when Patricia, Patrice and...' He started to open the notebook.

'Ernie,' I supplied.

'Bert,' Pavlik corrected with the hint of a grin. 'When they were kids living in Southern Illinois. Nothing that was followed up on.'

'Patsy and her boyfriends,' I said.

'Maybe,' Pavlik said. 'But there's no record of any abuse.'

'Damn.'

'Hey.' Pavlik massaged the back of my neck.

'This is *good* news.'

'Not if it happened but nobody knew about it. I was hoping to give Sarah and her attorney some ammunition.'

'She's retained counsel?' Pavlik said. 'That's good.'

The way he said it made me sit up and twist to face him. 'Does she need it?'

'If she hopes to keep the kids,' Pavlik said.

'Oh.' I settled back.

'Why?' he persisted. 'What did you think I meant?'

'I'm not really sure,' I admitted. 'Things are so confusing.'

'Like what?' Pavlik resumed massaging my neck.

I settled back against him. He smelled of Dial soap and some other clean scent – deodorant, aftershave, cologne. I didn't know what, but I wanted me some. Actually, I wanted me *him*.

'What's confusing?' Pavlik restated.

'Life.' I said. 'But in particular, what's been going on at the Junction.'

'Kornell's accident and Sarah's car?' Pavlik said. 'Two pieces of bad luck, I'll grant you, but—'

I jumped up, remembering I'd wanted to tell him about the Firebird. My head caught Pavlik under the chin.

'Are you OK?' I asked.

'Fine, fine,' he said.

'You have tears in your eyes,' I pointed out.

'They're watering.' He swiped at his eyes. 'A natural response to having one's jaw driven into one's nasal cavity.'

Huh. I didn't know that. Probably because he made it up. Pavlik was a manly man.

'I'm really sorry,' I said, rubbing his chin.

'Not exactly the way I thought I'd see stars with you tonight.' He cupped my face and kissed me lightly.

'If you want to see stars, perhaps you should visit the Thorsen Planetarium,' I murmured.

'Shows every night?' He was kissing my throat now.

'I wish,' I said involuntarily.

Pavlik chuckled and moved down to my collarbone. 'Maybe we can arrange for a private viewing.'

A warm breath tickled the back of my neck.

Unfortunately, it smelled of steak scraps and kibbles. 'Go away, Frank.'

The sheepdog didn't obey, preferring instead to lick the nape of my neck.

'C'mon, Frank,' I said. 'Go away.'

I looked at Pavlik.

'Are you thinking what I'm thinking?' he asked.

'Threesome?' I said. 'Even I'm not that desperate.'

I slapped my hand over my mouth, appalled by what I'd said. Not so much the threesome part, though I did draw the line there. More the 'desperate' part. Men want what they can't have. Hell, we *all* want what we can't have.

'No.' Pavlik looked taken aback. 'I was thinking he must need to go out.'

'Oh. Sure.' I jumped up, wanting to get out of the room as quickly as possible. 'I'll take him.'

As I started toward the door, Pavlik caught my hand and pulled me back to him. 'I want you,' he breathed into my hair. 'Take care of the dog. Then let's go to bed.'

'Is that a toothbrush in your pocket,' I asked, rubbing up against him, 'or are you just happy to see me?'

'Both.'

Twenty-Two

It wasn't until we were in the kitchen the next morning that Pavlik and I returned to the subject of the accidents at the Junction.

'Should have brought your razor.' I set a mug of coffee in front of him, then ran my hand over the stubble on his chin.

'You sure it's five o'clock shadow?' he asked as I sat down across from him with my cup. 'Maybe it's the bruise from when you clocked me.'

'It's more like a nine a.m. shadow,' I said, 'and I'm sorry about jumping up like that.'

'What were you so excited about?'

I tried to think back. God, a little sex, and it pushed everything else out of my mind. We had talked about Patricia's family, and then Pavlik...

I had it. 'You called the offing of Sarah's Firebird an accident.'

'It collided with a building. What would you call it?' He took a sip of coffee.

I leaned earnestly toward him. 'Sarah says that she parked across the street next to the piano teacher's place.'

'Right.' Pavlik was dumping cream into his

254

mug. 'She told the police officers that.'

'But what she didn't tell them was that she pulled *forward* into the spot. How did the car end up across the street and turned a-hundred-and-eighty degrees?' I crossed my arms and sat back.

Pavlik took another taste and started piling sugar into the cup. 'Don't take this the wrong way, but Sarah might not be the most dependable chronicler of her activities these days.'

Now how could I take that the wrong way? Sarah, on the other hand, *she* might. 'I know Sarah's been a little – and unusually – emotional,' I said. 'But I think she'd remember parking her "baby".'

'Maybe.' Pavlik shrugged and tried the coffee one more time. 'Whoa,' he said making a face. 'Both cream and sugar, yet this stuff still tastes like pencil lead.'

Now *that*, I could take the wrong way. 'What do you mean?' I said, lifting my cup. 'This is Kenyan. It's one of my ... ugh.'

'Pencil lead, right?'

'I don't understand,' I stood up and went to the coffeemaker. 'It tastes like it sat all night, but I just made it this morning.'

'Did you empty out what you brewed last night?'

'Last night?' I stopped short. Of course. I had started the coffee last night, but we'd gotten side-tracked. And front-tracked. And...

'I always set up the pot the night before,' I

said, dumping the coffee grounds and starting over. 'This morning when I came down, I just hit the "brew" button, but there was nothing in it. This must have sat all night.'

I poured water into the reservoir, fresh grounds into the basket and punched the button again. Then I turned to Pavlik. 'So, what is Sarah on?'

'What do you mean?' He was looking me straight in the eye, still answering a question with a question.

I gave it right back to him. 'Are you saying you don't know what I mean?'

'Didn't I say that?'

I was out of questions. So I tried a simple noun. 'Lithium?'

Pavlik flinched, a first for me.

I sat down across from him. 'I saw it in your notebook, along with the other notes you made when I was in your office. At first I thought it was Lithuania and had something to do with where they thought the cocaine might have come from. But you had written "flour" and "talcum" on a different section of the page.'

'The talcum is why the guys on the scene suspected cocaine,' Pavlik said. 'They could pick up a slight flowery scent and thought the cocaine had been cut with it. As it turns out, the "cocaine" was flour, just like you thought. Smart.'

I had no intention of letting Pavlik distract me with compliments, so I just folded my arms.

'And the lithium? They found it in Sarah's drug test.'

'I can neither confirm nor deny.' Pavlik sat back and folded his own arms.

God, don't you hate it when your body language is quoted against you? 'But you did suggest I keep an eye on her.'

Lithium was used to treat bipolar disorder, but that was pretty much the extent of my knowledge. I took a shot. 'Sarah is bipolar. I thought you knew that.'

Pavlik's jaw dropped. 'How long have *you* known?'

'Maybe two seconds.' I was thinking about Sarah's behavior over the last week or so. Certainly more mood swings than usual, but Sarah was always a little unpredictable. 'What do you know about bipolar ... ity?'

'Bipolar disorder,' Pavlik corrected. 'Previously called manic-depression. My ex-wife suffers from it.'

Pavlik had been divorced about a year when I met him. His ex Susan and their young daughter lived in Chicago.

'I'm sorry,' I said. 'I didn't know.'

'Five million people in the US are bipolar,' Pavlik said. 'Susan was misdiagnosed for nearly five years.'

'How can that be, if it's so prevalent?'

'Unlike some people who get nasty during the manic stage, Sarah felt great. It was only when she was depressed that she saw the doctor. It didn't occur to either of us that the good times were the other side of the same coin. That she might be too happy or too energetic. We just figured the meds were working. Little did we know that the anti-depressants were probably fueling the manic swings.'

'And lithium somehow treats both the manic and depressive sides?'

'It's a mood stabilizer, though it has more effect on the manic stage. It helped Susan a lot.'

'I'm glad.' I reached across the table and covered his hand with mine. 'I hope it does the same for Sarah. How long will she have to take it?'

'Bipolar is a lifetime illness, but there are some types that are more severe than others. Susan has Bipolar Two, which is milder than One. Even so, she'll need to stay on lithium until the grave.'

As might my friend. 'So it would be good if Sarah had Bipolar Two, like your Susan.' By good I meant better than B-One.

'Hey.' Pavlik turned his hand over and took mine. 'She may even have Cyclothymia.'

Sounded like something you caught from bicycle seats. 'Cyclo-what?'

'It's a bipolar-*like* disorder. You still have the mood swings, but they're relatively mild. Most people who have it are never diagnosed. They just come off as ... well, moody.'

'Cyclothymia, thy name is Sarah.' Or so I hoped. 'But do they still prescribe lithium?'

'I think so, though some people don't have to take anything.'

'Could the lithium – or the disorder, itself – make Sarah forget to set the parking brake? Or that she backed the Firebird in?'

'I don't know, honestly.' Pavlik shrugged. 'I'm no expert on lithium or bipolar, Maggy. But you *are* an expert on Sarah. That's why I thought you should keep an eye on her.'

And I'd abandoned my post. For what?

Oh, yeah. I ran my fingernail across the palm of Pavlik's hand.

'If the lithium is in her bloodstream, it should be helping, right? She seemed better yesterday.'

'We actually found traces in her urine. Lithium therapy takes a couple of weeks to kick in, but yes, it should help. Don't worry.' His eyes were that unreadable gray this morning. 'She'll be fine.'

After Pavlik left, I loaded the dishwasher and then sat down at my computer. I googled 'bipolar'.

The first article I clicked on was useless, but the second had some good information and seemed to be from a reliable source.

The manic phase of bipolar apparently could exhibit itself as irritability, overspending, euphoria or even hypersexuality, among other things. Depression could range from being 'a little down' to inexplicable grief and thoughts of suicide.

'It can be everything and anything,' I said to Frank as he plodded in from the corridor and laid his big fuzzy head on my lap. I rubbed between his ears. 'No wonder it's not diagnosed. How am I going to be able to tell what's normal for Sarah?'

Frank lifted his face and yawned.

'Last time you get onions with your steak,' I said, fanning the air.

Frank sighed and padded away. He circled twice and then settled down on the fireplace hearth, butt toward me.

'I know, I know,' I called after him. 'Nothing you do is ever right. I'm ungrateful.'

And talking to a sheepdog. Maybe I was the one who should be on medication.

I slipped the list of symptoms out of the printer tray and read it over. Irritability was pretty much a given for Sarah. The others I'd rarely if ever seen her exhibit, except for grief over Courtney, Sam and the Firebird this week. And that 'grief' *was* 'explicable'.

'I've got it,' I called to Frank. 'If Sarah is anything *but* irritable, I'll worry. Simple.'

Frank lifted his head in obvious agreement. Then he went back to sleep.

I turned my attention to the other things I needed to accomplish today. It was too bad that the problems had shadowed the reopening of Uncommon Grounds, but we were moving forward thanks to Ronny.

Which reminded me, I had to give him the list

of equipment and furniture we salvaged from Uncommon Grounds and stored at Caron's. She and Bernie had extra garage space now that their son was away at college. Me, my house was about as big as Caron's garage and my garage the size of their golden retriever's dog-house.

I double-clicked on a document entitled 'Inventory', and there it was:

5 tables, one with a broken base
9 chairs
1 coffee brewer, dented
8 Lucite bins for coffee beans
A 12-pack of toilet paper
4 sleeves of to-go cups
2 sleeves of lids for to-go cups

I'd better bring one hell of a lot of expertise to the partnership, because I sure wasn't bringing much else. I printed out the list to give to Ronny and checked my watch.

A little before noon. With luck Ronny would be at the depot.

Since it was Saturday, the Junction was quiet as I pulled up.

I caught a glimpse of Christy through her front window, but Penn & Ink was dark. As I slowed to turn into the depot's driveway, I could hear the faint strains of jazz coming from Art's place. At least the street wasn't completely deserted.

There were no other cars in the lot when I parked. That meant that Ronny either wasn't working today – understandable for a Saturday – or had run out to lunch. I'd had the foresight, though, to put the list in an envelope with his name on it. I'd stick it in the door.

As I walked up the driveway to the front of the depot, I glanced toward the flower shop.

Still no indication anyone was taking care of it. The strip of what was supposed to be grass between our drive and the other building was a mass of yellow dandelions and thistles, a hose snaking through the weeds. A spigot dripped rusty water down the brick siding. Not exactly great advertising for a floral designer.

I reached in to twist off the faucet and pick up a couple of roof tiles that must have blown off during the storm earlier that week. Rounding the shop, I leaned the tiles against the front door and stepped back to survey for other damage.

The windows were grimy, with the exception of the one farthest from the depot and partially obscured by a flowering shrub. As I got closer, I realized that the window wasn't clean, it was mostly missing.

I edged in behind the bush and balanced on my tiptoes. As I peeked in, I was careful not to cut myself on the shards that still framed the opening in a sunburst of glass.

The window hadn't blown out in the thunderstorm. A rock was lying on top of one of the two grocery bags sprawled in the corner. A big rock, capable of both breaking the window and pummeling the bag where it had landed.

'Now why would someone do that?' I said.

'Just being assholes.'

The voice startled me. I peered out from behind the bush to see Art Jenada. His hands were balled and on his hips as he surveyed the window. 'This place is a deserted eyesore, an open invitation to vandals.'

'Who owns it?' I asked, coming out to join him.

'Got me. That good-looking florist was renting it, but she's been gone for a year.' Jenada picked a fragrant blossom out of my hair and handed it to me.

I stepped back, feeling vaguely uncomfortable. 'Is there any way of finding out?'

'The owner, you mean? Mike might know. He seemed mighty interested for a while.'

'Mike? You mean Michael Inkel?'

'He prefers either Mike Inkel or Michael Ink. Michael Inkel isn't – I don't know, classy enough.'

'I guess I can understand that. He is a writer, after all. A name is important.'

'A tech-writer. He writes catalog copy and the instructions that are folded into the box. They don't put the author's name on the front of those.'

I'd been in public relations and written my share of news releases and copy, so I bristled a bit at that. 'It's good work and it pays well.'

'Did, when Mike worked for a corporation. Now that he's freelancing and things are tight, he's trying too hard to keep up appearances. Drives Rebecca crazy.'

Whatever drove Rebecca crazy was OK by me. 'Why?'

'Didn't you hear him when he introduced the two of them to you?'

'Sure. He said she's a graphic artist and he's a writer.'

'Correct. The implication being that she's picking typeface and drawing taco ads. The reality is that Rebecca has exhibited her water-colors all over the country.'

'But not anymore?' I knew we were getting far afield, but I'm a sucker for neighborhood gossip.

'It's hard to make a living at it. And don't get me wrong, she's not ashamed of the commercial work. She just doesn't think Mike should be either.'

Or promote himself at his partner's expense. 'Did you say they were looking into buying this building?'

'More than a year ago. And I had the feeling he was more interested in the florist than the shop.'

I was impressed. Rebecca wasn't the only creative one on the block. Jenada had raised gossip to an art form.

'Why? Are you looking to expand your

empire?' He waved at the depot. 'With that place and the florist shop, you'd have the whole block. Once the commuter train starts running, it should be a goldmine for you and your friends.'

The same thing Ronny had said, but all of a sudden I didn't like Jenada's tone. 'A coffee-house and a florist shop? Neither is exactly a license to print money.'

'I'm talking tear-down,' Jenada said and then looked sorry he had. 'I mean, any business might be a goldmine, what with the train coming back and all.'

I followed his finger to the railroad tracks where Kornell had died and where Sarah's car had been parked. There was no baking flour on his hands. Now.

The Junction was the only commercially zoned area in town, with the exception of Brookhill Drive where Uncommon Grounds had been. The rest of Brookhills was residential, the only 'tear-downs', the original ranch-style homes, making way for mini-mansions.

But a whole block, that would be room enough for most anything, including even a hotel or training center. Maybe one that catered to the business trade. There was plenty of parking and the new train would provide easy access to downtown.

Jenada was right. A full block could be very valuable to anyone who could get his floury hands on it.

'You climbed into Sarah's car, didn't you?' I asked abruptly.

I hoped that stating the non-sequitur question as fact, like when I told Pavlik I knew Sarah was bipolar, would yield results. Confirmation.

Jenada took a step toward me. Apparently he hadn't read the script. 'What are you talking about?'

I held my ground, despite growing trepidation. I did, however, back-pedal in a different way.

'Sorry,' I said with my best self-effacing smile, 'I tend to jump subjects. I meant when the Firebird crashed into the depot. I thought you told me the emergency brake was on.' God, I was good.

'The brake?' Jenada rubbed his forehead. 'Let's see. No, in fact, I'm sure it wasn't.'

OK, so he was good, too.

'Besides,' Jenada continued, cocking his head, 'the brake *had* to be off. How else could the car have rolled across the road and up on to the porch?'

All right. So he was *really* good.

Jenada let it hang there.

I cleared my throat. 'I thought it might be possible the brake failed or maybe was burned out. Could you tell if the gearshift was in "park"?'

'That I'm not sure of,' Jenada said. 'The transmission stick is between the seats, so I couldn't see it without getting in.'

266

'Which you didn't.'

'Correct.' He had a little smile on his face. 'Why would I?'

He was right. If he had disengaged the brake, turned the car around, put it in neutral and, maybe, for good measure, given it a push, why would he get *back* into the car after the crash?

Which, of course, raised the question of how the flour – his flour, I was sure – had ended up on Sarah's driver's seat.

After Jenada left me, I walked slowly to the front door of the depot.

Art Jenada had been angry because Kornell Eisvogel hadn't renewed the lease for his catering business.

I knew how that felt, though I hadn't killed my landlord over it. Somebody else had, but that was a whole different story.

I didn't think that the lost lease would be sufficient reason for killing Kornell. It might be enough, though, for Jenada to haze us. If you could call a classic car totaled on your front porch and a sabotaged deck railing 'hazing'.

Let's say Jenada wanted a business near the commuter station. He already had that. There was nothing to stop him from opening a competing restaurant across from us in the space he was currently leasing. God forbid.

On the other hand, maybe the stakes were higher. Maybe Jenada did want the whole block. But even if he dissuaded us from reopening Uncommon Grounds, even if Sarah decided to put the depot on the market and he bought it, he *still* wouldn't have the rest of the block.

I stopped short and turned back to look at the florist shop.

Unless Art Jenada already owned it.

Twenty-Three

I intended to shove the envelope containing the salvaged inventory from the original Uncommon Grounds under the door. 'How can a place this old *not* have a crack somewhere,' I said under my breath.

'Weatherization.' Ronny was behind me. 'Back in the seventies, they were so concerned about energy efficiency that people were getting sick because the houses were too snug.'

I handed him the envelope. 'Hey, do you know who owns the place next door?'

'Uh-unh.' Ronny slid his finger under the edge of the flap. 'Why?'

'Somebody threw a rock through the window and I thought the owners would like to know. Maybe I'll stop at Town Hall. Somebody there can probably tell me.'

Ronny was looking over my list.

'I know it's short,' I said sheepishly. 'Between the ceiling and the water damage, not much could be saved.'

'Perfectly understandable. Besides you bring something far more valuable.'

'My expertise?' I guessed. I was looking at

what Ronny was wearing. Jeans, T-shirt and work boots. And he was carrying a clear plastic document file.

'You *are* Uncommon Grounds. You bring the name, the reputation and the customers.' He looked down at his shirt. 'What are you staring at?'

'Your clothes,' I admitted. 'You look so...'

'Normal?' Ronny asked with a grin.

'Well, yes.'

'Ha!' Ronny said, striking a pose. 'I laugh at normality and drop ice cubes down the vest of mediocrity.'

I recognized the paraphrase. 'Rowan Atkinson in *Blackadder*. I loved it.'

'Me, too,' Ronny said. 'But back to the clothes. I have to take weekends off because there are only so many decades.'

'This way you don't have to repeat as often.'

He looked offended. 'Please. The decades may repeat, but I never do.'

God help us, Ronny must have another pair of polyester pants at home.

'You are a marvel, partner.' I was going to ask what day the fifties had been rescheduled to, but Sarah pulled up in her Firebird, and—

Wait a minute...'

'Wow.' I said as she parked in front of us. 'Mario is a miracle worker after all.'

I circled the car. 'It looks better than ever.'

Sarah's turn to be offended. 'What do you mean?'

I couldn't say the right thing to anyone today. Though as I observed to Frank, 'irritable' was a normal condition for Sarah and a reassuring characteristic of her for me.

'I meant that Mario did a wonderful job. It was a compliment.'

'This is *not* my car. I'm test driving it.'

Ronny was taking a walk around the car himself. 'Maggy's right, though. It looks identical.'

I hadn't said the Firebirds looked identical. I said this one looked better and I'd stand by that. Not repeat it, perhaps, but stand by it.

Mollified, Sarah turned off the engine. 'Mario found it for me. It has four thousand miles on it.'

'What? Did some little old lady from Pasadena own it?'

'Oconomowoc, but yeah, that's pretty much the gist of the pedigree.'

Oconomowoc was west of Brookhills. 'So all this is original?' Ronny asked, touching the hood.

'Except the paint.' Sarah climbed out and wiped off the fingerprints Ronny might have left. 'That faded over time, so Mario restored and clear-coated it.'

'Beautiful job.' Ronny looked like he wanted to touch the car again. Sarah eyed him and he withdrew his hand.

'Are you going to buy it?' I asked.

'I'm thinking about it, yeah,' Sarah said.

'Just be careful about doing that on the

271

rebound,' Ronny warned. 'When my favorite platform shoes wore out, I found a new pair online in my size.' He shook his head. 'What a mistake.'

'They didn't fit?' I guessed.

'They were made of cardboard. Fell apart the first Disco Day.'

'And the moral of the story is?' Sarah asked dryly.

'Grief clouds one's mind.'

At Ronny's answer, Sarah teared up. Apparently the lithium hadn't kicked in completely.

Seeing her turn away, Ronny put his hand on Sarah's shoulder. 'I'm not saying you *shouldn't* buy it, Cuz. But if you'd like me to look it over first—'

'Mario said—'

Ronny held up his hands. 'I'm sure Mario is very competent. Much more so than me. I'm just saying that if you want a second opinion, I'm available.'

'That's what Mario suggested,' Sarah said. 'He told me I shouldn't take his word for the condition of the car, since he's the seller.'

'What a good guy,' I chimed in.

'I have to go see the lawyer about our partnership agreement,' Ronny said. 'But I should have time to look at the car on Monday. Do you think Mario could bring it to your place first thing in the morning? It would save me considerable time.'

'Sure,' Sarah said, pulling an envelope out of

her pocket. 'Here's the deed.'

'Great,' Ronny said, opening the document file he still held. He pulled out a paper and showed it to us. 'Here's my proof of funds and I'll put this,' he took Sarah's envelope, 'with it.'

Ronny looked around. 'What did I do with your list, Maggy?'

'It's in your back pocket,' I said, 'for what it's worth.'

'Don't underestimate your value,' Ronny said, now putting all three documents into the file. 'As I told you before, Maggy Thorsen brings "Uncommon Grounds" and its reputation to the enterprise. That's priceless, right, Sarah?'

She was examining an imaginary nick on the finish of the Firebird II. 'Right.'

What, no smart remark? But then Sarah was distracted by the reincarnation of her beloved baby.

'I think that's just a little tar,' I said helpfully. 'Probably kicked up when you turned off Brookhill Road. They were patching holes there yesterday.'

Sarah rubbed at the mark with her cloth and then beamed at me. 'Came right off. Thank you.'

Yeah, the meds definitely hadn't kicked in. She was being way too nice. Unless this was the real Sarah.

I looked at her smile.

Nah.

'What's that?' Sarah asked, pointing at my hand.

I realized I was still clutching the pink blossom Art Jenada picked out of my hair.

'This is from that shrub in front of the florist shop. It got stuck in my hair and Art Jenada picked it out.'

The bloom was pretty much mangled. I took a sniff. 'It's already lost its scent.'

'What were you doing in the bushes with Art Jenada?' Sarah asked.

'I wasn't "in the bushes" with him.' I explained about the broken window and our subsequent conversation.

I finished with, 'He accused me, or actually us, of wanting the florist shop.'

'Who'd want the place?' Ronny nodded at the ramshackle building next door. 'It's an eyesore.'

'That's what Jenada maintained,' I said. 'But then he said the whole block would be a "goldmine", for whoever owned it.'

'They better have a trunkful of money,' Sarah said. 'This place is structurally sound. I'm not sure about that one.'

'I wouldn't even walk in there,' Ronny agreed.

'Jenada wasn't talking about fixing it up. He was talking about tearing it down, along with the depot. He said the land itself would be more valuable as a result. I'm not sure he's wrong.'

Sarah looked at me for a long moment.

'Nope,' she finally said. 'We're stretching ourselves financially to open the depot. Where would we get the money to buy the flower shop?'

We turned in unison to Ronny.

'Don't be thinking of me,' he said, holding up his hands. 'The seventy-five is all there is.'

Sarah sighed. 'Fine. Let someone else with vision do it.'

'Like Art Jenada,' I said.

'Do you think he really wants the place?'

'I think he wants both places. Ours and the florist. And,' I paused dramatically, 'I think he might engage in a little vandalism to get them.'

'The rock through the window?' Ronny asked. 'Why would Jenada do that?'

'To make the place look worse, so no one else would want it? But I was thinking more about the things that have happened here at the depot. The loosening of the railing. Sarah's car.'

'My Firebird?' Sarah picked up a discarded plank from the damaged deck. 'I'll take the bastard's head off.'

'You will not,' I said. 'We have no proof.'

'Which is a reason not to go to the police,' Sarah said. 'It's not a reason why I shouldn't smack him one. Or two.'

'Calm down, Cuz,' from Ronny. 'Going vigilante isn't going to help anything.' He turned to me. 'What makes you think Jenada is involved?'

'Flour and talcum were found on the Fire-

275

bird's driver's seat, and he claims he didn't sit in the car.'

'Talcum?' Ronny asked. 'I thought you said it was just flour.'

'I did, but then I saw the lab results on Pavlik's notepad. The police thought at first that the suspected cocaine had been cut with it.'

'Good thinking, I guess.' Ronny said.

'But if Jenada did it,' Sarah said, 'wouldn't he have covered by saying he was in the car later?'

'Not if he didn't realize why I was asking.' I never minded patting myself on the back.

'Pretty stupid of him,' Sarah grumbled, taking the wind out of my sails. 'What else you got?'

'This.' I held up the blossom. 'It doesn't smell.'

'So?' Ronny asked, looking puzzled. 'Why would you think it did?'

'Because I smelled flowers when I was with Jenada,' I said triumphantly. 'It wasn't the blossom I smelled, it was *him*.'

'Jenada was wearing perfume?' Sarah seemed to no longer dwell on her home planet.

'No,' Ronny said, finally getting it. 'Talcum powder.'

Twenty-Four

'Why the hell would Jenada be wearing powder?' Sarah said. 'He sure doesn't look gay.'

She realized what she'd said and held up her hands apologetically. 'I'm sorry. I didn't mean anything about Eric.'

Definitely *not* our usual, insensitive Sarah.

'Not to worry.' I turned to Ronny. 'My son is gay. And,' I grinned at Sarah, 'he doesn't "look" gay, either.'

'Anyway,' I continued. 'I'm not sure why Jenada would use powder. Maybe he dresses up as his mother and sits in a rocking chair.'

'Psycho,' Sarah said.

'Right,' I said approvingly. 'The original, though, not the remake.'

'No, I meant you,' she said. *'You're* the psycho.'

Now that was just unkind.

'Maybe he has jock itch,' Ronny offered. 'Or the pain and heartbreak of athlete's foot. I've been known to use powder when nothing is available.'

Art Jenada and jock itch on Sarah's driver's seat. Not a pretty picture.

'Another thing,' I said. 'When I rang Jenada's bell that day, he didn't answer. Then when I was walking away, he finally came out. He could have just made it back from where Sarah's car was parked.'

'Did you talk to Pavlik last night?' Sarah asked. 'Tell him someone turned my car?'

I said I had. I didn't add that Pavlik suspected she'd done it herself.

'So they're going to investigate?' Ronny asked.

'It's not Pavlik's case,' I said. 'It's the Brookhills municipal department and they've decided it was an accident.'

'Accident,' Ronny echoed with a poker face.

'Then it's up to us to take matters into our own hands,' Sarah said, raising the plank again.

Ronny took it away from her. 'I have to go talk to the lawyer now. Promise me you won't do anything stupid.'

'Who says it would be stupid?'

'I do,' Ronny said. 'Do you want to end up back in jail?'

Sarah shook her head. 'Big Martha kept smiling at me.'

'A woman in the cell with you?' I asked.

'I don't know.'

Maybe Pavlik was right. Sarah's memory was faulty. 'You don't know if she was in the cell?'

'No, I don't know if she was a woman.' Sarah shivered. 'And I don't want to find out.'

* * *

278

With Ronny on his mission to the lawyer, Sarah and I were alone. I wanted to ask her about her own visit to the family law attorney, but not while we were standing on the street in front of the depot.

'What are you doing now?' I asked her.

She gestured toward the Firebird. 'I need to take her back.'

'This one's a girl?'

'It's easier when you have one of each. They don't suffer from comparison.'

Oh. Well, that made perfect sense.

'Want me to follow you to Mario's?' I said. 'Then we can drive on to my house. Maybe have an early dinner? Grill out?'

Sarah shook her head. 'You're being nice to me again. Why?'

'Do I need a reason to be nice?'

'Usually.'

I was really sick of having my courtesy questioned. I thought about telling her 'why'. And then, I did.

'I know about the lithium, Sarah.'

'Who told you?' she demanded. 'Was it that spineless snitch Caron?'

'You told Caron?' They were both traitors: Sarah for telling Caron, and Caron for not coming clean with me. Just 'happened' to see her at the psychiatrist, my ass.

'I just happened to see her at the psychiatrist,' Sarah said. 'I had to tell her. Besides, I wanted to compare drugs. There's something so liberating about knowing other people are crazy, too.'

'You're not crazy,' I said. 'You have a mood disorder.'

'Mood, schmood.' Sarah smiled. 'The drugs are good.'

I started to ask her how long she'd been on them, but decided to defer.

'I want to hear more,' I said, 'but let's wait till my house. You can drop off the car and then we'll stop at the store to buy something to grill.'

'I have a better idea,' Sarah said. 'You go home and let Frank out and feed him. Then come over to my house. Bring wine if you want it.'

'How are you going to get home?' I asked.

'Mario.'

The way she said it made me wonder whether she and Mario were more than hot rod-lover and mechanic. I'd have suggested that Mario join us, if I hadn't wanted to speak to Sarah in private.

Besides, there was only so much car talk I could take.

'What are we having?' I was onboard with not cooking or having to straighten up my house. I did, though, need to know which color wine to bring.

'Pizza,' Sarah said, 'or whatever is in the refrigerator.'

I didn't necessarily want pizza again, but I'd also seen the inside of Sarah's refrigerator. 'Pizza is just fine. I'll bring red.'

'Just enough for you,' Sarah said, climbing into the driver's seat of Firebird II. 'I've had to give it up. The lithium, you know.'

'But you had some the other night,' I pointed out. 'In fact, the other *two* nights. And Jim Beam yesterday.'

'Big mistakes and I paid for them, believe me.' She started the car. 'I scuttled my rum and Cokes. Who knew they considered wine "alcohol", too?'

With a wave, Sarah took off.

As she departed with a roar, I saw the curtain behind Art Jenada's front window twitch.

Somebody, and I think we all know who, had been watching us.

When I approached Sarah's house nearly an hour later, a white van was pulling away.

'Did Mario just leave?' I asked, hooking a thumb toward the disappearing truck.

Sarah swung the front door wide and stepped aside to let me in. 'We discussed having Ronny check out the car. Mario is going to drop it by tomorrow morning at eight thirty.'

I imagined the conversation:

Sarah: 'I want my cousin to look at the car. Monday all right with you?'

Mario: 'Sure.'

I didn't quite see why that required a house-call, but if Sarah had found a kindred spirit in Mario, I was all for it. And her. Or them.

Sarah picked up a Schultz's grocery bag that

was sitting next to the threshold.

'I thought we were ordering pizza?' I said. 'You don't have to cook.'

'I'm not,' Sarah said, shaking the sack at me. 'These are Auntie Vi's things. Mario found the bag in the trunk of my Firebird.'

'You should have invited him to join us,' I said, knowing full well it was too late.

'I did. He had plans.'

'Don't you think you should have cleared it with me? After all, we might have private stuff to talk about. Partner stuff.'

'You just suggested I invite him.'

'I was making a gesture. Showing support of your relationship with him.'

Sarah looked skyward. 'And I'm the one on drugs.'

I followed her out to the kitchen, wanting to take advantage of the opening. 'So, how long have you been on lithium?'

Sarah was going through the stack of takeout menus next to her phone. 'Just a week. That's why I slipped up on the wine.'

And the Jim Beam. But, being the sensitive friend that I am, I plunked my bottle of Syrah on the counter and went digging through Sarah's cupboard drawers for a corkscrew.

'Last one on the left,' she supplied.

'When did you realize you were ... having problems?' I finished rather lamely, even for me.

'You mean when did I know I was a crazy?'

282

'Stop that,' I snapped. 'This isn't something you should kid about.'

Sarah turned, Pizza Palace menu in hand. 'No. This is something *you* can't kid about. I have it, so I can kid about it. I can say anything I damn well please.'

Her hand was shaking a bit when she picked up the phone. 'What do you want? Pepperoni, mushrooms and banana peppers?'

'Go ahead and get onions.' It didn't rise to the level of anchovies, but this was a more generous concession than it might appear. The topping agreed with Sarah about as well as it did with Frank. Urging Sarah to eat onions was akin to sacrificing myself on the altar of flatulence.

Sarah turned around, phone to her ear. 'Really?'

'Really. And I'm sorry. I've just been worried about you.'

'Before, is when you should have—' She held up her finger and placed our order.

When she hung up, I asked, 'What? No infinite holds? No singing of pizza songs?'

'Nope. I think you may have imagined the whole thing.' She grinned at me. 'I've been really worried about you, Maggy.'

My, my. Weren't *we* feeling chipper?

'Point taken. We're all nuts. So what were you saying about "before"?'

'Just that now I'm getting treatment and it's helping. So what's to worry about?'

'Nothing,' I said. Except the depot, her late step-uncle, her even 'later' car, and her teenage foster kids. But if Sarah could see a silver lining, so could I.

I went to hug her and she held up her hands to ward me off. 'Let's not get carried away, OK? I don't like you that much.'

'You *are* feeling better,' I said, delighted.

'Well, yeah. Kind of.' Sarah set out a wine glass for me and a Coke for herself. 'I still have the mood swings, but they're not as wide as they were.'

'Great.'

She shook her head. 'I have to tell you, Maggy. It scared the hell out of me when I cried.'

'Me, too,' I said, following her out to the living room, where we settled down to await our pizza.

I took a sip of wine. 'Did you see your lawyer yesterday?'

I was treading carefully, trying not to bring up unpleasant things in a way that might upset my friend.

'I did,' Sarah said, sliding a coaster under my glass as I went to set it down.

'And?'

'He told me I do have rights in this situation.'

'Terrific,' I said, glad there was positive news. 'What's he suggesting?'

'First of all, he's going to contact Patrice and inform her that I am still Sam and Courtney's legal guardian and they are still minors. She is to have them call me immediately.'

'They haven't replied to your messages yet?' That was just plain wrong. How thoughtless could Sam and Courtney be?

Then again, both *were* teenagers.

'No, they haven't. And my calls go right to voicemail, like their phones are turned off. I did try texting, like you suggested, but not a peep.'

Nor a 'tweet', presumably. 'What will you say to them when you do get the chance?'

'I'm going to tell them that I love them. That their mother loved them, too, and she wanted me as their guardian, not an aunt they never knew.'

'Pitch-perfect,' I said. And remarkably sensitive.

'That's all I can do. If it doesn't work, my lawyer is going to demand Sam and Courtney return here while the whole issue of custody is considered.'

'Even better,' I said. 'Once they're here, face-to-face—'

'Unless Patrice blocks it.'

'If they don't come to Brookhills, would you consider going to Cape Cod?' I asked it hesitantly. I was trying to imagine the scene as Sarah pounded on Patrice's door and came up only with Armageddon.

'Damn right, I will.' Sarah stood just as a Volkswagen with a 'Pizza Palace' placard turned into the driveway.

'That's the spirit.' As Sarah went to the door to pay the pizza guy, I got out plates and napkins.

Fighting Patrice, buying a new car, throwing in with me on Uncommon Grounds. Sarah didn't need any help. She seemed to be doing wonderfully.

Which meant that maybe my generous offer of onions as an additional topping was precipitous of me.

Three slices later, I had a suggestion. 'Want to sit outside?'

'That bad?' Sarah asked with a wicked grin.

'Mere preparation.' I picked up my glass and led the way to her brick patio.

'It really is beautiful out here,' I said, surveying the spring flowers in the beds skirting the bricks. 'Did you do the plantings yourself?'

Sarah snorted and waved me toward the umbrella-topped glass table. 'You've known me how long now?'

'Just a couple of years, when you think about it. We became friends only after Patricia was killed.'

'Huh.' Sarah cocked her head. 'I guess that's true. It seems so much longer.'

It did. No matter which way she meant that.

'And what about Patricia?' I asked. 'How long were the two of you friends?'

'We met just after she moved to Brookhills, so about four years. Before she died.'

Sarah took two fingers and touched her lips, then tilted back and puffed heavenward. Blowing a kiss to Patricia up there somewhere or, more likely, another pretend smoke ring. When Sarah talked about the past, it always seemed to dredge up her old habit.

'Did Patricia tell you anything about her family life?'

'Nope.' Sarah looked sideways at me. 'Why? What do you know?'

'Nothing, I –'

'Spit it out Maggy. Just because I'm on drugs doesn't mean I won't rough you up.'

An idle threat. Perhaps.

I reluctantly filled her in on what Caron had told me about Patricia's childhood. Then I told her what Pavlik had found or, to be fair, not found.

'Huh.' Sarah tapped her index finger on the table like she was knocking the ash off a cigarette.

Not exactly the response I'd expected. I didn't want to color her thoughts with my own take on the situation, though, so I kept quiet.

'Huh.'

But now I couldn't stand it. 'All right. "Huh", what?'

'Granted, Patricia was not wrapped particularly tight,' Sarah said slowly, 'but I can't believe this is something she would make up.'

'She never said anything to you?' I asked.

'Nothing. No indication whatsoever.'

287

'Yet Patricia wanted you to have custody of the kids over blood relations on her side of the family tree.'

'True.' Sarah had a rueful grin on her face. 'Guess it shows "tight-wrapping" was not exactly a prerequisite for guardianship.'

I punched her shoulder. 'That's not what I meant. You're plenty wrapped.'

'You wouldn't just say that, would you?'

Quite honestly, I probably would.

But I was telling the truth in this case. Sarah, sans mood swings, was one of the most dependable people I knew. 'Of course not.'

'Liar.' The grin faded. 'Thing is, Patricia, whatever her background, wasn't abusive to Sam or Courtney. I'd bet my life on that.'

'So you're saying all is well with Patrice, too?'

She shrugged. 'Innocent until proven guilty, Maggy. Pavlik didn't find anything. Even I came up empty.'

I looked at her.

'My kids were staying with her,' Sarah said. 'You'd have to guess that I'd check the family out the best I could.'

'Like how?' I asked. 'Google them?'

'I started there and found Patrice's name on a list of her church board members.'

That was a good sign, I guessed. Though God knew – and I concurred – it wasn't conclusive. I'd had a run-in or two with crazies intertwined with their churches like yarns in a sweater. 'Did you actually talk to anyone?'

'Their pastor. The church organist. Oh, and the woman who does their flowers. All passed Patrice with flying colors.'

I had to give it to Sarah. She was thorough.

'Even so,' she continued, 'I'm going to call my attorney in the morning and tell him what you told me.'

That Caron told me.

That Patricia told her.

I felt like we were kids again, playing a game of telephone.

Maybe it was time to grow up.

Twenty-Five

The next day was Sunday. As it turned out, it was the day of rest before ... well, the rest.

By the time Monday morning dawned, my Escape had been washed, the lawn cut and a plan made.

Art Jenada might well be the one behind all the 'accidents', but if I didn't have proof, the harassment wouldn't stop. And, so far, if you didn't count Kornell's crash – maybe a true accident – no one had been seriously hurt.

Unfortunately, I couldn't count on that continuing as September first approached. It was time to protect ourselves.

Jenada said he didn't know who owned the building the florist had rented. I had no reason to doubt the caterer any more than I had reason to trust him.

So I didn't.

I found Laurel Birmingham, town clerk, unlocking the door of our municipal hall at eight a.m. sharp.

'Morning, Laurel,' I said as I came up behind her.

She jumped, hand to her breast. 'You scared me to death, Maggy. What are you doing here this early?'

'I need to find out who owns a property. Can I do that with you or do I have to go to the county courthouse?'

The courthouse was five miles away, but boasted the advantage of having Pavlik's office nearby. If I needed to go over there, maybe he'd buy me breakfast.

'Come on in.' Laurel swung open the door, but blocked my way while she reached to turn on the corridor lights.

'Sorry. There are no outside windows in the passageway, so it's pitch dark,' she said, letting me pass by.

Laurel is tall and well-proportioned, with what my mother had called an hour-glass figure. Laurel's cellphone would stay put. In fact, she'd probably have to send divers in for it.

'Thanks,' I said, willing myself to be tall. 'I wouldn't want to break a leg on the cow.'

I patted the snout of a life-sized, plaster Holstein displayed in one corner. The animal was mostly white, but instead of the requisite black patches, hers were red and shaped like apples.

'Careful.' Laurel was sorting through her key ring for the one to the Clerk's Office. 'That thing's worth ten thousand dollars. It's here on loan from an art museum in Manhattan.'

New York lending Wisconsin a cow. How wrong was that?

I followed Laurel into the office and waited on the public side of the counter as she went around back, dropping her purse on a desk. Then she came toward me and straightened her nameplate.

'Can I help you?'

'Funny. And I hope so.'

I explained about the broken window in the store next door to the depot.

'Did you report it to the police?' Laurel asked.

'I didn't even think about that,' I admitted. 'Is it too late?'

'No, and it would be a nice favor to the owner. That way they'd have a police report for the insurance company.'

If their insurance coverage was like mine, another twenty windows would have to be broken before the deductible was exhausted and coverage kicked in.

Still, it was the right thing to do. Plus, it would get me the information I wanted without having to explain why. Laurel might be a fount of data, but this wellspring flowed both ways.

'Who does own it?' I asked.

'If I had a dollar for every time someone asked that question.' She brought her laptop computer to the counter.

'People always want to know who owns the property next door to them?'

'No, not just any property,' Laurel said, slipping on her reading glasses. 'I'm talking in particular about the one next to the depot. A hotel chain is looking to build in the Junction area.'

Ah-hah.

As Laurel spoke, she was tapping at her keyboard. Now she swiveled the laptop so the screen faced me. 'I keep telling people this is all public record and available online. Anyone can access it, you just need the address or the owner's name.'

'I don't have the owner's name,' I said.

Laurel rolled her eyes. 'But you do have the address, right?'

'Umm.'

'Oh, for God's sake.' She turned it back and tapped some more. 'At least the last guy had the address.'

'And who was that?' I asked it in what I hoped was a casual, I'm-just-marking-time kind of way.

Laurel eyed me over her glasses. 'Why do you care?'

'I don't.'

'Then why are you asking?'

'Just marking time until you're done.'

'Right.' She was searching through the paper on the counter. 'I think I still have the sticky-note with the address. It has his name on it.'

She selected a miniature sheet of lined paper and held it up. 'Here it is.'

'Seven-fifty Junction Road,' I read. 'And,' I looked up at Laurel, 'From the Desk of Art Jenada?'

She hit enter and positioned the laptop again so I could see the screen.

Why would Jenada look up the ownership of his own property? Unless...

I pulled the computer closer to me.

Site Address: 750 Junction Drive
Property Owner: Eisvogel, Kornell

Son of a gun.

Twenty-Six

'This can't be right,' I said more to myself than to Laurel. 'He's dead.'

'Then the property will go to his heir or heirs.' She reclaimed her computer. 'The hotel people have probably already tracked them down.'

'Him,' I corrected, 'and they probably have. But I have next dibs on the guy.'

They say you always find what you're looking for in the last place you look.

Well, duh.

So, of course, I didn't expect to find Ronny in the *first* place I looked.

On the way to the depot I called Sarah, only to get her voicemail. I couldn't remember the code to bypass it, so I had to wait through the long-winded menu of 'Kingston Realty – if you want this, press that'.

When I finally heard the beep, I left my own long, meandering message – too long, apparently, because the phone beeped back at maybe the four-minute mark and cut me off. When given the option, I pushed the '7' key to delete, intending to re-record more succinctly.

The thing was, though, how does one say, 'I think your cousin has been playing us. He will inherit the florist shop from Kornell and may have killed him to get both that and the depot. You might be next, so give me a call when you get the chance. Toodle-oo.'

By the time I'd worked out the perfect message, I was at the depot. There was no sign of life when I pulled up in front. I checked my cellphone. Nine a.m. No wonder Ronny wasn't here at the Junction; he'd still be at Sarah's place.

I tried her again and was rewarded with the same Kingston Realty greeting and menu. Not wanting to waste more Ronny-free time, I flipped my phone closed before the outgoing message ended and exited the Escape. As I did, something caught my attention.

The florist shop. Something was different.

I approached. Same dirty windows, but the broken one had been boarded up. I assumed the police hadn't done it, because I hadn't called them. And I didn't see Art Jenada doing manual labor that benefitted someone else. Besides, he saw the florist shop as a 'tear-down'.

So that left Ronny. Was there something valuable inside? Or maybe just something he didn't want anyone to see?

The window was covered by a 4-foot by 4-foot sheet of plywood. It had been a hasty job – nails instead of screws, like the sabotaged deck railing, and not many nails even at that.

I looked around for something to slip under the edge of the board and pry it off. I tried a branch from the flowering bush, but it was too flexible. As I went to toss it away, I realized the twig, like the blossom that had snagged in my hair, had no scent. So if Jenada was not the talcum-wearing culprit, where had the aroma come from? I certainly hadn't imagined it.

Had I?

I returned to the Escape and got its tire iron. Then I went back to the window. The job didn't take much effort with the right tool. I pried one side free and the weight of the wood did the rest.

As the plywood fell away, I got the familiar whiff of flowers. No, I hadn't been imagining it.

Levering myself up on to the windowsill, I was reluctantly grateful to Ronny for clearing out the glass shards before boarding the thing up.

This visit, it was the morning sun that was slanting through the filthy windows, illuminating the check-out counter and skanky fake flowers.

I swung one leg over the sill, catching my knee on a stalagmite of glass that had been missed.

'Careless, Ronny,' I said, as I felt blood – but no pain – run down my leg. I dearly hoped I wouldn't stumble across a body, as was my habit. The DNA evidence alone would put me away for life.

Once in, I opened my cell to try Sarah again. If I bled out, I wanted them to find my body before it started to smell.

As I selected her name from my address book, I circled the room, trying to locate the floral smell. My nose led me to the grocery bags on the floor.

The rock that had been used to break the window was still atop one of them. I nudged it aside.

That bag and its twin, sitting cockeyed nearby, were both from Schultz's, just like the bag Mario had salvaged from the trunk of Sarah's Firebird.

Two Schultz's sacks. Ronny had come into the depot with them. This was just after Sarah's car had taken its last lamented dive on to the porch. Ronny had – supposedly – returned from the senior home and the bags – supposedly, too – contained things from the room Vi and Kornell shared before she went into the Sunrise wing.

Cellphone still clutched in one hand, I picked up the crushed bag and dumped out the contents.

A sweet-smelling white cloud enveloped me.

'Silken Petals,' I said, almost choking on it.

'Vi's favorite,' a voice from outside the cloud said.

As the talc cleared, a form started to take

shape.

Tight black pants, white socks, black shoes, open shirt. Inked-on sideburns. Slicked-back hair with a lock dangling down.

Apparently, Elvis *was* in the building.

Twenty-Seven

'Did you buy all these for Vi?' I still had my cell in hand and faintly registered the Kingston Realty message starting. I slid the phone, open, into my pocket hoping Ronny wouldn't hear the outgoing announcement, too.

'I did. Every one of them.' He even sounded like Elvis Presley. Low-pitched, southern twang. 'But they kept disappearing. Vi especially loved the sprinkle bottles, so she could just turn them over and tap the powder out. Arthritis, you know.'

'No, I didn't know.' Edging away, I tried to string Ronny along. 'Did the arthritis contribute to her fall?'

'My father "contributed to her fall". The bastard killed the only person who ever loved me.'

I thought it best not to expand on that just yet. 'You said Vi's Silken Petals kept disappearing?'

'That witch in the souped-up wheelchair was taking them. Everybody knew that. Her room was next to Vi's and my father's, so I took them back.'

A beep from my pocket.

'Clara Huseby is dead, you know.' I said it

loudly to cover the cell sound. 'An accident with her wheelchair. Sarah and I found her.'

'So I heard.' Ronny was squirming in his pants, like they were chafing him. Or maybe it was his homage to the pelvis of Elvis.

Now Ronny smirked. 'That wheelchair was giving Clara all sorts of problems. I tried to fix it, but...' He shrugged.

'You *are* good with your hands. Did you inspect the car Sarah wants to buy?'

'I did. Looks like just the thing for her.'

I'd have bet it was. Ronny probably turned Firebird II into a death trap. And he already had the deed to the depot. If Sarah was out of the way, even without the partnership papers sign-ed, he could forge the deed with nobody alive to question the signature.

Except ... me.

I needed to warn Sarah. Get enough damning information on tape so that when the recording ended and she received it as a voicemail, Sarah would know not to drive the new Firebird.

Somebody knowing where Maggy Thorsen was would be a good thing, too. Blood still trickled down my leg, but I had a feeling that was the least of my current worries.

I coughed like I was clearing my throat. 'Sorry,' I said loudly, 'but when the bottle broke, the talcum got in my throat. I don't know if the florist kept the water on, but I could use something to drink.' There. That should tell Sarah where I was.

'The water's disconnected,' Ronny said. 'My father, the cheap bastard, had it turned off.'

'So cheap he wouldn't pay a mechanic? Is that why Kornell asked you to fix the Buick's fuel line?' I asked.

'Please. He never wanted me to touch his precious classic.'

'More precious than his own son?'

'At least this one.' More squirming.

I knew he was thinking about Tommy. 'Even so, you did your best to fix Kornell's car.'

'What can I say? I'm a saint.'

And I was sweating bullets. 'The Buick's clock was off, too. I mean in addition to the fuel line.'

'A real shame.' Ronny attempted to stick his hands in his pockets, but the pants were too tight. He settled for hooking his thumbs in the belt loops.

'And the depot clock? That was wrong, too.'

'A timely convergence, you might say.' Ronny didn't sound so much like Elvis anymore. 'But still, the chances of anything happening?' He shrugged.

'Yet *every*thing did,' I said. 'It must have seemed like a sign from God to you.'

Ronny's thumbs slipped out of the belt loops. 'Not a sign from God, Maggy. Just an accident.'

'But a very lucky accident.' I needed to move things along before the recording ended. I knew I risked agitating him, but I had to take the chance. 'You inherited this place from Kornell and when you realized – thanks to me telling you Wednesday – that the depot wasn't part of the package, you decided to throw in with Sarah and me, figuring you'd get the property one way or the other.'

I hurried on before he could interrupt. 'You probably rigged up the bad electrical wires and plumbing yourself. The hose under the sink was a nice touch – you cut it from the garden hose outside. No wonder Jenada was able to obtain a permit for his restaurant. Everything was fine until you got hold of the place.'

A very Elvis sneer.

'You rammed Sarah's Firebird into the building, too, didn't you?'

'Don't be silly,' Ronny said. 'I just turned the car around for her.'

'And forgot to set the parking brake?' As I said it, I finally heard a faint beep from my pocket, followed by a woman's voice signaling that the message had reached its maximum length. If I did nothing, the voicemail would automatically go to Sarah's phone.

Ronny shrugged. 'I suppose I might have. Don't quite remember.' He bent over and lifted the rock I'd left on the floor.

Bad sign.

I held up my hands, playing for time. 'One thing that I don't know, though, is how the flour got in Sarah's car.'

A grunted laugh. 'There was a floury apron on the porch railing,' Ronny said. 'I might have

303

shook it over the seat before I followed Art into the depot.'

'You knew the apron was Art's?'

'It seemed a good bet, don't you think?'

'So you set him up?'

'I just wanted to cause a little confusion.' Ronny gave an Elvis pout. 'I figured any white powder would give the emergency workers pause.'

He hefted the rock like he was weighing whether it would crush my skull. If Ronny's MO was *staging* accidents, what was he going to do? Bean me with the rock and say I fell on to it climbing through the window?

That could work, come to think of it. Meaning, I probably shouldn't mention it to him.

Instead, I said the next thing that came into my head.

'What about Vi?' I was edging away. There was a simple thumb-turn deadlock on the door. I'd stand a better chance going out that way than through the window. 'Did you kill her, too?'

Unlike my other accusations, this one seemed to shake him. 'My father killed her. I told you that.'

'Your father?' I was still moving.

Only problem was that Ronny was shadowing me. 'Yes, my father. He used to hit me, did you know that?'

I decided to take another shot in the dark. 'Of course he hit you. You killed his son. Who could blame—?'

'I was his son, *too*,' Ronny roared. 'It was an accident.'

'Was it, Ronny? Was it really?' The florist shop's door was less than four feet away now.

'Stop that,' Ronny shouted, raising the rock.

I wasn't sure if he meant talking or moving, so I ceased both.

'Get back over there.' He was indicating the corner where I'd started, near the bags and far from the door.

Back to square one.

All I could do now was hope Sarah got the message. In the meantime, I'd keep Ronny talking and, last resort, take him down. Let's hope Sarah was right, and I did outweigh the twerp.

While I had been dwelling on other things, like how I would beat the crap out of the nutcase if I got hold of him, Ronny remained fixated on his brother.

'It was an accident,' he repeated. 'Maybe I left the door open, but Tommy was the one who wandered out.'

Ronny seemed to be calming down. I did not view this as good news. My chances of taking him were better if he wasn't thinking clearly.

'My father should have watched Tommy, if he loved him so much.' This last sounded like the whine of a five-year-old.

'And the ball?' I asked, trying to stir him up again. 'The one that Tommy chased into the road?'

'Tommy wanted it,' Ronny said softly. 'It rolled into the street.'

'You threw it.'

A flare of anger. 'I kicked it.'

'That first time was a revelation, wasn't it? You realized you could kill, but not be blamed.'

I'd struck a nerve. 'I *was* blamed,' Ronny screamed, free hand rolled into a fist. 'I was blamed my whole life.'

'By your father, but not by anybody else,' I said measuredly. 'Not by Vi or anybody you cared about. You were just a little boy, after all. If anything, it made Vi love you more. "Poor Ronny, it's not his fault."'

'That's right.' Ronny stuck out his chin. 'It wasn't my fault.'

'You took no responsibility and had no remorse. Then or now.'

'Remorse for what?' Ronny was visibly trying to calm himself again. 'I left a door open and kicked a ball. Out of the goodness of my heart, I did some repairs on an old lady's wheelchair. Fixed my father's fuel line. Reset a clock or two. Turned a car around for my cousin and neglected to set the parking brake.'

He shrugged, rock still in hand. 'What can I say, Maggy? Some people are just accident prone.'

I retreated behind the Schulz's bags and snuck a glance out the window. Still no Sarah. I was on my own. 'Did you loosen the porch rail to throw us off?'

'Maybe.'

'Poor little Ronny,' I intoned. 'Fell off the porch and hurt himself.'

His face changed and he took a step toward me. I might have pushed one too many buttons. Time to back off and appeal to his ego.

'I have to hand it to you,' I said, tipping my head. 'You do a great Elvis. Circa nineteen fifty..."

'Fifty-seven.' Ronny gave a little butt wiggle and a smidge of pelvic thrust.

I gestured at the bulge in his pants. 'What do you use for it?'

Ronny looked down at his crotch. 'A rolled-up sock.' He adjusted said sock with his non-rock hand. 'As long as the pants are tight enough. Bell-bottoms, now they're a problem. The boner falls out.'

'Embarrassing,' I said. 'But I meant what do you use for the jock itch.' I leaned down and picked up a container of Silken Petals. 'Maybe if you put a little of this on your ... sock,' I twisted open the top, 'it'll help.'

Ronny stuck his free hand out. "These tight pants *are* murder.'

I held the powder just out of his range. 'And the polyester. No wonder you wore shorts the other day.'

'And boxers.' The Elvis clone took a step toward me. 'Had to air the boys out.'

'But maybe a little too much air?' I was

careful to keep the container out of reach. 'How'd you keep the sock in?'

A sheepish grin. 'That was a problem.'

Ahh. 'Fell out as you were exiting Sarah's car, huh?'

But Ronny was getting impatient with the conversation. 'I told you I moved her car. Now give it.' He made a grab for the container.

Always one to accommodate, I thrust the bottle in his face and squeezed hard, crushing the dispenser and sending up an explosion of Silken Petals powder.

Ronny dropped the rock and fell back, coughing and rubbing at his eyes.

Taking advantage of the distraction, I made a dash for the door. As I turned the deadbolt and went to push, a hand grabbed my shoulder from behind.

I tried to shrug it off and keep going, but Ronny was stronger than he looked. The little bugger even spun me around and shoved me back into the room. Ronny's head was covered with powder, his eyes streaming, the tears making flesh-colored rivulets down his cheeks.

I retreated to get my balance. Then, as Ronny came toward me, I moved forward as well, going on the offense. I could see he was startled.

As the distance between us closed, I zigged. Ronny zigged.

I zagged and Ronny zagged. We were like two people trying to pass each other on a sidewalk.

I faked another zig, knowing the man would anticipate it. When he did, I zagged instead.

As Ronny tried to change directions, I stepped around and kicked out the back of his left knee. As he went down, I heard two things. The rip of his pants and the thud of his head against the rock on the floor.

Holy shit.

It had been self-defense, right? Ronny was the one who attacked me. And dropped the rock there. This was his fault, not mine.

Even as I had the thought, Ronny groaned and turned over.

All remorse gone, I took off for the door again and this time pushed it open, in my haste nearly tripping over the roof tiles I'd left there myself.

Then I ran like hell.

Twenty-Eight

'Elvis really has left the building,' Art Jenada said.

We were on the sidewalk, watching as Officer Heckleman led Ronny out of the florist shop. Firefighter Brady was snapping photos.

Ronny had a gash on his forehead but apparently he'd live. After over-powdering (sorry) him, I ran across the street and directly into Jenada. He gave me a towel for my bloody leg and then called 911. The two of us armed ourselves with catering knives and stood guard outside the shop until the police arrived and disarmed us. Then they went inside and found the real bad guy.

'I can't see,' Ronny screamed as Heckleman and he passed us. 'And I probably have a concussion.'

'I'm sorry,' I called after him. 'It was an accident.'

Ronny didn't laugh.

'Not a fan of ironic humor, apparently,' I said to Jenada.

'Isn't that your friend the sheriff?'

I turned the direction Jenada was looking to

see Pavlik's car pull up to the curb. As Heckleman eased Ronny into the rear seat of the municipal squad, the sheriff took a moment to fully appreciate Ronny's fashion statement. Then he proceeded up the sidewalk toward us.

'Michael Jackson?' Pavlik asked, hooking a finger toward Ronny.

'No. The King, 1957. Elvis did the white sock thing first.'

Pavlik pointed to the still-open door of the florist shop. 'So I guess we could say that Elvis has—'

'Forget it,' I said. 'Already been done.' I introduced the sheriff to Art.

'We met at the last disaster, I think.' Jenada stuck out his hand. 'Or maybe the catastrophe before that.'

'The train crash,' Pavlik agreed. 'It's so hard to keep count.'

They looked at me like this was *my* fault.

'Listen, I'm the hero here. I disabled the bad guy. And,' holding up my phone, 'got the confession on voicemail and sent it to Sarah.'

'Let's hope she got the message and didn't delete it,' Pavlik said. 'But you're right. You are the hero. Great work. Just don't repeat it.'

'Promise.' After all, the chances of again coming across a man dressed like Elvis when I had a bottle of talcum powder in my hand were probably slim to none.

'What happened there?' Pavlik was pointing at my leg. The paramedics had removed the towel and replaced it with an embarrassingly small bandage. They said I might have bled out, but it would have taken a week or so. And a clotting disorder.

'I'm fine. Just a scratch.' I looked around. 'Where's Sarah?'

'Haven't seen her,' Pavlik said.

'You mean the woman with the baggy suits?' Jenada asked. 'Nasty disposition, no more Firebird?'

'That's her,' I confirmed.

'Haven't seen her either.'

Jenada waved at Christy, who was waiting timidly across the street, wringing her rubber-gloved hands. 'Gotta go. I think she wants me.'

Jenada winked in my direction and crossed the road to her. Penn and Inkel were making their way over to Christy as well, with Rebecca making sure Michael didn't cross the street to the crime scene. It would be interesting to see how that relationship progressed. Or not.

'Quite a crew you're going to have here at the Junction,' Pavlik observed. 'This line-up puts Benson Plaza to shame.'

'And just think,' I said. 'We'll still have Amy and Tien. Add Sarah to the mix...'

An unfamiliar car roared up. The driver slammed on the brakes and screeched to a stop in front of us, laying down a strip of rubber.

'Cool skidmark,' Sam Harper said, jumping out of the passenger side of the car.

'Sam, you're home.' I hugged him. 'You look

like a surfer dude.' I tousled his sun-bleached hair.

'Skidmark? Eww.' Sam's sister Courtney climbed out of the backseat.

'Not *that* kind of skidmark, stupid,' Sam said.

'Don't call your sister stupid.' Sarah came around from the driver's side.

I hugged Courtney and complimented her on her tan.

'Fake Bake. I'm not an idiot like my brother.' She threw him a look.

Happy homecoming. I turned to Sarah. 'They are back – that's wonderful.'

'Sure.' I could see her resisting the urge to grin. 'One hour off the plane and they're already fighting.'

'Hey, just be glad they have each other. Eric used to pick fights with me.'

Pavlik had gone off to talk to Heckleman, so I led Sarah to one side, so the kids wouldn't overhear. 'So, what happened?'

'Sam and Courtney called, finally. I asked them to come home and they did.'

'Simple as that?'

Sarah shrugged. 'I may have told Courtney the hot guy she likes called. Next thing I know, she wants me to book them the next flight home.'

Sarah was trying to act irritated, but couldn't quite carry it off.

'That's all?' I asked. 'What about Sam?'

'Sam? I said I was buying a new car.'

I looked at her.

Sarah shrugged. 'I can't help it if he assumed *he* was getting the Firebird.'

'That's downright cruel,' I said. 'Shame on you.'

'Hey, they're home. Besides, I talked to Mario and he offered to help Sam rebuild my poor Bird.'

I didn't think it was the right time to ask about the parts that already had been harvested.

'Speaking of Mario and the car, did you get my message?'

'Yeah, but I didn't listen to all of it. I was at the airport, picking up the kids.'

Oh-oh. 'You didn't erase it, did you?'

'Nah. Should I ask what's going on here?'

'You were supposed to be saving my life,' I said. 'Ronny is a little whacked.'

'A *little* whacked?' Sarah pointed to the squad. 'He's doing Elvis in whiteface.'

'That's talcum powder. Silken Petals, to be exact. I used it to blind him.'

For a change – and a welcomed one – Sarah seemed at a loss for words.

I said, 'Your cousin—'

'Step-cousin.'

We were back to that, eh? 'Your *step*-cousin has been behind all the accidents. Your unc ... Kornell owned the flower shop and Ronny wanted it. He engineered the accident with the train and when that was successful, it made him overconfident.'

'Overconfident?'

'I think he felt like this was all preordained. Consider his history: He left a door open and kicked a ball. Presto, his pesky little brother is out of his life forever.'

'He did that on purpose?' I don't think I'd ever seen Sarah so astonished.

'I think so. Maybe just to get Tommy into trouble. But Ronny admitted kicking the ball into the street because Tommy wanted it.'

'Ronny was a kid,' Sarah protested. 'Kids make mistakes.'

'Of course they do. And kids learn from their mistakes. In Ronny's case, though, he learned that he could "make mistakes" – like not tightening Kornell's fuel line or Clara Huseby's wheel—'

Sarah started to interrupt, but I tamped her down with my palms, '—and feign ignorance. Ronny would set things in motion and then walk away.'

'Like someone leaving a bomb in a train station.'

'Exactly, except in this case Ronny seemed able to convince himself that he wasn't responsible.'

Even as I said it, I was thinking about my knee-jerk reaction to Ronny's imagined death. Maybe self-justification was as natural an instinct as self-defense was. After all, nobody wants to admit – even to themselves – that they've done something wrong.

Ronny, though, had perfected the art.

'But what did he expect to accomplish here in the Junction?' asked Sarah.

'When Kornell died, Ronny thought he'd inherit half the depot. When I told him that wasn't true—'

'He didn't already know?'

'No, don't you remember? Kornell said he hadn't told his son anything. Given that, Ronny thought he'd get both the florist shop and Vi's interest in the depot when his dad died.'

'But even if that were true, I'd still have the other half.'

'He intended to buy your share with his inheritance and make a killing by selling the whole block to a hotel chain. When he realized he didn't own fifty per cent and you recognized how valuable the property was, Ronny knew he couldn't afford to buy you out.'

'So,' Sarah shaking her head, 'instead, he bought *in*.'

'Exactly. Ronny asked for the warranty deed, supposedly to give to his lawyer. I don't have to tell you that it wouldn't be hard to forge a new one and get some shady notary public to witness it. If you weren't around to contest it—'

I interrupted myself. 'You didn't let Ronny touch the new Firebird, did you?'

'Why? You think he sabotaged it?'

'It worked with Kornell. Was Ronny alone with the car?'

'Are you kidding?' Sarah said. 'Mario hovered over him the whole time, pointing out the features.'

'That's probably why Ronny gave up and came back early. He caught me nosing around in the florist shop.'

'I chased both Mario and Ronny out, so I could pick up the rental car and get the kids at the airport.'

'I'm so glad they're home,' I said, squeezing her shoulder.

'Me, too.' Sarah took a deep breath and let it out slowly. 'Feels like things are getting back to normal.'

'Yup,' I said. 'It's all downhill from here.'

'I thought it was uphill that was good.'

'Nope.'

'But—'

'Don't think about it,' I warned. 'Your head will hurt.'

The squad car containing Ronny started to pull away. He tried to wave, but the handcuffs defeated him.

'By the way,' I said, watching him go. 'Ronny shook the flour from Art's apron on to the seat of your car.'

Sarah looked sideways at me. 'And the talcum powder?'

'Do you really want to know?'

'Probably not, but when has that ever stopped you?'

Good point. 'Remember when Ronny sug-

317

gested that Art might be using the talc for jock itch?'

'Yessss,' Sarah said cautiously.

'Well, it was Ronny who had the jock itch.'

Sarah wrinkled her nose. 'But how much was he using? I mean we're talking about it seeping through his trousers.' An odd expression swept over her face. 'I hope.'

I imagined Sarah, imagining Ronny hopping in the Firebird sans pants. Should I let her ... dangle? I giggled.

'Oh, God,' Sarah groaned. 'It'll cost a fortune to have Mario reupholster.'

I relented. After all, the old Firebird was going to be Sam's car. 'Ronny's sock fell out of his shorts.'

Sarah looked like she wanted to smack me one.

I explained. 'Ronny stuffed his pants with a sock. Don't you notice how well-endowed he seemed to be for a guy so slight in build?'

'No, I didn't notice. He's my cousin for God's sake. Why would I be looking at his wee-wee? And while we're at it, why were you?'

'I'm naturally observant.' I cleared my throat. 'Anyway, Ronny restole your aunt's Silken Petals from Clara the Klepto when he went to the Manor.'

Sarah didn't say anything, still seemingly concerned about the wee-wee situation.

'Presumably,' I continued, 'Ronny was feeling chafed and powdered his sock. He said

318

when he climbed out of your car before sending it down the hill, the sock fell out.'

'Into my driver's seat.'

'Yes.'

'Anything else disquieting you want to tell me?'

'Probably. Come to dinner and I'll fill you in on the rest.'

'Not tonight, Maggy. I thought we'd have a family dinner.'

'I *am* family,' I said, sounding like Kornell the first time – and the last time, come to think of it – that I'd seen him.

'Besides,' I continued. 'Your kids don't have time for you. Look at them.'

Sam and Courtney were on their phones across the street, chattering away.

I said, 'Believe me, those two are going to be scheduled solid. They won't be home, except to sleep, for days. There's a lot of catching up to do.'

'They weren't gone for even a week,' Sarah said indignantly. 'It's not right—'

I overrode her. 'It *is* right for the kids, Sarah, and also for you. You had it pegged last week. Sam and Courtney *are* going to leave eventually. You need to have a life that's not built solely around them.'

Sarah looked weepy.

I poked her in the arm. 'We're not going to start all this nonsense over. Dinner is at my house tonight. If the kids want to come, they're welcome. If Pavlik wants to come, he's welcome.'

Shit, the whole world could come. I'd just get a bigger pizza.

'Fine.' Sarah was watching the squad car containing Ronny disappear in the distance. 'Just one question.'

'Yes?' I said gently. After all, this had been a tough day for my friend.

'Where in the hell are we going to find a new contractor?'